I0823583

CALIFORNIA CABALLERO

Center Point
Large Print

Also by William Colt MacDonald and available from Center Point Large Print:

Peaceful Jenkins
Mascarada Pass
Showdown Trail
Guns Between Suns
Law and Order, Unlimited
The Gun Branders
Marked Deck at Topango Wells
West of Yesterday

CALIFORNIA CABALLERO

William Colt MacDonald

CENTER POINT LARGE PRINT
THORNDIKE, MAINE

This Center Point Large Print edition
is published in the year 2025 by arrangement with
Golden West Inc.

The text of this Large Print edition is unabridged.
In other aspects, this book may vary
from the original edition.
Printed in the United States of America
on permanent paper sourced using
environmentally responsible foresting methods.
Set in 16-point Times New Roman type.

ISBN: 979-8-89164-729-9

The Library of Congress has cataloged this record
under Library of Congress Control Number: 2025941594

1

OLD CASTAMETO'S DAUGHTER

Late morning sunshine beat down with a white, brilliant glare on the dusty plaza in Santa Lozana. Surrounding the plaza on four sides were squat, adobe houses—a few painted in vivid pink or ochre—and a number of ramshackle wooden buildings. At one side was a two-story, false-fronted, frame structure bearing across its front elevation a sun-faded sign proclaiming it as the Santa Lozana Hotel. The other buildings were dwellings, a handful of *cantinas*, a couple of gambling resorts. Life moved but sluggishly through Santa Lozana at this hour of the day, and shop doors were tightly closed against the heat.

On various sides of the open square, narrow streets led the way between buildings to other sections of the town. To the north and east of Santa Lozana rose the peaks of the Santa Ana Mountains whose higher ridges appeared to support a long, pyramided bank of fleecy clouds in the otherwise unbroken expanse of sapphire sky. The four sides of the plaza were spotted here and there with bits of dusty-green plant growth; at one end a huge pepper tree, to the lacy branches of which still clung tenaciously a number of crimson berries from the previous autumn's ripening, provided cool shade to a group of loungers seated on a wooden bench resting against its gnarled and twisted trunk. Other loungers—Spaniards, *Americanos*, Indians and Mexicans—were sprawled nearby in various attitudes on the sparse grass, chatting listlessly and drawing on the inevitable cigarettes.

Across the plaza, the door of a *cantina* swung open, and a lean, black-haired individual appeared against the dark interior of the building, halted in the doorway, resting one shoulder carelessly against the casing, and coolly surveyed the sun-drenched plaza. Slight as the action was, it held, demanded, the attention of the loungers beneath the pepper tree. Spaniards, Mexicans and Indians observed the bronzed man framed in the *cantina* doorway, without appearing to look at him. The *Americanos* stared frankly and openly, certain traces of exasperation appearing on their unshaven countenances. One said, "There's Dilliard, now."

His companion spat a long brown stream. "Cursed renegade!"

The first man said, "You got the nerve to call Dilliard that to his face, George?"

"I ain't that crazy," came the hasty answer. "And don't you go repeatin' me."

"You a-skeered of Dilliard, George?"

George considered the question and finally

replied in the negative, adding explanation, "It's just that I been leery, ever since I was a younker, 'bout messin' with dynamite."

"Plumb sensible, I figures you. Especially in view of what happened to Herb Dorman this mornin'."

"Herb's jaw was bad swollen, last I seen him."

George's companion nodded comprehension. "Looks like to me as if Dilliard didn't give a damn if he busted his knuckles."

"If you're askin' me, fellah, I'd opine Dilliard didn't give a damn 'bout *anythin'*—and I reckon his knuckles is tougher than Herb's face, at that. Leastwise, Herb's got proof o' that fact."

The two men chuckled over the absent Herb's predicament and again gave their attention to the man standing before the *cantina* door. The smiles were erased from their faces as they took in Dilliard's lean, whipcord length in its woolen shirt and dark trousers worn long over boot-tops. A wide-brimmed, flat-crowned felt sombrero rested rakishly on Dilliard's black hair which curled slightly at the back of his neck where it touched the faded red bandanna.

Dilliard was smoothly shaven, with good features and steady eyes of slate-gray. Unconscious of the scrutiny from across the plaza, he stood frowning thoughtfully, completely lost in his abstractions. After a moment he allowed the loosely-swung door of the *cantina* to close softly at his back and became aware of the group clustered beneath the pepper tree, his glance flitting swiftly across the faces of the loungers.

The eyes of the *Americanos* shifted before that penetrating gaze, shifted to the Colt single-action forty-five, slung, butt-forward, at Branch Dilliard's left hip. The six-shooter was of the cartridge loading type. In a land where the cap-and-ball revolver still reigned supreme, this new model weapon, just commencing to make its appearance in California, had, on the previous evening, efficiently carried out its part in preserving the lives of Branch Dilliard and one other, the latter a Mexican, one Antonio Aguilar.

Tony Aguilar had been drunk, no doubt as to that, and a fool in the bargain to try to best four tin-horn card sharps at their own game in one of Santa Lozana's gambling joints. Standing at a sidewall bar in the gambling establishment, Branch Dilliard had watched the playing cards pass from hand to hand, while the gullible Tony was being steadily and mercilessly rooked of his scanty store of money. Had Tony swallowed less *tequila* that evening he would have realized, as Dilliard did, that the game was crooked. Dilliard didn't like it; he swore under his breath, then endeavored to shrug off the Machiavellian tactics of the scoundrelly quartet with the thought that, after all, it was only a "greaser" being victimized.

However, even that thought failed Branch when the Mexican, his alcohol-befuddled brain finally managing to flash a warning to its owner, protested the matter of five queens in the deck. To this the four gamblers had replied with drawn guns, the action proving just a bit too much to be compatible with Branch Dilliard's innate sense of fair play. Branch had taken an active hand in the affair, sustaining the charges of the game but fright-paralyzed Tony, and thus drawing upon his own person the combined anger of the four tin-horn gamblers.

The resulting action had been brief: a flash of swift shots; two sorely-wounded gamblers; two more, their arms flung high in frantic surrender. From near the wall, someone had shot out the lights, plunging the room into darkness. Some further shooting ensued, while Branch Dilliard took time to reload his gun in the shelter of an overturned table before emerging, victorious, into the night air of the plaza, half carrying the suddenly sobered Tony.

The following day, nothing was to be seen nor heard of the four gamblers; they had disappeared, and the gambling house where they had operated had been closed. But in his swift gun work, the lean-jointed, black-haired *vaquero* from Texas had produced an effect that would long remain vivid among the loungers resting in the plaza of Santa Lozana. And *that* is more than a little in a town that had, from its very inception, bragged loudly of its toughness.

There were other results. Along with gaining a reputation as a fast man with a six-shooter, Branch Dilliard had also earned the undying gratitude of Tony Aguilar. Two things Tony possessed of which he was inordinately proud: a rather futile command of the English language and a sweetheart whom he hoped, in some not too distant day, to make his *esposa.*

It was to escape the overwhelming thanks of Tony and his sloe-eyed Teresa the morning following the shooting affair, that Dilliard had secluded himself in the cheap *cantina* from which he had just emerged. And in the *cantina* Branch Dilliard had overheard certain whispered words which presented for his consideration a new and vexing problem.

Dilliard's eyes narrowed in the shade of his wide hat brim. "I won't do it," he told himself doggedly. "It's none of my business. First I get mixed up with this Mex boy, Tony, last night. Now it looks like I'm bein' forced into more greaser affairs. Just about one more move in the direction I'm headin', and I'll be settlin' down to *frijoles*, a *serape* and a church steeple hat for the rest of my days. Nope, not for me. I'm goin' to get out of this country. Texas suits me plumb down to my boot heels."

Dilliard's lean jaw set grimly; he gave the

brim of his hat a savage down-jerk. "Damn it," he complained, "it appears like I just get shoved into other folks' troubles. Some folks—well, it would be all right. But why in the name of the seven bald-faced steers should I risk my hide for a Mex girl? At best I'd probably just get mixed up into some greaser politics that are none of my business. Texans and Mexes just don't mix agreeable—not since the Alamo. 'Course, that was a long spell back. Just the same, the old enmity seems to get renewed every so often."

Branch's lip curled a trifle scornfully as he glanced across at the group beneath the pepper tree. His cogitations resumed: "Not that the *Americanos* in this town are anythin' to brag about, either. Taken by and large they're sheep lousy. And some of 'em got the nerve to criticize *me* for helpin' Tony against men of my own race. Oh, my God! Men of my own race! If those four tin-horns weren't the sneakinest, buzzard-lovin' sort of snakes—well, me, I reckon I prefer Tony. *Americanos*! Cripes! I'm ashamed of the lot of 'em. They're jelly-spined, yellow-backed, afraid to tell me what they think—exceptin' that one hombre, this mornin', who called me a renegade to my race."

Dilliard laughed shortly, glanced reminiscently at a set of bruised knuckles on his right fist, then thrust that hand into a pocket in search of cornhusk cigarette paper and tobacco. "I wonder how his jaw feels 'bout now," Branch mused while he rolled the cigarette with long, deft fingers. Meditatively he lighted the smoke, slowly shook his head with decision as delicate spirals of gray curled from his nostrils. "Nope. I'll keep out of it. Reckon I'll pull out today. I might take a *pasear* up to San Francisco before I head back to Santone. I understand 'Frisco's quite some town. Anyway, I ain't goin' to mix into no more greaser affairs."

A rider, resplendent in tight green jacket and velvet trousers trimmed with silver braid, reined a magnificent piece of horseflesh across the plaza and disappeared down a side street. Branch's eyes followed the horseman until he had passed from view, taking in the high-horned saddle, fancy stamping on the skirting, silver-mounted bridle and huge eagle bill *tapaderos*, the wings of which nearly brushed the earth. There'd been something proud, jaunty, defiant about the slim figure beneath the huge, high-crowned, embroidered sombrero, that Dilliard couldn't help but admire.

"These California buckaroos sure do themselves proud when it comes to rigs," Branch commented to himself, "both for themselves and their ponies. Danged if that Don didn't look plumb elegant. I'd admire to own an outfit like that." Branch grinned suddenly. "Maybe I should turn Mex for a spell. That'd sure give the folks back in Texas a shock. Nope, I reckon I got too much sense to do anythin' like that. Men should stick to their own kind. There ain't any doubt on that score."

And then, abruptly, Branch Dilliard reversed his decision. His gaze, returning from the rider who had passed, strayed across the plaza to the second floor of the Santa Lozana Hotel with its paint peeling under the brilliant glare of the hot March sunshine. A movement of shutters being thrown back from a window caught and held Branch's attention. For a brief moment a slim white form appeared in the opening.

Branch Dilliard blinked, suddenly caught his breath. He had gained a fleeting impression of coiled hair the color of cornsilk, dark eyes, full red lips, "and—and—" Branch added mentally, before the girl, with a disdainful curving of nostrils withdrew to her room, "a lot of frothy, white lace."

A hot, choking sensation filled Branch Dilliard's throat. There was a queer, mad thumping in the region of his left breast. Dilliard gazed dumbly at the empty window, but the girl didn't reappear.

"Why—why—" Dilliard told himself, "she's beautiful! Just like a girl out of a book. I—I didn't know they really made 'em like that. No Mexican, that girl—not with hair like that."

His blood pumped hotly as a new thought entered Dilliard's mind: "Sa-a-ay, she must be old Castameto's daughter—whoever he is! The old Don I overheard those two skunks talkin' about." Dilliard swore softly under his breath, "And I said it was no business of mine what happened. I didn't know I could be so dumb. It *is* my business, what happens to her—plenty! If I let those measly coyotes go through with what they're plannin', I won't ever dare call myself a white man again."

The Texan's gaze came reluctantly away from the empty window. He noticed that his cigarette had gone dead. He struck a match, his eyes sweeping swiftly around the plaza. To Dilliard's surprise, nothing had changed; the loungers beneath the pepper tree still dozed or chatted idly. Here and there a man sat slumped in the shadow of an adobe building. Branch Dilliard grinned sheepishly. "I don't know what I expected, but I know everythin' isn't the same with *me* as it was. I reckon maybe I'd better go talk with Tony and see what he knows—if anything."

Stepping to the footpath that passed the *cantina*, Dilliard strode quickly halfway around the dusty plaza. His gaze was still riveted on the empty window in the Santa Lozana Hotel when he turned into a narrow, unpaved street bordered on either side with blocky adobe houses. At the first corner Dilliard turned to the right, into the *Calle de los Caballeros*. The Street of the Gentlemen Riders it may have been, but it differed but slightly from the thoroughfare the Texan had just left. It curved a wide, dusty path between twin rows of adobe shacks, past open doorways, many of which were peopled with Mexican women and children. A mingled odor of cooking and mesquite smoke permeated the atmosphere.

The *Calle de los Caballeros* was a winding street, a colorful street. Vividly painted *ollas* were suspended beneath shaded porch roofs where contact with any vagrant breeze could contribute to the cooling of their contents for thirsty mouths. Gracefully curving strings of dried chili hung in scarlet profusion against white walls. Before one house, a middle-aged Mexican woman, surrounded with bowls and platters, was industriously engaged in shaping *tortillas* for the noon meal.

The door-to-door chattering of dark-eyed women ceased abruptly as Dilliard came striding along the middle of the street, his gaze fastened straight ahead where the thoroughfare ended, a hundred yards distant, in a series of crude corrals, several of which contained shaggy ponies. The glances that followed the Texan's broad shoulders were admiring. Already the *Calle de los Caballeros* knew of the previous night's service rendered Antonio Aguilar by the bronzed *Americano* from distant Texas, and the Mexican race is not prone to consider lightly a kindness to one of its people. Dilliard strode on; he was nearing Tony's house now.

2

GOLD FOR GUNS

The Texan found Tony Aguilar seated on the shady side of the last house from the end of the street. Beyond were the corrals and past those railed enclosures was open country stretching to the mountains. The Mexican was slim-hipped and round-faced, with a wisp of black mustache adorning his upper lip. His cotton clothing was worn but clean. In his arms he cradled a guitar, its plucked strings giving off the melodious strains of the plaintive "El Sonoreño." From the open window above Tony's head came an appetizing aroma of meat and chili peppers in the process of stewing.

As Tony's eyes fell upon Dilliard, "El Sonoreño" came to an abrupt, discordant, twanging conclusion. The guitar banged to earth. Tony leaped to his feet, hands outstretched in gracious welcome, his vivid green and yellow *serape* flung hastily aside.

"Tony—" Branch commenced.

"To our *casa* at las' you have arrive'," Tony's teeth flashed whitely. "All morneeng, Teresa an' I have look, but eet ees like finding the needle in the camel's eye—how you say? Or ees it the needle in the camel's back? Maybee eet is a straw—no?" A frown troubled Tony's brown features a moment, then his eyes cleared. "I hav' eet! You are like finding the camel in the straw stack! But, now, at las', you come. Ah, my savior, my deliverer from the den of Daniel lions—"

"That's plenty, Tony," Branch said as his hands were being pumped vigorously. "I came to see you—"

"Ah, yes! *Sí, sí,* Señor Don Branch," excitedly. "Like wet storms after the drought you are ver' welcome, like—like—" Tony paused for further, mouth-filling similes.

"Antonio!" A soft voice floated through the open window.

"Teresa!" Swift Spanish now. "Come quickly. It is the Señor Branch who has arrived. He has come for our expressions of gratitude—"

"*Cuidado*!" Dilliard's Spanish was as voluble as Tony's. "Stop! Wait a minute! I came to see you about—"

There came a rush of bare, brown feet through the doorway of the house. Dilliard caught a swirling impression of flying black hair, velvet-dark eyes in a round, comely face, white cotton skirt and blouse. Two bare arms were flung warmly around Branch Dilliard's neck, his head was jerked down, moist kisses were implanted lustily all over his features. Teresa had arrived on the scene!

"Dang it!" Dilliard burst out, his face crimson,

as he caught and held the joyous Mexican girl's strong wrists. "Stop it! *Al instante*! You are *demente*—both of you. I came here to—Stop it, I say! Now, listen, Teresa—Tony—Teresa—"

Dilliard's protestations were futile. Teresa was a whirlwind of gratefulness. Ensued further glowing kisses, fervent handclasps, and considerable ardent eloquence on the part of both Mexicans. Only by threatening an immediate departure was Dilliard able to still the storm of thanks his arrival had precipitated.

Teresa, sudden alarm showing in her features, stopped midway during a renewed assault on the Texan. "No, do not make the departing, Señor Branch," she begged, her English little better than Tony's. "Ah, we theenk we hav' los' you. We hav' make the utter, entire search an' your person ees not to be locate. We are cas' down like the stone in the mud. Tony, he tries the cheer-up weeth hees music. You hear what he plays? 'El Sonoreño'! Such an *imbécil*! He would wring tears from the cow—no? An' then you come—so beautiful—you, who we theenk is los'—ah, Señor Dilliard—"

"Whoa, there!" Dilliard stepped back from Teresa's renewed advances, his forehead dotted with nervous perspiration. "Now look here," he continued earnestly, "we went through all this business last night. I've been thanked enough. Let's have no more of it—"

"Ah, but it was you, Señor Dilliard, who save with your six-shootaire my so beautiful Antonio. Nevair can we thank you enough."

Again the girl made a rush toward Branch. Branch held her off with one hand, fighting to make himself heard through the torrent of words issuing from Teresa and Tony.

Tony was grinning broadly now. "This, my Teresa, her kisses knock you—what they say?—flat. No?" proudly. "That ees eet! Flat like the carpet from the floor!"

Branch chuckled. "You get the general idea, Tony. Yes, flat. Like a *tortilla.* But no more, please."

"That ees eet," enviously from Tony. "Flat like the *tortilla*! What fine comman' the *Americano* language has of you—"

"*Tortilla*?" Teresa blinked, then beamed, fell into Spanish again: "But, of course, you have come to eat with us." Spinning swiftly, the girl rushed into the house. There ensued immediately a great clatter of dishes.

Branch followed Tony into a neat, white-walled room with a hard-beaten earth floor. Luckily, there were three straight-backed wooden chairs, a board table. In one corner a mesquite wood fire burned in a small fireplace; blackened pots bubbled and steamed. Across the room was a cot on which were neatly folded blankets. A brightly colored *chimayo* adorned the back wall and, below it, a wooden stool held a bucket of water. A small cabinet in another corner displayed a tiny statue of the Virgin Mary, a crucifix and some bright bits of ribbon.

The meal was already prepared. There were *frijoles*, *enchiladas*, *tortillas*, a huge platter of *farsanta*; a bowl of small, pickled peppers brought tears to Dilliard's eyes as he reached hastily, frantically, for a cup of water to soothe his tongue. Tony roared with laughter, while Teresa giggled at the *Americano*'s inability to cope with the fiery peppers. The food was tasty, highly-flavored, appetizing. It came out, during the meal, when Teresa produced a bottle of *vino*, that the dinner had been arranged in Dilliard's honor.

"An' then," Tony explained, "when we look for you to make the invite, you are not to be foun'."

"Sure lucky I showed up then," Branch grinned through a mouthful of food. "Whew! If I eat any more, I'll be bogged down like a snow-bound cow critter."

"Bugged down? What is thees?" Tony looked questioningly to Teresa, then at the cot and blankets across the room.

Teresa frowned, then flushed hotly. "You see one?" she demanded of Dilliard, dark eyes moving rapidly from bed to table. "Always I keep the clean house. I—"

"You don't understand," Dilliard laughed. He

put the words into Spanish, laughter broke out, Teresa looked relieved.

Eventually, the meal reached a conclusion. Dilliard loosened his belt with a contented groan and got down to the reason for his visit, asking, "Tony, do you know anyone named Castameto? He was spoken of as 'old Castameto.' "

Tony's mouth dropped open, his eyes widened. He and Teresa exchanged quick glances. Tony nodded, gulped. "It mus' be," he admitted miserably. "How shall I face him, Teresa! We should have returned long since."

"Have I not always insisted that was the correct way?" Teresa said quietly.

"That you have," Tony conceded. "You see—" turning again to Dilliard and breaking into his distinctive style of Americanese, "—eet ees the lashing of the tongue wheech the *patrón* would geeve me. The return I have pos'pone of so many times, now I do not—"

"Hey," Dilliard broke in, "what are you talking about? I asked if you had ever heard of a man named Castameto, and you start talking in circles. What's it all about?"

"The Señor Don Castameto, he is here, in Santa Lozana?" Tony asked cautiously.

Dilliard shook his head. "Not that I know of. In fact, I don't think he is. I only heard his name mentioned."

"Ah, that ees different." Tony brightened, deftly

twisted a brown cigarette and settled back in his chair. Teresa hitched her chair closer, struck a match for him. Tony drew two meditative puffs into his lungs, exhaled. "Eet mus' be the same," he said finally. "Don Salvadore Castameto. It mus' be."

"But do you know him?" Dilliard persisted patiently.

"Know him? Hah! Do I know him? One time I hav' ride for heem—what you call?—work hees cows. Señor Branch, you mus' understand, een thees country I am one gran' *vaquero*. I am, those days, what you call the cattle-boy. For t'ree-four years I work the cattle of the Rancho Sicamoro—"

"That's it," Dilliard said, "the Rancho Sicamoro. I heard it mentioned. Big spread, isn't it?"

"Beeg?" Tony laughed. "Beeg is no name. Not even Don Salvadore knows 'ow beeg. Maybee one hondred t'ousand acre—maybee one hondred feefty t'ousand. What difference eet makes? Feefty t'ousand, hondred feefty t'ousand. All the same, here in California. Nobody pay any attention. There ees land for everyone, and there are no fences like I hav' hear is the custom in your Texas country."

Dilliard winced. Fencing was a sore subject with cattlemen in those early days. "Yeah, they're gettin' so they fence some," he said reluctantly. "But what about this big spread of Castameto's?"

"As I am telling, I was once the *patrón*'s bes' *vaquero*. No one was my equal in the ropeeng, the rideeng, the tyeeng—"

Dilliard laughed at the young Mexican's enthusiasm. "You got plenty proof of that, I suppose?"

"Proof? What is thees proof? I do not need proof! I admeet all I say is truth."

"You're modest," Dilliard chuckled. "How come you left the Rancho Sicamoro flat on its back thataway?"

"Flat on hees back? Oh, you mean, all upset. I understand. You mean I would be missed."

"Somethin' like that."

"Of that is a certainty. You see, Señor Branch, eet was this way, I meet trouble."

"Trouble on the Rancho Sicamoro, eh?"

Tony nodded, his face fell. "Eet was like thees. I'm tie my rope around a man's shirt an' drag it over the earth. The shirt ees get very dirty and torn. Don Salvadore is ver' angry. He spiks to me like a father—a ver' angry father. Een those days I am so hot of the head, I'm lose my temper. I peeck up my saddle, and without saying the *adiós* I make my depart."

"Hmmm," Dilliard considered. "Seems like a lot to make a fuss over. Castameto must have thought a heap of his shirt."

"Eet was not the *patrón*'s shirt. Eet belong to a man name' Beeljones."

"I suppose then," Dilliard puzzled, "this Bill Jones was a friend of Castameto's."

Tony shook his head. "Don Salvadore had never before laid the eyes on the man. But he became ver' angry when he saw the blood on the torn shirt and thees gringo—excuse, Señor Branch—thees Beeljones layeeng so white and quiet—"

"Blood on the shirt?" Dilliard interrupted, frowning.

"*Seguro!*" Teresa put in. "You understan' when Tony is dragging that shirt at the end of hees rope, while he rides ver' fast over the rough ground, thees Beeljones is inside of the shirt!"

Dilliard stared, then burst into sudden uncontrolled laughter. "So that was it," he said finally, "you dragged Bill Jones at the end of your rope."

"Eet ees no matter for laughing," Tony said aggrievedly. "Thees Beeljones, I catch him stealing one of the *patrón*'s horses. Like I say, I am hot of the temper. I theenk I teach heem a lesson when I drop my rope around hees shirt and drag him over the groun'. I teach heem lesson, all right. He nearly die. The *patrón* was ver' angry, saying I should have let Beeljones have the horse in a country that has so many. But the feelings of me are injure'. When eet is certain that Beeljones weel make the recover, I'm leave right now, *pronto*, at once."

"In other words," Dilliard grinned, "you got out."

"*Sí*, that is correc'. I come to Santa Lozana. I see Teresa. I'm theenk I am stay here—at leas' for long time. I'm think I ain't nevair go back to the Rancho Sicamoro." Tony beamed proudly on Teresa, passed one arm about the girl's shoulders. "You ain't blame me—no? My Teresa eet ees who ees learn me to spik the so-good *Americano* language. I'm think I could not do without my Teresa."

Teresa blushed. Followed swift whisperings between the pair that heightened her color and Dilliard's embarrassment.

Dilliard said, "Say, if you don't mind, cut out the turtle-doving and tell me about Don Salvadore, will you?"

The pair separated reluctantly. Tony said, "Ah, the *patrón*. I'm wish sometimes I hav' nevair leave heem. I tell you, Señor Branch, nevair have so good an hombre draw hees breath. Hees heart ees as beeg as hees *rancho*—"

"An' it is time," Teresa said, "that Tony should return to the *patrón*'s house. Plenty of trouble have come to him. It is to be regret that nozzing can be done."

"And I reckon," Dilliard said, "he's got more trouble due. Unless," grimly, "I take a hand."

"What is this?" Tony asked quickly.

"Castameto has a daughter, hasn't he?"

Tony nodded vigorously. "I remember her before she goes to the East—to your Boston. Ah," enthusiastically, "she was beautiful! Almos'—" hastily, "—almos' so beautiful as my Teresa. Is it not so, Teresa *mia*? You hav' seen her once."

Teresa augmented Tony's information. "It is true like you say, Antonio. The Señorita Castameto is like—like—" English wasn't sufficient; Spanish was resorted to: "She is like a silver flame in the dusk."

"Or a pale yellow rose of Monterey," Tony said softly.

Branch nodded slowly. "She's all of that."

"What?" from Tony. "Where have you seen the *señorita*?"

"Here—in Santa Lozana. She arrived by carriage from San Pedro, late last night—early this mornin', rather. Tomorrow morning, shortly after dawn, when she has rested, the journey to the Rancho Sicamoro will be resumed."

"And thus she could join her *padre* by tomorrow night—" Teresa commenced.

Tony broke in quickly, "How is it you know all this, Señor Branch?"

"I overheard some talk in the Cantina of the Golden Cock a spell before I came here—"

Teresa's disgusted sniff interrupted, "Bah! Small wonder we could not find you when we searched. To think of you entering that den of vileness. Do you not know the Cantina of the Golden Cock is fit only for pigs and dogs? Murder and gambling takes place—"

"That joint is all that you, say," Dilliard agreed. He didn't add that he had gone to the Cantina of the Golden Cock to escape the thanks of Tony and Teresa, knowing they would never dream of looking into the place for him. "No matter, I just wandered inside. I heard two men talking. They'd been drinking and didn't have enough sense to keep their voices down. I heard certain plans being made. Tony, do you know two hombres in this town named Bisbee and Corill?"

Tony swore in Spanish and nodded vigorously. "This Bisbee is a bull of a man with red whiskers? *Sí*, Wirt Bisbee. And Clem Corill, a small black snake with poisonous eyes?"

"You called the turn, Tony."

"*Sí*, I know them. *Hombres muy malo*! Ver' bad! Corill is of the worst. In the town of El Vaca he killed a man, but there is no justice in El Vaca while Drake Scabbard is in control. Both men worked for Scabbard at one time. A week ago they arrived in Santa Lozana—"

"Drake Scabbard? Seems like I heard his name too," Dilliard frowned. "Is he here? What about him?"

"Scabbard rarely rides out of El Vaca. If he is here I have not seen him. Of all black-hearted men he is the blackest. It is Scabbard who would ruin Don Salvadore Castameto." Tony's eyes flashed angrily. "Ah, I would like the chance to t'row a rope aroun' Drake Scabbard's shirt."

"Tony," Teresa said, "the Señor Branch was telling us something."

Dilliard went on, "I was telling you I heard Bisbee and Corill talking in the *cantina.* They got pretty careless in their *habla* and I heard a good deal more than was intended for an outsider's ears. But here's the bad news: there's a plot afoot to kidnap the Señorita Castameto."

Tony blinked. "Kidnap? What is this kidnap? Nap? Sleep—no? The *señorita* is no longer what you call the kid, but what is this scheme to make her to sleep?"

Dilliard explained in Spanish. Tony and Teresa gained their feet, gesticulating angrily. Teresa spouted indignant Spanish, intersprinkled with mouth-filling words of American profanity of whose meaning she was completely ignorant.

"*Por Dios*!" from Teresa. "It must be stopped!"

Tony gulped, "*Madre de Dios*! *Madre de Dios*!" Dilliard finally succeeded in calming the pair and bringing them back to a sober realization of the necessity of sane thinking. Tony cooled down after a time, offered Dilliard a *cigarro*, lighted its companion for himself. Dilliard's teeth clamped down on the cylinder of tobacco. Silence fell on the room, fragrant smoke weaving graceful patterns above the dish-cluttered table. Tony broke the silence first.

"What is to be done? I think I shall ride to warn the *patrón*."

"We lack time for that," Dilliard said. "There's a deputy-sheriff some place in Santa Lozana."

Tony swore softly.

"No good, eh?" from Dilliard.

"No good at all. Cowardly, a cheat, a robber, a bully."

Further silence between the three. The *cigarro* was half consumed before Branch Dilliard reached a decision: "Well, I reckon it's up to me. Now, I got to figure out how to do it."

Tony's eyes widened. "What? You would the rescue attemp'? You—yourself?"

"I don't see any other way."

Tony sighed, looked longingly at Teresa, shrugged hopeless shoulders. "Then," he announced dramatically, "you mus' count on my body also. But we shall be kill'. That is certain! Already, Señor Branch, you hav' make the enemies in Santa Lozana. When you save my so worthless skin, las' night, you made into danger the hide of yourself. Those men had frien's. Two of those frien's are Bisbee and Corill."

"It is gossiped about the plaza," Teresa spoke slowly in Spanish, "that by his actions last night, the Señor Branch has made himself a renegade from his own people, that he aided a Mexican against *Americanos*. There has even been talk of a reprisal. The talk smolders hotly, only that, but a move in defiance of Corill and Bisbee will be sure to fan into life the fierce flames of revenge."

Dilliard scowled impatiently. "I heard somethin' of that talk, myself, this mornin'. That renegade talk doesn't bother me. I'm not worryin'. All I'm thinkin' about right now is the Señorita Castameto—and the job ahead. We've got to make plans, and make 'em fast!"

3
DRAKE SCABBARD

The sun commenced to shift, throwing a broad patch of yellow light through the open doorway. None of the three talked to any extent for a time. Tobacco smoke drifted lazily through the window in the side wall to seek the outer air. Once Teresa departed and returned with a bottle of wine. The conversation gradually picked up; various plans were discussed, examined for flaws, discarded. The situation appeared more hopeless every minute.

The patch of sunlight on the floor, near the doorway, commenced to assume diagonal lines. The shadows in the street lengthened. Somewhere near the corrals a horse neighed shrilly and a dog started barking. While the three talked, the sun dropped below the low hills far to the west of Santa Lozana. An evening breeze stirred the air, bringing a chill touch from the coast lands.

Tony shrugged hopeless shoulders and fell silent. Dilliard's mind felt tired, worn. Teresa looked from man to man, before speaking a trifle timidly: "You can think of nothing?"

Dilliard slowly shook his head. "Nothing that might work with any degree of certainty, Teresa."

"Something will occur to us," Tony said doggedly. "The *buen Dios* will not allow us to fail."

"Look you—" again Teresa hesitated before continuing, "it may be I have thought of a plan that might succeed."

Tony looked hopeful, "My Teresa, she is ver' smart. I think we should give the heed—"

"By all means," from Branch. "Let's hear it."

Teresa commenced to speak, at first, slowly, then as she gathered courage, the words came swifter and swifter, as though she, herself, were already convinced her plan was the sure way to success in rescuing Castameto's daughter.

In silence, Dilliard and Tony heard her through to the end. As the girl talked, the frown lifted from Dilliard's features. He swore softly under his breath. Tony commenced to look anxious, but he kept his mouth closed. Finally the girl fell silent.

There was an odd, triumphant light in Dilliard's eyes now. "By gosh! Teresa, it might work at that—" He stopped suddenly, his face fell, he shook his head in abrupt decision. "Nope, nothing doing. I can't let you run that sort of risk."

"The Señor Branch is right, Teresa *mia*," from Tony. "Your idea is a courageous one, but—"

"Antonio! *Silencio*! Be quiet! It is for us to decide the best way—not the safest. Besides—" shrugging her slim, brown shoulders, "—where is the risk?" Teresa's white teeth flashed an encouraging smile. “Of danger, there will be none,” she insisted. “Antonio could follow behind and see all that takes place. It is you, Señor Branch, who will have the most danger—”

“I’m not worrying about my part,” Dilliard said anxiously. “It’s you and Tony—you and Tony will have to decide.”

Teresa turned on Tony. The two talked excitedly for several moments, crackling Spanish passing between them. Now and then Dilliard put in a word or two. Tony’s protestations became more and more feeble as the girl’s voice became stronger.

Finally, Tony turned to Dilliard, shrugging his shoulders, throwing his arms wide in a gesture of surrender. “I geeve up! Señor Branch, you see before you the example of the so beautiful woman making the defeat to the *inteligencia* of the male animal of the breed. Of the certain we shall all be kill’—”

“Tony, hush!” from Teresa. She turned to Dilliard. “It is settled then?”

Dilliard nodded slowly. “It’s all right with me, if Tony is satisfied.”

“I am satisfy’,” Tony conceded.

Teresa rose to light a candle placed in a bottle. It was dark outside now.

“Just a minute, Teresa,” Dilliard said. “Don’t light up yet. Maybe it will be better if nobody looks in here and sees me talkin’ to you two. If any of your neighbors should spot us, and then see us tomorrow—"

Teresa nodded. "Perhaps it is better to leave the room dark. But for the neighbors, have no fear. They know you to be our friend. Tomorrow morning, not one of them will be about to see anything. Should any of the *Americanos* come asking questions, our neighbors will have seen nothing. That part, Tony and I shall take care of, after you depart. But a little light we must have."

The girl threw some mesquite knots on the embers in the fireplace. Dancing flames flickered against the white walls. Teresa regained her chair. The three talked earnestly for some time. Teresa brought out some cold beef and brewed coffee at the fireplace. An hour passed.

Finally, Dilliard rose to his feet. "Well, it's all settled then." His tone held grim decision. "My horse is in the stable, at the rear of the hotel. You'll have another horse all ready, eh, Tony?"

"*Sí*, *sí*, Señor Branch. All shall be in readiness."

Dilliard turned to the girl, putting on his hat and saying, "Teresa, I won't be forgetting this. You're white—white all through."

"It is nothing, Señor Branch. For my Antonio, you have already done much more."

"That's open to argument," Branch told her, "but we won't talk about it right now." He turned back to Tony. Gold coins clinked between them. "I'll pro'bly need another six-shooter. Buy yourself a gun too. No, you won't be able to get a ca'tridge gun, like I'm totin', in Santa Lozana, but I reckon I haven't forgotten how to handle a cap-and-ball. I haven't any too many ca'tridges left, anyhow. I'd hate to run short of loads."

"Tomorrow morning, then," Tony's voice came through the flickering lights in the room.

"Tomorrow morning," Dilliard replied, and added, "*Adiós*."

"*Adiós*," Tony answered.

Teresa's soft voice came from just over Tony's shoulder, "*Vaya con Dios*."

Dilliard returned slowly to the plaza. A few Mexicans still held down the benches, huddled in their serapes. Rectangles of light glowed from the adobe buildings surrounding the square, and scattered about the plaza, beneath flaming torches, chili and tamale vendors dispensed their wares to high-sombreroed Mexicans. Smoke and a pungent odor of burning wood floated on the chill night air. Voices in various tongues drifted softly through the gloom to be broken now and then by the raucous tones of boisterous *Americanos*.

Dilliard slowly circled the plaza, lost in thought. Prompted by some sudden impulse, he directed his steps toward the Cantina of the Golden Cock and stepped inside. Loud voices assailed his ears. The small barroom was packed with the scum of Santa Lozana. The odor of stale liquor, tobacco, and unwashed bodies made Dilliard's nostrils quiver.

Smoke floated like a heavy pall, almost obscuring the low ceiling. The floor was thick with cigar and cigarette butts and dust. The place was dimly lighted with three kerosene oil lamps suspended on rusty brackets about the walls. In one corner a Mexican plucked listlessly at a guitar, his notes being drowned in the din made by the *cantina*'s customers. Opposite the bar, at a table, a group of Mexicans waxed noisy over their dicing. At a second table five *Americanos* of hang-dog aspect quarreled, in whining tones, regarding the merits of various poker hands.

The bar was lined with men. Near the front door, Dilliard spied the two men known as Bisbee and Corill. Bisbee was bulky-shouldered, the lower half of his face covered with matted red whiskers. Corill was slim, swarthy, with beady, shifting eyes. Both wore boots, sombreros and the rough clothing customary to the country. Dilliard noted the cap-and-ball six-shooters swung at their belts, and wondered, idly, just how proficient the two were in the use of such weapons. After a moment he decided that, despite the loud, swaggering manner of Wirt Bisbee, Clem Corill was the more dangerous man of the two, the one to whom, on the morrow, if worst came to worst, should be devoted the closest attention.

The pair were deep in conversation with a

stranger who stood between them at the bar. Dilliard slowed his pace to look the stranger over. He heard Bisbee call him "Mister Scabbard," and decided this must be the Drake Scabbard mentioned by Tony as being the boss of a town named El Vaca.

Scabbard was clothed in the style of the day affected by the more well-to-do Californians—a long, square-cut coat, tightly fitting trousers that narrowed at the ankles of his boots, high-cut vest and the whitest of linen. Dilliard put his age at somewhere between thirty-five and forty. On one of Scabbard's hands, holding a long, slim, black cigar, gleamed a diamond ring.

Dilliard pushed up to the bar, next to Corill. After a moment a round, greasy-faced *mestizo* took his order for a drink. Dilliard tasted the fiery rotgut that served as whisky, set his glass down unfinished. No one paid him any attention. A few vagrant words from Scabbard caught Dilliard's ears, then Bisbee's reply.

"I tell you, Mister Scabbard, there won't be any slip-up. You just leave matters to me and Clem. . . . What? . . ." Then a short laugh, "Now, don't you worry about what happened to them two that met her. We already took care of them, tonight, 'bout half an hour before you got here. . . . Shucks, no! You needn't to have made that long ride. Just you trust us. . . ."

Scabbard interrupted in sharp tones. Bisbee

lowered his voice. Corill glanced cautiously around, started to turn back, and his gaze fell on Dilliard standing unconcernedly at his shoulder. Abruptly, Corill left the bar and passed behind Scabbard's back to say something to Bisbee.

Dilliard heard Bisbee rip out a smothered curse. The two talked steadily to Scabbard for several moments, their voices too low to carry to Dilliard's ears. Then they departed abruptly with quick good-byes to Drake Scabbard, leaving Scabbard at the bar a scant couple of feet from Dilliard, who was, apparently, lost in his own abstractions and unaware of anyone around him.

Dilliard heard Corill and Bisbee at the doorway. Their steps died away. A customer started to step in between Dilliard and Scabbard. Scabbard elbowed the man out of the way and closed the distance between himself and Dilliard.

"Stranger in Santa Lozana, aren't you?"

Dilliard looked up to find Scabbard surveying him with cool, appraising eyes, eyes that to Dilliard didn't seem quite natural. They were pale blue, hard, glassy in the feeble light cast by the lamp behind the bar.

Dilliard nodded. "I reckon."

"I thought you were. I hadn't seen you in town before."

Dilliard asked, "You live in Santa Lozana?"

Scabbard shook his long, narrow head. His features were abnormally pale, the skin stretched tightly over the high cheek-bones. Beneath his highly-arched nose, a thin black mustache drooped below either corner of a thin-lipped mouth.

"No," Scabbard was saying, "but I come to Santa Lozana quite frequently. I make my home in El Vaca—southeast of here, a half day's ride—if you push hard . . . Have a drink?"

Dilliard refused, gesturing to the nearly-full glass standing on the bar before him.

Scabbard laughed softly. "I don't blame you. This dive is pretty low. The liquor is poor. It just happened that I had to come in here tonight, looking for a couple of men who work for me on occasion. You probably heard me talking to them."

"Can't say I paid any particular attention," Dilliard said easily. He wasn't sure, but he thought a wave of relief flitted across Scabbard's white features at the reply.

Scabbard said, "I may have a little deal on—cattle. Perhaps sheep as well. I'm not certain it will go through, but I refuse to stay in Santa Lozana until it does. I'd rather make the ride again than stay at that measly hotel."

"I find it tol'able," Dilliard said.

"*You* might." There was a faint sneer in Scabbard's tones. "Cow man, aren't you?"

"When I work at it."

"Bring a herd through to California?"

"Not this time," Dilliard replied. "I delivered

a herd at San Diego three years ago, then went back. At present cattle prices in this country, there isn't much profit in trailing a herd here. By the time you figure certain natural losses on the trail, then fork over to the soldiers at Yuma four-bits each for wagons and ten cents a head for cows to rope-ferry you across the Colorado—well, like I say, the way stock prices are at present, it don't pay enough to make it worthwhile."

"You could swim your cows across the river."

Dilliard laughed. "Yes, if the river wasn't high. I swam some across and lost them. After that, I paid my ten cents a head, like any sensible man would do."

"I suppose," Scabbard nodded. "What part of the country you hail from?"

"Texas."

"What brings you to California this time?"

Dilliard stiffened a little, then said easily, "I'm just ramblin' around."

"Do you expect to stay?"

"I haven't made up my mind."

"Like California?" Scabbard persisted. Dilliard shrugged.

"What have you got against us?"

Dilliard smiled, faced Scabbard squarely. "I ain't so sure I like the people."

Scabbard nodded. "Yes, the country is overrun with greasers."

"I wasn't referrin' to *greasers*. It's what you

call the *Americanos* here. I never saw such an inquisitive bunch. Everywhere you go, it's the same. They're never satisfied until they've turned you inside out. 'Where do you come from? What are you doing here? How much money have you got? What's your business?' Back home, folks take you at face value and mind their own business."

Scabbard's white features flushed faintly. Dilliard's thrust had penetrated in no uncertain manner. Scabbard forced a short laugh. "You've got to admit I didn't inquire as to the state of your finances," he pointed out. "Grant me that much anyway. . . . But California's a great country—cattle, sheep, land. Too many greasers, of course, but we'll run them out in time."

"I suppose so," Dilliard said shortly.

"Look here, there's no use our quarreling about something that doesn't matter. I'd like to call you friend. I'm Drake Scabbard. Guess I neglected to give you my name before." He stuck out one hand, but Dilliard, engrossed in rolling a cigarette, affected not to see it.

"Name's Dilliard," Branch said noncommittally.

Scabbard drew deeply on his black cigar, held it for Dilliard to get a light, then said, "Dilliard, eh? You must be the man I heard about."

"Hope it was somethin' good?" Dilliard's eyes were steady on Scabbard's.

"We-ell," cautiously, "that depends on how you look at it."

"What did you hear?"

"About that little ruckus you staged, last evening, in that *cantina* across the plaza. They tell me you shot up some white men in taking the part of a greaser—"

"Who told you?"

"Why, I just don't know. I guess it might have been those men I was talking to when you came in here."

"I reckon they spoke the truth. I sort of hated to see four tinhorns ganging up on a defenseless Mex."

"You're too sensitive," Scabbard laughed. "The sooner the greasers learn that this country was intended for white men, the better it will be all around."

"Y'know," Dilliard drawled, "I always figured the Spanish were white."

"Depends how you look at it. Not the Mexicans—"

"I figure they're Americans if they were born here."

Scabbard commenced an impatient exclamation, checked himself, and ordered two drinks from the bartender. Men talked noisily all around Dilliard and his companion. The drinks were set out. Dilliard made no move to accept his glass. Scabbard downed his liquor quickly, made a wry face. Drawing a white linen handkerchief from his pocket he wiped his thin lips, saying, "Well, if you won't drink, I won't hold it against you. Don't blame you in fact. It's poor stuff. Come to El Vaca and I promise a different brand of mouthwash. But I do want to give you a piece of advice I hope you won't resent."

"Hop to it," Dilliard invited.

"Look here, Dilliard, you're new to this country. California isn't Texas. Conditions, customs, are vastly different. But it's just this. I hate to see you starting off on the wrong foot. You can't buck white men with Mexicans and get away with it. You'll be run out." Then Scabbard added, "If not killed."

Dilliard laughed easily. "Yeah, I saw it tried, once—last night."

"You were lucky. Next time you may not come off so well. If you stay, you'll have to conform. It's a rich country, as I said. A man can follow any line—cattle, sheep, minerals, land, farming. I'm interested in all of 'em. I'm getting rich. You could, too. You look brainy—"

"Thanks," ironically.

"I mean it. I want to see you started right. I'd do the same for any white man I took a liking to. You know cattle. I understand you handle your gun well. I can use you."

"For my cattle—or gun—knowledge?" Dilliard asked quietly.

"Maybe both. Look here, I'll be frank with you. The greasers must go. They're dirty, they'll steal you blind, they're lazy—"

"No American push and go, I suppose."

Scabbard missed the sarcasm. "You've hit it!" he exclaimed. "Now, you come to El Vaca. I'll give you a job—"

"I might get to El Vaca one of these days," Dilliard said, "but I wouldn't promise to take a job with you."

"I'd put you in the way of getting rich. I can use a man of your ability. But you've got to give up this idea that a greaser is as good as a white man—"

"Got to?" Dilliard's eyes narrowed dangerously.

Scabbard hesitated, then, bluntly, "That's the long and short of it, Dilliard. You'll have to come to your senses, if you stay in this country."

Dilliard laughed scornfully. "Scabbard, no man yet has dictated how I'll think or how I won't think. I'm too old now to change my habits, and even if I wasn't—*you're not the man to give me orders.* Get that just as straight as you know how."

Crimson spots of angry color appeared on Scabbard's high cheek-bones. He swallowed heavily but managed to hold his voice nearly normal: "I see I've made a mistake. I withdraw my offer." Now his voice was low, venomous: "I can't advise you to come to El Vaca. In fact, I'd advise you to stay just as far away from my town as the devil will let you. Is that clear?"

"It's clear you're making threats," Dilliard said grimly.

"Take that as you like. I'm telling you. You're not due to last long in this country, Dilliard. You'd better get out."

Dilliard smiled contemptuously. What he said next he had a certain purpose in saying, "Scabbard, I'm planning to leave tomorrow, but you and your kind aren't scaring me out. I ain't never yet been snake-shy. But you mark my words, it's you and men like you that are due to get out—and aces to tens you'll go out feet first!"

Cold flames of rage glittered in Scabbard's eyes. He made a quick motion toward his right coat pocket, then checked the movement.

Dilliard laughed coolly. "Derringer, eh?"

Scabbard held his right hand well wide of his pocket and commenced to edge away from the bar. His words came through grated teeth, "Dilliard, it's a good thing you're leaving, or you'd have a score to settle with me. I'd settle right now, except that I've got to start back to El Vaca tonight. If you ever cross my path again, watch yourself. You'll—"

Dilliard said, "Oh, hell!" and pushed contemptuously past Scabbard. At the doorway of the *cantina* he paused, glanced back over one shoulder. Scabbard stood as before, white features contorted with angry passion. Dilliard laughed and stepped outside.

Two doors away, Dilliard stopped and sat down on an unoccupied bench. Two minutes later, he saw Scabbard leave the *cantina*, mount a waiting horse that stood in front of the building, and take a southeasterly course across the plaza, riding hard, to disappear in one of the streets that led from the square.

"So much for Scabbard," Dilliard laughed softly. "So he's got to get started for El Vaca tonight. He might have spoken the truth at that. Scabbard wouldn't want to be around here tomorrow morning, now that things are settled with Corill and Bisbee. I wonder where *those* two snakes disappeared to."

The plaza was nearly deserted now. Dilliard got to his feet, started across to see to his horse in the shelter back of the hotel, before turning in. Halfway across the square, he halted and glanced toward a certain window in the building. The shutters were closed but a thin sliver of yellow light penetrated between the boards.

The words of his Mexican friends recurred to Dilliard now; he thought, " 'A pale yellow rose of Monterey; a silver flame in the dusk.' Castameto's daughter is all of that. I reckon the English language can't compare with Spanish when it comes to expressing a man's feelings."

A moment later he continued on the way, murmuring, “Well, tomorrow tells the tale.”

He glanced at the sky and found it overcast with dark clouds. There was something chill, ominous, in the breeze that swept in from the far-off seacoast.

4
A WILDCAT FOR FIGHTIN'

Rain had come during the night, one of those hard, drumming rains that seep deeply into the sun-baked earth, like the warm glow of old wine spreading through a man's body; the sort of rain that brings life to the Southern California hills and swells to the bursting point the myriad buds of lupine and orange poppy.

With the coming of dawn the rain had ceased, though the filigreed branches of the red-berried pepper tree in the plaza were still heavy with silvery drops. Above the Santa Ana Mountains, to the east of Santa Lozana, the cloudless sky was touched with amethyst, the flush spreading swiftly like a bit of water color from an artist's brush touching an already dampened square of paper. The horizon brightened as broad streaks of orange-crimson lifted above the mountain peaks; soon the sky was a-glow with bright, warm tints, giving promise of the heat to come.

The first rays of the sun slipped quickly down into Santa Lozana, picking out green highlights on a huge, spear-pointed *agave* at one corner of the plaza and throwing into bold relief the puddles of water basined in yesterday's dusty square. Smoke curled in graceful spirals from the chimney openings of adobe houses; the fragrance of flaming mesquite was in the air.

Life was moving about the square now. A Mexican appeared in his doorway, glanced at the sky, scratched his thick thatch of blue-black hair, yawned and turned back, drawn by the aroma of hot coffee. Other figures, serape-shouldered, moved out into the footpath. A hen with a brood of small chickens picked futilely at the clinging adobe mud, until she and her tiny charges were frightened into a panicky rout by the mischievous whoopings of a nearly-naked Mexican youngster.

Before the entrance of the Santa Lozana Hotel waited an open carriage with two horses. A small crowd had gathered; some sort of altercation was taking place.

The Señorita Castameto, heavily veiled and clothed in flowing, voluminous skirts of some soft dark material, was demanding details relative to the whereabouts of the two men who had driven the carriage to the hotel the previous day. The pair at present attending the vehicle—two slovenly-appearing half-breeds—were not her men, not her father's employees. Why were *they* not on hand to attend their duties? The Señorita Castameto swore they should be punished for their absence.

The two breeds on the driver's seat sat in stolid silence, staring straight ahead, leaving all explanatory details to a pair of *Americano* riders, one of whom wore a matted red beard; his companion was slim and dark and had shifty eyes.

The *posadero* of the hotel turned to the Señorita Castameto, still standing in the doorway of the building—why did she hesitate? The baggage was already piled on the front seat of the carriage. What difference who drove the vehicle, or who accompanied it?

The hotel man appeared nervous, while he strove to assure the girl that the Señors Bisbee and Corill were most reliable men.

The *señorita* ignored the innkeeper's words and again demanded some information about her own men. With ill-concealed impatience, Clem Corill reined his pony away from the side of Bisbee's horse and gave fuller explanation: the regular drivers had imbibed too freely of *tequila* the previous night and, deciding to leave the employment of the Rancho Sicamoro rather than rise so early in the morning, had turned the job over to himself and Wirt Bisbee. It was to be the duty of the two *Americanos* to see that the *señorita* arrived safely, by nightfall, in her father's arms. They had harnessed the horses to the carriage and procured these two men to drive it; it would be a pleasure for Corill and Bisbee to ride at the side of the vehicle and act as bodyguards.

But now Corill assumed an aggrieved manner: he wasn't at all sure, in light of the *señorita*'s protestations and objections, that he and his pardner wanted the job. Where so much doubt existed, pay for the work might not be forthcoming. The *señorita* had better make up her mind.

The girl's every movement betrayed indecision. She eyed Corill and Bisbee dubiously, flung her hands scornfully toward the pair on the driver's seat. Her words were short, brief, vitriolic. The hotelkeeper's voice rose in argument. The *señorita* spoke quick replies in imperious Spanish. The man appeared to dwindle before the heat of her manner. He fell silent, looking to Bisbee and Corill to do any further persuading that might be necessary. By this time the knot of curious about the carriage had been augmented, the sounds of the altercation drawing the idle ones from all directions.

Impatiently, the girl abruptly decided to get into the carriage. Between the hotel entrance and the vehicle was a wide pool of rainwater. Immediately humble and anxious to please, the hotelkeeper stepped around the corner of the hotel, bawling loud orders. After five minutes had passed, two Mexicans appeared from the rear of the building, bearing planks to bridge the puddle.

On the same side of the square, at the corner

where it opened into a side street, Branch Dilliard watched the scene from the back of his horse. He saw Bisbee and Corill back their ponies to let the men with the planks accomplish their purpose.

"Dammit!" Dilliard muttered under his breath. "She's decided to go with those cutthroats, after all. I was hopin' she'd refuse." An afterthought crept in. "Or was I?"

Before dawn he had seen Tony and Teresa, gone over their plans a final time. No one noticed Dilliard quietly sitting in his saddle. Other horsemen were moving about the plaza by this time. All eyes were fastened on the group before the hotel. The sun was climbing fast, well clear of the mountains now.

Dilliard saw the two hotel servants appear with the planks. Some time was lost in the placing of the impromptu bridge. One end of a plank fell, striking the puddle; muddy water spotted the side of the carriage. Suddenly, the Mexicans burst into loud lament; the planks were not long enough to reach across the pool. A third length of board would have to be procured.

The Señorita Castameto took a part in the discussion that followed, speaking swift, impatient Spanish, giving suggestions, pointing out that no further planks were necessary. After a few moments her ideas were placed into execution. The planks were again lifted, placed parallel to the wall of the hotel. Now, by utilizing the boards for her movements, the girl could reach a comparatively dry stretch of earth and, passing around the rear of the vehicle, enter the conveyance from the outer side.

The crowd fell back so as not to impede her progress. The girl passed around the back of the carriage. Dilliard got into action. Touching spurs to his pony, he moved forward at a swift trot, then gained speed.

A pair of Indians stood near the step of the carriage. The girl ordered them away. They moved slowly, reluctantly. The girl brushed past, started to place one foot on the step.

A wild, Texas yell left Branch Dilliard's throat as he charged straight for the onlookers clustered near the carriage. The crowd scattered swiftly. Near the rear of the carriage, Corill and Bisbee turned in their saddles, saw Dilliard. It didn't occur to them that the Texas cowman was taking part in their plans. They backed their ponies, to allow Dilliard free passage.

Corill said, "Bet a plugged *peso* he's drunk."

"Sure gets started early," Bisbee laughed.

Dilliard was closing in now. Suddenly he swerved, directing the pony still closer to the carriage. The *señorita* had hesitated at his wild yell and turned to watch. Coolly, she judged the intervening yards between herself and Branch Dilliard's thundering horse, figured he would just clear her in passing. Quickly she put one foot in the carriage, drew the other to the step.

Dilliard nodded approval of the girl's movement, even as he closed in. He caught a brief glimpse of startled faces. Excited cries rang 'round the plaza:

"The *Americano* is drunk!"

"The gringo from Texas has gone *demente*!"

"Look! He rides like a fiend out of hell!"

The latter, Señorita Castameto was quick to admit as she saw Dilliard rise in his stirrups. A startled cry welled in her throat: the crazy rider would crash into the carriage. The girl shrank back, bracing herself against the collision.

Of what happened next, she was never quite clear in her mind. There came a wild drumming of swift hoofs in her ears, then she felt Dilliard's right arm sweep around her waist, felt herself lifted bodily in the air. Wind rushed into her face as Dilliard drew the girl up before him, on the saddle. His pony hadn't even broken stride in the mad rush.

Then they were away, leaving behind a cursing Corill, a dumbfounded Bisbee and a large number of startled natives. Corill acted first, hand sweeping down to his six-shooter. Bisbee was quick to follow suit.

The vicious *pin-n-ng* of a leaden slug whined past Dilliard's right ear as his horse dashed across the square. Two more reports sounded simultaneously.

Dilliard shifted the girl's weight to his left arm. His right reached to his gun-butt. Knee-guiding his pony, he half-turned in the saddle and released three swift shots.

He heard a horse scream, caught the thud of its splashing as it went down in the mud. The plaza was a torrent of voices now. Other shots flew high over Dilliard's head, as Corill urged various bystanders to take a hand in stopping the Texan. A fat man wearing a deputy-sheriff's badge waddled out of a *cantina*, jerking his gun and firing widely.

Dilliard didn't shoot again; he was moving too fast for accurate marksmanship. Straight for the opposite corner of the plaza he rode. Passing the giant, spear-pointed century plant, he noted a hole appear as though by magic in one of the broad green leaves. Almost instantly the report reached his ears.

"Gettin' too close for comfort," he chuckled grimly, driving in his spurs.

The girl's veil had blown to one side. Dilliard met her eyes for just an instant, flushed, and lowered his gaze at the scorn that burned into him.

"I'll tell it all—later," Dilliard protested. "No time for explanations now. There's nothing for you to be afraid of—"

"Gringo pig!" the girl flashed out.

Dilliard snapped, "Have it your own way. No time for arguing now."

He swung the pony swiftly to one side as they left the plaza and darted down a side street. The girl's form was warm in his arms, as he moved with the motion of the speeding horse. Back of them an excited hue and cry rose on the air.

The *señorita* was struggling to get free now. Dilliard clutched her tighter than ever, fighting to pinion her arms. One hand wrenched loose from his grasp. Dilliard felt raw streaks of fire rip down his right cheek, noticed the fingernails of the girl's left hand were tinged with crimson.

This, in its way, was good. Dilliard could understand rage, conflict. Passive resistance had him stopped, crippled him. He grinned through the blood coursing four wide channels along his right jaw, seized and gripped tightly the belligerent hand.

"I'll bet you're a wildcat for fightin'," he muttered, rocking to the motion of the horse.

Something else came back to him in that mad rush through narrow streets, twisting, turning, doubling back to elude the pursuit he was certain was under way, something else that touched his grim mouth with humor . . . a silver flame in the dusk . . .

"Or silver daggers in hot sunlight," Dilliard amended silently.

The girl had ceased struggling now. From back on the plaza came faint yells calling confused advice. Horses were being procured and saddled to follow the first batch of pursuers.

Dilliard glanced at the girl in his arms, voiced a silent prayer that his plan might be successfully carried through. A moment later, turning into an empty street, the Texan spotted an anxious Tony awaiting his arrival. Dilliard brought the pony to a long sliding halt that jerked the beast to rear haunches, then stepped down from the saddle, holding the girl.

Tony forced a white smile. "I'm hear shooting—and men like they have gone *loco*. I'm guess you are lucky, like the four clovers—no?" He glanced at the *señorita*, then quickly averted his gaze, reluctant to meet the girl's scornful eyes.

Dilliard panted, "So far we've been lucky—yes. Get in that saddle, Tony. Let that horse have his head and he'll do things for you. Give those coyotes a run they won't forget."

Tony nodded, left hand clutching the bridle.

Dilliard turned swiftly to the girl, saying in Spanish, "Only a little farther to go now. Will you walk, or must I carry you? There's no time to argue the question. Make up your mind—quick!"

The reply came in chilling accents from behind the veil and in English—almost perfect English, "Don't touch me! Don't touch me again! I'll walk."

The street was momentarily deserted, only the two men, the girl and the horse being in sight between the crooked double row of adobe dwellings which appeared to be lifeless. Tony was in the saddle now, taking Dilliard's place. He spoke to the pony, got under way like a shot from a gun, turned at the first corner.

Dilliard looked after him but a moment. "Give 'em a run they won't forget, Tony," he repeated softly. He caught a fleeting glimpse of the rider as Tony directed the horse diagonally into an alley to drop from view.

Then Dilliard turned back to the girl. "This way," he directed, indicating a passageway between two houses. The way was choked with tall brush. Dilliard held the branches aside, impelled the girl before him, then followed. The brush closed behind them.

Dilliard halted, pulled the girl down in the shelter of the screening brush and waited. Running footsteps, pounding hoofs, sounded along the narrow street. A score of men flashed past, yelling madly. Bisbee and Corill led the way, Bisbee mounted on a different horse than the one he'd had in the plaza. Peering out, Dilliard saw the pursuers take a different route than that followed by Tony. He chuckled with satisfaction.

Dilliard had been holding one hand over the *señorita*'s mouth. Now he felt it torn savagely away. He wasn't looking at the girl but he felt her concentrated hate boring into him.

"Sorry you feel thataway," the Texan muttered

humbly. Then, shortly, "C'mon, we haven't any time to waste."

They negotiated the passage between the houses, emerged near the corrals in the *Calle de los Caballeros*. From this point it was only a few steps further to the house of Tony and Teresa. Teresa was standing in the doorway, anxious-eyed, when Dilliard and the girl arrived. There was no other sign of humanity along the winding street.

Teresa's voice trembled: "It hav' work, eh, Señor Branch—?" she commenced.

"Part of it, anyway." Dilliard was breathing heavily. He glanced at the *señorita*, decided that this was no time for argument. "Inside," he ordered briefly, jerking his head toward the doorway.

Teresa stood back. The Señorita Castameto hesitated, then entered, her head held high. The Texan was right on her heels, closing the door as he moved in.

Teresa was silent. Now came the difficult part of the plan. The *señorita*'s head raised defiantly as she faced the man and Mexican girl. Dilliard hesitated, his mind fumbling for a beginning. Abruptly, he discarded his groping for proper phrasing and came to the matter at hand.

"You'll change clothes with this girl," he ordered.

That precipitated a storm of protest. The

Texan wasn't surprised at the *señorita*'s refusal; that was to be expected. What he hadn't anticipated was the sudden torrent of fiery Spanish that greeted his proposal. Dilliard felt the hot blood creeping up his features. Teresa shrank back, her own round face mantled with a blush of shame.

"It is not so, Señorita Castameto," Teresa commenced. "When you understand you will—"

Dilliard cut in, speaking impatiently, "We haven't time for explanations, Teresa. We're wasting precious moments now. This girl will just have to take our word for things—" Abruptly, he broke off, turned to the *señorita*: "It's necessary that you change clothes with Teresa. You won't be hurt. We're doing this to help you. Please hurry—"

"No! I refuse, gringo pig!"

Teresa's pleadings were ignored. Dilliard swore under his breath. Precious minutes were fleeting past. The *señorita* remained adamant, defiant. Her refusals assumed a knife-like edge that cut and jeered at Dilliard's orders.

Abruptly, the Texan spoke in harsher tones than he'd employed before: "All right, *señorita*, you've had your chance. We can't waste more time. You'll either do as I say, or I'll take a hand and make you do it," he said brutally. "It's up to you. Make up your mind without further nonsense—and make it up *plenty pronto*!"

5

A GRINGO JOKE

A tense silence suddenly descended on the room as the Texan snapped his words. Castameto's daughter halted the fiery tirade tumbling from her lips and searched Dilliard's face. She saw tiny drops of perspiration dotting his forehead, but there wasn't a trace of pity, surrender, in his hard features. A quick glance at Teresa told the *señorita* she could expect no aid from that direction. No doubt about it, this *Americano* savage wasn't to be trifled with. It might be best to obey him.

Briefly, the *señorita* nodded agreement with the instructions. A long sigh of relief blew softly from the Texan's lips. Mentally he thanked his gods that his bluff had worked.

"You'll do it—without further trouble?" he insisted.

"I'll do it." The *señorita* motioned to the doorway. "Get out!" coldly.

Dilliard hesitated, gestured toward Teresa. "You promise not to make trouble for this Mexican girl, after I step out?"

"I shall do as you say," haughtily. "Just keep your dirty hands from me. When my father receives word of this outrage—"

“When your father hears of this *outrage,*” the Texan half-snarled, “he ought to get down on his knees and thank Teresa for the risk she is running. So far, you’ve acted the part of a little fool. Now try to help us by hurrying.”

Dilliard swung around, started for the door. Teresa suddenly found a new problem, “Wait! Señor Dilliard, what of the *zapatos*?”

Impatiently, the Texan paused, frowning, “Well, what about shoes, whose shoes?”

“It is like this, Señor Dilliard,” Teresa explained. “Of the shoes I have none. The *señorita—*”

“The *señorita,*” Dilliard said shortly, “will just have to go barefooted, Teresa, as you do. And you’ll *just have* to make her shoes fit you. Let’s lose no more time. Hurry!”

He opened the door, stepped outside, closed it at his back. Sounds of movements came from inside, then voices. Teresa was doing her utmost to explain the situation, but a sharp word from the *señorita,* who refused to believe the Mexican girl’s words, sent Teresa into silence. From certain things that he heard, the Texan knew the two women were exchanging clothes without any further objections from Castameto’s daughter.

“Well, she quit kickin’ up a fuss about that, anyway,” Dilliard muttered thankfully. “Pro’bly got an idea she’s fallen into a scorpions’ nest, but too scared to fight any more. Still, I got to admit she didn't look scared any. Just plain mad!"

The Texan moved around to the back of the house where a saddled horse stood ready beneath a thatched *ramada.* Standing in the shade of the horse shelter, Dilliard waited in silence, smoking a cigarette, which wasn't half consumed when he heard the creak of saddle leather, and Tony reined his pony into view around the corner of the house, a few yards distant.

Horse and man were breathing easily, indicating that Tony hadn't been pushed too hard. Tony swung down from the saddle, in the shade of the *ramada.*

"What of the *señorita*?" he asked.

Ruefully, Dilliard passed one hand down his damp cheek with its four livid streaks reaching to the jawbone. "She put her brand on me."

"Almos' the earmark, too—no?"

"She's a wildcat for a fight—gentled down a lot, now, though."

Tony smiled broadly, commenced an old Spanish proverb, "Until the tigress has found her mate—"

Dilliard interrupted, "You sure you threw those hombres off your track?"

Tony nodded vigorously. "There is no doubt of that. Half a mile to the northeas' of Santa Lozana, I dropped down, from sight, into the Arroyo Chico, keeping well out of the mud from las' night's rain. Those hombres hav' been follow the sounds of my horse. They don't guess where I go, quick like the lightning, when the horse sounds is stop so quick."

"Did they cross the arroyo?" Dilliard asked quickly.

"Farther down from where I am hide on the side of the ravine, in the thick, high brush. They crossed at a poin' where the mounts would not get flounder' in the mud. From behin' a mesquite bush, I'm watch an' hear the two *Americanos* try for decide where I go. Almos' I'm hearin' the wheels make the revolve in their heads. It was all ver' fonny. Finally, they give up, turn back. I'm think by now they have return to the plaza—"

"Tony, if they'd had sense enough to look for your horse's tracks, instead of listening for sounds, it might not have been so funny."

"What you say is true," Tony remarked sagely, "but I'm not fear to outwit soch *imbeciles*—"

A sudden call from Teresa interrupted the words. Tony and Dilliard returned to the front of the house, Dilliard leading his horse. Teresa stood in the doorway, clothed in the *señorita*'s garments which fit her snugly, but well enough for the occasion. Her words came from behind the veil:

"I'm ready, Señor Dilliard."

A wave of admiration for the Mexican girl's cool nerve welled up in Branch's throat. It was fortunate the two women were so nearly the same height. Dilliard's gaze strayed over Teresa's shawled shoulder to the slim figure in white cotton standing within the dim shadowed interior of the house. The Texan caught his breath. Again came that choking sensation in his throat. Teresa's crude garments seemed to enhance rather than diminish the *señorita*'s blonde beauty.

Her feet were bare, the cotton skirt reaching but a little below the white knees. The cornsilk hair was gathered tightly about the small, defiantly set head. Teresa had added a blue and gray striped *serape* to the costume, which the girl clutched with one hand.

Dilliard's gaze met the dark eyes of Castameto's daughter. Her eyes met his coldly; no fear there, no surrender; nothing but a slow, steady burning of haughty contempt. For this, Dilliard was thankful. At that moment, had Castameto's daughter shown one sign of weakness, voiced one word of entreaty, the Texan couldn't have refused her anything she might have asked. And all the driving force at his command was necessary for the movements now to come. There must be no weakening, no further loss of fleeting, precious moments.

Dilliard, jerking his eyes reluctantly away from the slim white form, turned to Tony, "You've arranged for a third horse on which to follow?"

"About that there is no need of hurry. I still have money. All that can be arranged after your departure." Tony's eyes swept along the deserted street. "You notice those neighbors about which you were so much concerned—there is no sign of them."

Dilliard nodded. "You handled it fine, Tony—all of it—you and Teresa." The Texan's bronzed features were tense with the strain of the situation. He put his left foot into the stirrup, swung up to settle into his saddle. Tony and Teresa were deep in conversation, gathering last clinging moments. Tony's voice broke a trifle. Finally he lifted Teresa up to the saddle. Branch held the girl before him. His voice was a bit hoarse when he said, "Teresa, it's your show from now on, everythin's up to you. Feelin' skeery?"

"What is thees skeery?" Teresa laughed nervously. "Eef you mean am I frighten'—pouf! Of what is there to be frighten'?"

The Texan was staring straight ahead. "Maybe we'll find out," he stated grimly. Then over one shoulder, "Tony, I'm countin' on comin' right back."

Further talk wasn't necessary. Dilliard started the horse, moved quickly along the narrow street and turned toward the plaza.

By this time, affairs in the plaza had quieted down considerably. The day was too hot to remain long in a state of excitement. The loungers had returned to their benches; many of them were already half asleep. The carriage still waited before the hotel, the heads of the horses, as well as those of the two breeds on the driver's seat, hanging low. No one had had any authority to say what should be done with it; the proprietor of the hotel had returned to other duties within his establishment.

At the opposite end of the square, Corill and Bisbee had dismounted in the shade of the pepper tree and stood leaning against their horses, deep in perplexed conversation, doubtless wondering what to do next. They didn't see the Texan's horse enter the plaza with its double burden.

Dilliard pushed his mount swiftly along, reached the carriage before the men on the driver's seat were aware of his arrival. Hearing a slight noise, one of them turned to see the Texan depositing the veiled Teresa on the leather-upholstered back seat. His eyes widened in astonishment, a startled exclamation left his lips. His companion turned with unaccustomed swiftness. Abruptly, someone across the square raised a surprised yell.

Dilliard laughed easily, explaining to the two on the driver's seat: "The *señorita* has not been harmed. It was all just a little *gringo* joke, *amigos*, to win a wager. I have won and I am satisfied. When you return, I shall buy you many drinks of *tequila.* You may now proceed to the Rancho Sicamoro."

Bowing deeply to the supposed *señorita* in the carriage, Dilliard laughed a careless "*Adiós*!" and turned his pony away from the vehicle. By that time, Corill and Bisbee had mounted and come tearing across the plaza. In a moment they had drawn rein, one on either side of the Texan.

Bisbee growled angrily, "Just a minute, Dilliard! What's your hurry?"

"Didn't realize I was hurryin'," Dilliard replied quietly, slowly backing his horse from between the two. "I've explained matters to your two boys drivin' the carriage. I haven't hurt the lady. Had a bet with a fellow that I could do what I did—shucks! I've won my bet and I'm plumb satisfied—"

"I ain't," Corill snapped. His hand commenced to slide toward the gun at his belt. Bisbee quickly reined his horse to one side, placing Dilliard between them a second time. "I ain't satisfied—not by a long shot," Corill added.

"That," Dilliard said coldly, "is just too damn bad. We can take the matter up more thorough, any time you've got a minute to spare. And, if you've got that minute right now, why not jerk that iron you're itchin' for?"

Corill's angry gaze locked with Dilliard's. For the space of a quarter of a minute he held his own before the cold, challenging stare of the Texan. Then Corill cleared his throat, lowered his eyes. Slowly, his hand came away from his gun.

Dilliard had made no move to draw; that hadn't been necessary with Corill. Something about the lean, bronzed Texan had shaken Corill's nerve, something cold and hard and ruthless he'd read in Dilliard's slate-gray eyes.

"Oh, hell," he gulped tonelessly, and backed his horse a pace.

Dilliard said flatly, "You showed good judgment, Corill. This business was all in fun, but just in case you were scoutin' for a ruckus, I wouldn't object to a mite more fun—at your expense. It's up to you."

Corill said, "Oh, hell," again, without raising his gaze, and backed his horse another step.

Dilliard laughed coolly, and, hoping to carry the business through on sheer bluff, touched fingers to the brim of his felt hat and made as though to turn his horse away. "*Adiós*, Señorita Castameto. May you have a pleasant journey—"

"Dammit," Bisbee growled, "you ain't gettin' off that easy, Dilliard. Is he, Clem—?"

"We got a job on," Clem Corill snapped pettishly. "We'll take care of Dilliard when we come back—"

"*Silencio*!" Teresa spoke impatiently from her seat in the carriage. "Is it necessary that we wait and broil in this sun all day?" To the two breeds on the driver's seat, "And what do you wait for, fools? Drive on! Must I be forced to listen to quarreling gringo pigs, while you wait, idle, like bad beans in a cold pot? Don Salvadore will take care of the *Americano* when word of this outrage reaches his ears. It is not your problem. Drive on, I tell you!"

Electrified into action, one of the men jerked on the reins. The other plied a vigorous whip. The startled horses leaped into swift movement. The carriage rolled off, leaving Dilliard still facing Corill and Bisbee.

"There goes your valuable package," Dilliard laughed softly. "Better get started before you're left behind."

Corill was inclined to agree. "C'mon, Wirt," he said sullenly. "We got important business. We'll take care of this hombre later."

But Bisbee, not having faced Dilliard's steely eyes as had his companion, wanted to argue the matter. He swore at Corill, adding, "Go on, if you're skeered, but not me. This has got to be settled now. Dilliard shot my horse when he was busy pullin' this joke of his. He's cost me a fresh nag. He ain't goin' to—"

"Look here, you two," Dilliard's voice abruptly turned chill and hard, "take my advice and get goin' *pronto*! If you're lookin' for trouble—"

That was as far as the Texan got with his speech. A vile curse rolled from Bisbee's lips. There came a swift blur of action as he threw caution to the winds and reached for his gun. Dilliard had caught the swift motion toward gun-belt. His own weapon came out and up in one, smooth, eye-defying movement.

The two weapons roared almost in unison. Bisbee's bullet went high and wide as he swayed back in the saddle. His open mouth uttered a shrill, high-pitched cry of pain before he toppled from his horse's back.

The Texan's gun was already covering Corill, who had started to draw.

"Hold it!" Dilliard snapped. "I don't reckon Bisbee's dead, but I might not aim so careful with my next shot. I've suggested twice that you *vamos*! I'm through hintin' now. Make yourself scarce. Quick!"

Yells sounded around the plaza. The little fat man with the deputy's badge came running from a house. Corill cast one nervous glance at Bisbee, now in a sitting position in the mud, then nodded shortly to Dilliard: "You've got the drop this time, Texas man, but we'll meet again, and I'll be rememberin'—"

"You won't do any rememberin' either," Dilliard said grimly, "unless you turn that horse and make yourself scarce—"

"What's going on here?" It was the little fat man with the deputy-sheriff's badge.

Dilliard eyed the man coolly. The deputy had vacillating eyes of an indiscriminate color which peered at Dilliard uneasily. He was entirely chinless and wore a very dirty shirt.

Dilliard said, "I just had to shoot me a skunk."

"Now, looky here, feller," the deputy commenced. “You can’t run rough-shod over Santa Lozana. You’ve caused enough trouble—”

“Want to make anythin’ out of it?” Dilliard said coldly.

The deputy swallowed hard. He wasn’t craving trouble with this tall Texan. “I’m the law here,” he blustered.

“That’s fine.” Dilliard’s tones were crisp. He gestured toward the groaning Bisbee. “You better arrest that hombre for pulling on me—”

“Did he pull first?” the law-officer asked eagerly.

“Hell, didn’t you see him?” Dilliard said impatiently.

“Reckon I did at that, come to think of it.”

“That’s a lie—” Corill commenced.

The fat deputy scowled, employed Dilliard’s words of a few minutes before, “Want to make anythin’ out of it?”

“You know who the liar is, Corill,” Dilliard said steadily. “You know Bisbee went for his iron first. You’re lucky you didn’t get what he got—”

“Bisbee,” the deputy said pompously, “I’ll have to arrest you. Get up, you ain’t hurt much.” He tugged the white-faced Bisbee to his feet, and without waiting for further argument dragged the wounded man off across the plaza, followed by a jeering group of Mexicans.

“And that’s that,” Dilliard said shortly, eyeing Corill. “Corill, your carriage has disappeared.

You better hurry if you want to catch up to it. Or did you decide to stay?"

Corill muttered something unintelligible under his breath and took the hint. Plunging in his spurs, he turned his pony and went racing off in pursuit of the carriage and the girl he supposed was old Castameto's daughter.

Dilliard glanced around the plaza. Peace had again settled over the town. Bisbee and the deputy were just disappearing through the doorway of a building.

Dilliard heaved a long sigh as he reined his pony toward the street that led to Tony's house. "Anyway, it's worked so far," he said gratefully. "Now, if only nothin' happens to Teresa—"

He stopped short on that thought, not caring to dwell on the various possibilities a discovery of the exchange might bring.

6
KILLERS' LEAD

Once away from the square, Dilliard raced his horse back to Tony's house. A saddled horse waited before the door. Tony stood in the doorway, his face ashen. It lighted with sudden relief as the Texan hove into view. Dilliard pulled to a halt, without dismounting.

"*Poder de Dios*!" Tony's voice trembled as he dashed out and caught at Dilliard's hand. "What has happened? My Teresa . . . ?"

"Teresa's all right, Tony. She's on her way, and they never suspected a thing—"

"But I heard shots—"

Dilliard nodded, related briefly what had happened in the square. ". . . Corill rode after the carriage," he concluded. "Last I saw of Bisbee he was on his way to the hoosegow."

Tony scowled, "By nightfall he will be free again. That deputy-sheriff is of the no-good."

"Bisbee may get free, but he won't get around for a spell—not with a smashed shoulder. These ca'tridge guns pack a wicked punch."

Tony smiled broadly, "Then our scheme—eet hav' work?"

"So far," tersely. "Teresa's what matters now.

As soon as we leave, I want you to ride after that carriage, see that nothing happens to Teresa."

"*Sí—sí—*"

"Remember, stick to that carriage like a leech. Don't let Corill or the others learn you are following, but, until you see me again, don't you lose sight of that carriage."

"*Seguro*, I stick to the leash on that carriage."

Dilliard didn't bother to correct that impression. He said, "The *señorita—?*"

"Is inside of the house. I have explain' that she is to make the ride with you. I have try to explain all of this mad business, but she refus' to listen to truth. She tells me I am one lying peeg? Me, Antonio Aguilar, the bes' *vaquero* what evair rope on her father's *rancho*! I'm don't think I'm like that."

"Tell her her horse is ready and I'm waiting," Dilliard said.

Tony entered the house. A moment later, the girl emerged, her head held high, dark eyes full of hate for the gringo savage who had abducted her. She drew the *serape* over her head, held it close to her face. Tony tried to help her mount the horse at the side of Dilliard's pony but withered before the scornful glance she bent on him. Assistance hadn't really been necessary; in an instant she was in the saddle.

Tony turned, red-faced, to Dilliard, repeating instructions he had furnished the previous evening: ". . . and follow the Arroyo Chico for the firs' mile," he finished. "After that it will be of the entirely safe to ride to higher ground."

His words died to silence as Dilliard led the *señorita*'s horse past the corrals at the end of the *Calle de los Caballeros*. From this point the earth dipped abruptly, carrying the riders below the level of town.

A little later, the two horses dropped into the Arroyo Chico—a narrow twisting ravine that carried them swiftly away from Santa Lozana. Occasionally the matted brush bordering the sides of the arroyo forced them to progress along the mud at the bottom, but, for the most part, the horses had good footing.

In time, Dilliard felt it safe to move to higher, open country. The ponies scrambled up the sides of the arroyo, carrying their riders out to a long stretch of rolling hill-land. Half an hour passed before Dilliard glanced back from the backbone of a low ridge. Santa Lozana was four miles away by this time. Only the roofs of the highest houses and the top of the red-berried pepper tree in the plaza showed above the gradually rolling terrain.

"We'll be able to make better time now," Dilliard stated, endeavoring to make casual conversation.

The girl just looked at him, didn't reply. Dilliard flushed and fell into silence. . . .

All morning the Texan and the *señorita* pushed

steadily on, with no conversation between them, getting ever higher into the foothills of the Santa Ana Mountains. Though not delayed as they had been in negotiating the bottom of Arroyo Chico, Dilliard was finding it difficult to make fast time. The *señorita* rode side-saddle, Teresa's short, cotton skirt gathered as closely as possible about her bare white ankles. Dilliard had tried, once more, to explain matters to the girl, but had been met with a rebuffing silence. Dilliard had again fallen silent, reflecting grimly that before many hours he'd be able to offer positive proof attesting the worth of his actions.

The girl rode a few yards in advance, only turning her horse when Dilliard gave directions. Tony had mapped out the course the Texan was to follow; Dilliard was quick to recognize certain landmarks the Mexican had indicated.

The sun was high, now, throwing down hot waves. The *señorita* retained the gray-and-blue *serape* over her head, but Dilliard wasn't missing a certain painful redness of her bare feet. He drew a clean bandanna from his pocket, reined alongside the girl and dropped the bandanna over her ankles. If he had expected any expressions of gratitude for his actions, he was doomed to disappointment. The girl eyed him coldly, but kept and arranged the offering so it would do the greatest good.

At noon the two riders dipped down a hillside

in Conejo Canyon to make a short camp at a thin, trickling branch of some unnamed creek. The water was clear and cold. The *señorita* disdainfully refused the cold *tamale* Dilliard proffered, but drank water from the stream and bathed her face and arms. Then they mounted and moved on.

Had the situation been different, Dilliard would have enjoyed the journey. As it was, he experienced a certain pull toward this new, strange country. Many of the hillsides they crossed were a riot of color—orange poppies and lupine and violet brodiaea spread vividly painted tapestries along the rolling slopes. Below, on the more level stretches, huge gnarled live oaks spread their magnificent low-hanging branches, the lack of underbrush beneath giving it all the appearance of a wide park. Not a fleck of white showed in the turquoise sky.

Now and then Dilliard recognized clumps of sage and prickly pear, but the former seemed more green, the latter much larger, with vivid yellow flowers jutting from the great spiny pads, than in his native Texas. At times the horses breasted their way through great fields of wild, yellow mustard.

It must have been about two in the afternoon when Dilliard again sent the horses up into the higher hills. Reaching the summit of a long, rock-crested ridge, Dilliard directed the girl's attention to a dusty, wheel-rutted road in a canyon far below.

"By this time," the Texan said quietly, "we should be ahead of that carriage. I'm asking you to keep quiet, and watch that highway down there. Things will be happenin' presently. But no matter what takes place, don't make a sound. That's for your own good as well as mine. With luck, nobody'll see us up here."

The girl didn't answer. Dilliard dismounted, then helped the *señorita* down from her saddle, wincing as he sensed her involuntary drawing away.

The horses were screened from sight by great outthrusts of rock. Around Dilliard and his charge grew thick clumps of greasewood and mesquite. The girl glanced across the canyon to the opposite hillsides; there wasn't a soul to be seen—just rocks and trees and brush, blended by distance into bright green velvet. Overhead spread the spaceless blue sky, with a lone buzzard flapping lazily near the top of a small peak. That was all the girl could see, that and the roadway below, until Dilliard spoke cautiously.

"See? Down there."

Following the Texan's pointing finger, Castameto's daughter saw a slight movement near the edge of the road. A man appeared, as though by magic, from the brush bordering the highway, then dropped from sight again. Soon, a few feet distant from the first man, a second appeared.

Gradually, the *señorita* made out other forms moving below her, most of them huddled in the rank brush that grew profusely along the road.

Dilliard said tersely, "Am I a liar? Did Tony and Teresa lie?"

"But—but, *señor*, what do they wait for?"

"Your carriage—*you*."

The girl swallowed hard, glanced at the Texan. Her face was white. Perhaps, after all, this gringo savage had spoken the truth. Sudden fear clutched at her heart as she shrank back behind the protecting screen of mesquite.

From around a bend in the road came the quick *thud-clop-clop* of horses' hoofs, the squeak and rattle of the carriage. The waiting men on the road below quickly scattered out of sight, leaving the highway barren of movement.

Dilliard whispered, "The play's about to start. I'm askin' you to watch what happens."

The girl's eyes searched Dilliard's, some of the belligerency dying from their dark depths. She didn't say anything; just leaned forward to part the brush with one white hand to obtain a better view, as she crouched behind the sheltering mesquite.

By this time the carriage had appeared, the veiled Teresa sitting stiffly on the back seat. The two breeds on the driver's box were peering ahead, along the roadway. A certain tenseness in their attitudes betrayed that they weren't entirely ignorant of what was to happen. Riding at the side of the carriage was the man named Corill. Corill's harsh tones floated clearly up the slope as he ordered the two breeds to slow the pace a trifle. Again, the girl turned and studied Dilliard's grim features.

Without turning, Dilliard said, "Look!"

It all happened in the next few moments. The *señorita* saw fringes of white fire ruffle the brush near the road, heard quick shots, voices of yelling men. The carriage horses went to their knees, crashed down, tangling the harness.

There were further shots: one after the other, the breeds on the driver's seat pitched woodenly to the dust and lay still, faces turned to the white hot sunshine. The *señorita* wasn't missing the look of shocked surprise frozen on the features of one of the breeds, nor did she overlook the fact, through all the blur of action, that Corill, while appearing to fight off the assailants, was loosing all of his shots skyward.

Men swarmed into and over the carriage. Teresa was lifted from the seat, struggling frantically. Corill kept up the pretense. He cursed wildly, reining his horse about, making a good deal of racket with his gun. Finally, he spurred away from the carriage and along the road, quickly disappearing around the next bend. Shots, aimed high, pursued him from the guns of certain men near the carriage, but no attempt was made to follow Corill.

Powder smoke drifted slowly. There were sounds of many voices. Horses were brought from the brush where they'd been hidden. The *señorita* saw Teresa forced to mount one of the animals. The other men were in saddles now, moving across the roadway, ascending the slopes of the opposite hill, urging the horse that carried Teresa to greater efforts.

Dilliard said quietly, "Well, what do you think now?"

The girl didn't reply. She crouched as before, her fascinated gaze glued to the carriage, the dead men, in the road below.

7

A NEW BARRIER

Five minutes passed. The riders on the opposite slope were climbing higher now.

Dilliard said apologetically, "It wasn't a nice sight for you, but it was the only way I could make you understand. You wouldn't listen, before."

The girl nodded, wrenched her gaze away from the scene below, and gained her feet. She seemed stunned by what had taken place, as though still incapable of believing that the killing, and the capture of Teresa had actually occurred.

Dilliard said, "Those coyotes across the canyon are reaching higher ground. A few minutes more and they'll be level with us. We can't take chances of being seen."

He went to the horses, moved them back down the ridge, out of sight of those ascending the slopes on the other side of the roadway. The Texan noted it wasn't necessary, this time, to tell the girl to follow him. He walked on, leading the horses, the girl picking her way through the long grass behind him. Stopping beneath a spreading live oak, a quarter of the way down the hillside, Dilliard waited for her to catch up.

The girl approached him slowly, full comprehension of the deed in the roadway dawning on her now in all its hideous certainty. Her face was white, white touched with twin, burning points of indignation. Her full lips trembled with hot anger.

"But—but they were *Americanos*!" she exclaimed incredulously.

Dilliard said, hard-voiced, "I'm apologizin' for that, too. I'm not very proud of my own blood right at this moment."

"Señor—Señor Dilliard, I—" The girl paused, unable to continue. Her sense of justice demanded that many things be said. She had wronged the gringo and his Mexican friends. Yet the humiliation of admitting, to this common *vaquero* from Texas, that she had perpetrated an injustice, was a trifle more than the *señorita*'s strain of noble Spanish blood could sustain.

Dilliard misinterpreted the girl's hesitation. "Haven't forgotten I told you my name?" Laughing eyes betrayed the firm lines of his mouth and chin. "I didn't think you'd heard me."

Impulsively, Castameto's proud daughter forgot her stern resolutions. "No," she replied steadily, "I haven't forgotten your name. I remember, also, many other things. I should have believed you. But it all seemed so—"

"I'm not surprised that you didn't believe us."

"But I've been—been a little fool. You see,

so much that is bad has happened of late." The girl's English was almost perfect, carrying just the barest trace of a Spanish accent that Dilliard found fascinating. She went on, "I am traveling to my *padre*'s rancho. My—"

"I know—the Ranch of the Sycamores."

The *señorita* nodded, continued, "My brother was—my brother died—but that was some weeks back—" Again she hesitated, her dark eyes moist.

Branch Dilliard tried to make it easier for the girl: "I know that too," he cut in. "Your brother, Ramon, was killed. Your father's in trouble for avenging his death. You are on your way home from Boston, where your father had sent you to school. You came by sailing vessel to the Isthmus of Panama, across the isthmus by carriage. Then another ship to California, to the port of San Pedro—"

"You know all this?" Surprise tinged the girl's words.

Dilliard nodded. "From San Pedro you were traveling by carriage to the Rancho Sicamoro. Part of this I learned from Teresa and Tony. The rest—about the kidnapping and so on—I overheard by accident in a *cantina* in Santa Lozana. The two *Americanos* who were to accompany your carriage had been drinkin'. They talked too loud."

"But what of my own men who met me, with my father's carriage, at the boat in San Pedro, and who drove me to Santa Lozana? They were good men. I do not understand—"

Dilliard looked grim. "They—they were detained," he evaded the question. It wasn't necessary to explain that Corill and Bisbee had added bloodshed to their other crimes of violence. The girl would learn about that part soon enough. Dilliard pushed on hurriedly, "Why they wanted to steal you I don't know, unless the matter is somehow connected with your father's troubles. I imagine it was a matter of ransom—"

"But *you,* a stranger to the Castametos!" The *señorita* wasn't getting the idea at all. "You, an *Americano*, you risked your life to—"

"Reckon I didn't risk so much," Dilliard grinned.

"But you could have informed the authorities in Santa Lozana and let them handle the matter."

That had Dilliard stumped. He could have, of course, and perhaps prevented the whole happening. But he felt it doubtful. "That didn't quite occur to me," he said lamely, "or, if it did, I didn't trust the law-officer in Santa Lozana enough to take a chance. He's a pretty poor sort. I might not have been believed. Friends in Santa Lozana were scarcer'n frog's hair. It's a tough town at best. I had only Teresa and Tony I could depend on."

The girl nodded, without speaking, awaiting further explanation. The truth was, of course, that Dilliard had wanted a hand in the business himself. Now he hinted at something of the kind.

"Yesterday," he said quietly, "I saw you standing at your window in the hotel. It was just for a second or so, but that second or so sort of decided me I wanted to help you."

The *señorita* read more in his gray eyes than Dilliard had put into words. She met his gaze a moment, then glanced away, a slow flush stealing into her cheeks. She changed the subject, her mind returning to the hold-up in the roadway.

"The—the so-called bodyguard," she said, "what of him? Corill? That's the name you said. What of him? There were many shots but no attempt to hurt. He rode away—"

"On his way to break the news to your father," Dilliard told her. "He'll arrive with a long yarn about you bein' kidnapped."

"The two men on the driver's seat," the girl remembered next. "The guns fired straight in their case."

"A matter of double-crossing." Dilliard had to explain the word. "Oh, they were in on the plot, all right, counting on getting paid for their part of the job. But I reckon those other coyotes figured it would be easier to throw lead than pay money after the job had been done."

The girl was silent for a few moments, then, "Do we ride on, now?"

Dilliard nodded, "My work is finished when I

deliver you at your home. Nothing to prevent us from starting."

"My father will want to thank you. Not that—" she smiled and Dilliard's heart skipped a beat, "—not that I'm incapable of doing my own thanking, but—"

"Just believin' in me," the Texan told her steadily, "is all the thanking I'm wanting."

The girl's eyes were deep, inscrutable pools as she flushed and looked away. Dilliard was entirely missing the point that the Spanish dons of those early California days looked upon the *gringos* as an inferior race.

It may be the Spanish dons had much on their side to substantiate that belief: certainly the Spanish owners of large *ranchos* had found no particular cause to love the *Americano.* A considerable percentage of the men who first reached California shores, from east of the Rocky Mountains, were adventurers, seekers after gold, outlaws and schemers in nefarious projects, and they rode many rough-shod chapters across the early history of the Golden State.

"You haven't told me your name yet," Dilliard reminded the girl. "I know, of course, that it is Castameto, but—"

The girl smiled and commenced, "Señorita Mariposa Baca y Castameto de Hinojosa y Castilla la Vieja—"

"Whoa!" Dilliard grinned. "That's enough.

Don't bother with any more abbreviations. Lady, that's a mouthful! Let me see—" he struggled with unfamiliar phrases of Spanish, "—Mariposa means butterfly, doesn't it?"

"Butterfly, or—well, my *madre* interpreted Mariposa as 'night-light.' "

Dilliard thought of "a silver flame in the dusk." He said, laughing, "I didn't realize all I'd get when I asked for your name. I won't try to remember all of it. Reckon I'll just call you Mary, now that we're on friendly terms. Mary's shorter than Mariposa."

The Texan entirely missed the tightening that came to the girl's lips at this, to her, unbounded familiarity. After all, to Señorita Mariposa Baca y Castameto, descendant of a long line of noble ancestors, Branch Dilliard, of San Antonio, Texas, was only one more *vaquero gringo*, one more of the detested *Americano* invaders of a peaceful land.

The girl said coldly, "Señor Dilliard, wouldn't 'Señorita Castameto' be more in order?"

Dilliard jerked up at the look in her eyes. Comprehension came to him like a sharp slap across the mouth. He thought, "She's run a brand on me a second time, I reckon." Suddenly he grinned ruefully and nodded, "I reckon you're correct—Señorita Castameto."

The girl flushed at his tone. "I'm not forgetting I'm under obligations to you—"

"The sooner you forget it," Dilliard said shortly, "the better I'll like it. . . . Well, we'd best be getting along—Señorita Castameto."

Mariposa's dark eyes flashed angrily. She bit her lip, stared at Dilliard a long minute, then changed the subject: "What of the Mexican girl who occupied the seat in my carriage?"

"She'll be all right. You see, those hombres think they've captured the very proud Señorita Castameto. Until some business with your father is completed, they'll handle Teresa with silk gloves. No, I'm not sure what the business is. Ransom, maybe."

"But—but after those scoundrels learn of their mistake? What then of the girl?"

Dilliard studied the situation with a clear mind. "That," he admitted reluctantly at last, "has got my brain doing some queer tumbles too. I told Tony to follow the carriage, to trail Teresa, unseen, to wherever she was taken. I'm hoping he's on her track now. I figured to deliver you home—"

"Deliver!" Mariposa intruded hotly. "Am I some sort of package, an inanimate object, with no decision in its own affairs?"

Dilliard scratched his jaw—not the one bearing the fiery marks of the girl's fingernails. "You got decision, all right," he stated coldly, "but I'm not so sure I can say the same for your good judgment—Señorita Castameto."

His eyes clashed with her own blazing darker ones. The girl was furious, her short laugh harsh, jeering, as she gazed meaningfully at the four livid streaks down his cheek. Finally, she said insolently, "I lower, degrade myself, quarreling with a gringo savage. In this way, we reach no place. I have requested information regarding the welfare of the Mexican girl. I demand a reply—now—at once. I *demand!* Understand, gringo?"

"Your manners," Dilliard said hotly, "demand a damn good spanking, and for a plugged *peso* I'd give you one, here and now. For a minute I thought you had a trace of sense, but I was wrong. A dang good Mex boy and his girl have put themselves out to do you an important favor—"

"Aren't you forgetting yourself, Señor Dilliard?"

Dilliard shook his head. "You haven't given me a chance to do that. You put me in my place a spell back—at least, you thought you did. All right, I'm a gringo. What of it? I made a mistake—I admit that too—trying to be friendly with a little greaser spitfire—"

"Greaser spitfire! Gringo pig, you go too far! I warn you, I, Mariposa Baca y Castameto—" The girl panted hotly.

"Aw, forget it," Dilliard said wearily. The humor of the situation suddenly burst upon him and he laughed good-naturedly. "You said it all when you said we didn't get any place scrappin'.

You were mighty correct. Let's pretend you're always correct. We'll get along a heap better, until I can knock at the door of your outfit and say, 'Here she is. Not a hair of her useless head harmed.' "

"As you like, Señor Dilliard." The girl was suddenly calm again. "For the moment let us forget our differences. I've asked for information regarding the Mexican girl. I refuse to go on until you finish telling me of her."

"All right, all right," Dilliard said impatiently. "Like I told you, Tony's following her—leastwise I hope he is. I figured to unload you, then return and meet Tony at a place he'd designated. Then we'd see what could be done about getting Teresa out of the mess she's in on your account—"

"The mess, as you call it, might have been avoided if you had called at the hotel in Santa Lozana and told me frankly what was planned."

The Texan laughed scornfully. "And you'd have believed me, of course?"

Mariposa suddenly lowered her eyes; she hadn't any answer for that one.

Dilliard went on, "As I said before, I planned to join Tony, and we were going to see what could be done about rescuing Teresa. I'd even supposed your father might furnish enough men to help out on that job. I see now, if he's anything like you, I was pro'bly wrong. All right, Tony and I can do it alone."

Mariposa's dark eyes snapped, but she managed to control the fiery torrent of words that swelled to her lips. And that wasn't a particularly easy task. "If you asked," she said with bleak steadiness, "every man on the Rancho Sicamoro would be put at your command. The Castametos aren't entirely devoid of honor, as you seem to think. But what of the time?"

"Now what are you talking about?"

"Will you have time to secure the help of my father's men? Suppose the true identity of that Mexican girl should be discovered before you return. What then of her? She must not be harmed."

The Texan looked curiously at Mariposa Castameto. His reply was weighted with sarcasm, "That thought annoys you? After all, Señorita Castameto, Teresa is only a poor Mexican girl. There is no noble blood in her body—"

"Silence!" Mariposa snapped.

The Texan swallowed hard but remained quiet.

Mariposa went on, her voice coldly patient, explaining, "The Castametos always look to the welfare of their servants. To my knowledge, this Teresa has never been with us, but I recognized the man you call Tony; formerly he was one of our *vaqueros*. That makes Teresa one of our people. About her something must be done—at once."

"If you recognized Tony," Dilliard said, "I'll bet he never knew it."

"I thought we were talking about Teresa," haughtily.

Dilliard laughed shortly. "You're plumb insistent, anyway. You mean you want to see her safe?"

"I'd like that."

"Hadn't I better get you home first? Another dozen miles or so will do the trick."

"I know my own country, far better than you, Señor Dilliard. It will require more nearly fifteen miles to—do the trick as you call it. But first comes the welfare of our people—Teresa. She must not be harmed."

The Texan examined the proposition from all sides, his gray eyes narrowed in thought. Finally, "I calc'late it can be done," he said, half to himself. Then, to the girl, "It will mean waiting here alone."

"I'll wait."

"It may require some time."

"I've told you I'd wait," haughtily.

Dilliard nodded, tethered the girl's horse to a lower branch of the live oak, persuaded her to accept a couple of cold *tamales* wrapped in cornhusks and the canteen of water from his saddle.

"I might be a long time gone," he said tersely. "Now, I'm not givin' orders to a Castameto, but if I were you, I'd stay under cover in the brush—some distance from the horse. No telling who might show up here—I don't think anyone will, but you can't always tell. If I thought there was a speck of danger, I wouldn't be leavin' you."

The Texan swung easily up to his saddle, swept the soft hat from his black hair in a low, mocking bow, saying, "*Adiós*, Señorita Castameto."

Mariposa's reply was as haughty as his own and came with a cold shrug of white shoulders, "*Feliz viaje*, Señor Branch Dilliard. May you have a pleasant journey."

She watched him rein the horse through the mesquite, and then rose to follow him with her eyes, until he had reached the crest of the ridge and disappeared from view, her mind a turmoil of conflicting emotions.

She returned and sat down under the tree. Something was wrong. The Texan had acted for her best interests and she had snubbed him as though he were the lowliest *peon* on her father's ranch. And for a few minutes they had gotten on so well. But now, the barrier between them, abruptly dissolved after the scene of the hold-up, had been erected a second time. Just how that had happened, Mariposa didn't quite comprehend.

"He needn't have been so familiar," she tried to defend her actions, lip curling disdainfully. "So, he'd call me 'Mary,' would he? . . . Yet, was he wrong? He saved my life, it may be. Certainly, he risked his own. A brave man he most certainly is. And there is nothing of the savage about him, as I at first thought. For a gringo he is very good looking."

A faint flush stole up the girl's cheek, as she continued, "He has very good eyes, very true, honest eyes. I think, were our stations in life not so far apart, I might like him." Then, abruptly, "No, Mariposa, that is a very bad thought. Between a Castameto and a gringo can be only enmity. Always my *padre* has maintained that point. Besides, this Dilliard is crude, he is rough spoken, he has not the graceful manners of a Spaniard.

"But," she added as an afterthought, "he has a manner of his own, he is not so crude, nor rough. At times, he appears very gentle. It may even be he finds merit in the eyes of his own people—" She broke off suddenly, eyes wide with horror.

"Mother of God!" she gasped. "I didn't realize! We were so angry in our talk, I didn't think! I—I *am* a little fool! I have sent him alone to face those outlaws and rescue Teresa. He too was angry. I made my words sound like a challenge to his courage. *Madre de Dios*! No, no! I won't have it that way. He doubtless had some plan that could be carried through without danger. It must be that. He wouldn't be so foolhardy as to ride into that outlaw camp and demand the Mexican girl."

Mariposa wondered if she were lying to herself, summoning up possibilities simply to set at ease her own guilty conscience. She strove to turn her thoughts to other subjects, always defending her haughty manner in dealing with Dilliard.

Back on the New England seacoast, Mariposa had, usually, been accepted as an equal among the girls at the school she'd attended, though there were remembered snubs during her first year there, when various struggles with the English language had been met with thinly-veiled sneers. But all that had passed during the succeeding months of schooling, as she had adopted the customs and manners of the girls in her classes. Now, once more in her own country, that sense of democracy had faded, leaving in its place the fact, foremost in her mind, that she was the only daughter of Don Salvadore Baca y Castameto, a ruler of vast acres, *vaqueros*, and herds, by virtue of certain grants given, direct, from the Spanish throne in Madrid.

The girl insisted to herself that she hadn't intended to be cold and short with Dilliard's attempted friendliness. Something stronger than herself, heritage, had dictated the haughty manner, coupled with an involuntary resentment erected by her remembrance of Salvadore Castameto's warnings against any sort of intercourse with the gringos. Always it was the gringo who encroached on Spanish lands, gaining by hook or crook the possessions of Castameto's friends and neighbors.

Mariposa remembered her father's last letter. Tears welled in her dark eyes to be brushed impatiently away. Was the Ranch of the Sycamores, as well, to fall into the greedy, grasping hands of these *Americano* foreign invaders? The girl shrugged hopeless shoulders, murmuring "*Quien sabe*? Who knows?" But, somehow, she couldn't put away the idea that her murmured words had something to do with her mingled feelings toward Branch Dilliard. She was regretting now those four cruel scratches on his cheek.

8
THE OUTLAW CAMP

Dilliard's face was grim, set into harsh lines of thought, as his horse slowly descended the slopes that dropped from the crest of the ridge to the roadside. A rueful grin twisted the bronze mask that was his face, and he told himself, "Reckon she's pretty high-toned. At that, she needn't to have been so high and mighty. I'm a gringo pig, am I? Well, if she ain't a spit-firin' greaser—no, I'll take back the 'greaser' part. Not the other, though. Got a temper like a cat-clawed bob-cat. Mebbe that runs in the blood of these pure Spaniards. Just the same there was no call for her to be mountin' the high horse with me. I was just tryin' to be friendly like."

A new thought obtruded: was it just friendliness, or something more? The Texan toyed with that idea for a time, endeavoring to deceive himself, though he'd known from the beginning it was more than a friend he'd wanted to be to Mariposa Castameto.

He grinned weakly, "She'll be gettin' me down if I don't watch out," he muttered. "Still and all, there was no call for her to turn frigid just because I called her Mary. What's wrong with that name? Back home it was always a right solid moniker for a nice girl." What was it Teresa had called her—a silver flame in the dusk? The Texan laughed scornfully. "Sunshine on ice is more like her."

He swerved the horse around a huge clump of prickly-pear covered with yellow and crimson blossoms, and beheld, a short distance below, the carriage in the roadway, the dead horses sprawled in tangled and broken harness. The two breed drivers lay in the dust on either side of the vehicle, their eyes glassy under the hot California sun.

Dilliard resumed his abstractions: "I'll say one thing for Mary—pardon me, Señorita Castameto—she's got blued-steel nerve. Even seeing what happened, she was all for staying until she knew Teresa was safe. Oh, yes, 'the Castametos always look after their servants.' S'help me, Hannah, if that isn't the dangdest thing I ever heard tell of. Just because Tony once punched cows for old man Castameto, Mary takes it for granted Tony's whole family belongs to the same outfit. Darn little stuck-up wildcat! I wonder who she thinks she is?" He felt the hot blood rising to his face. "Gettin' hoity-toity with me, was she? Mebbe she thinks she owns me too, ordering me down to save Teresa. Not in so many words, but the way she said it—like she was darin' me to—"

Dilliard broke off suddenly, then, “Come to think of it, she might have had a certain amount of right on her side. Seems like I’ve heard the old Spanish Dons are like that. Once somebody works for ’em, they think it’s part of their duty to make ’em part of the family sort of. Well, dang her hide, she needn’t think I’m looking for corral and fodder for the rest of my days. I’ll get the little spitfire home, after Teresa’s took care of, and then pull out without so much as a good-bye. Never did like this California country. . . . Say, I wonder where Tony is?”

Dilliard had crossed the road by this time. Swinging down from the saddle, he examined the earth for sign. There were plenty of tracks but nothing to show that Tony had yet passed. The Texan pulled his horse to a halt beneath the spreading limbs of a big white oak and angrily twisted a cigarette. The cigarette was scarcely lighted when the sound of an approaching horse was heard around a bend in the roadway. A moment later, Tony loped into view, his horse covered with lather.

The Mexican’s eyes narrowed as his gaze took in the carriage and the two dead men. He greeted Dilliard stolidly, “You arrive in time, eh, Señor Branch?”

Dilliard nodded. “That short cut across the hills you told me about got us here first. We were in plenty time to see the whole show.”

"Teresa?" Tony tried to keep the words steady and was only partially successful.

"She wasn't harmed," Dilliard was glad to tell him. "Those skunks were right careful of her. Corill and Bisbee mentioned, that day I overheard 'em plottin', that they had never seen the girl. I doubt any of the other coyotes have either. So long as they believe Teresa is the Señorita Castameto, she won't be harmed. . . . I had you figured to show up before now."

"I was delay'. It require' longer than I hav' expect to buy a suitable horse. In Santa Lozana is mostly of crow-bait. . . . Where did you say those scoundrelly ones hav' take' my Teresa?"

Dilliard waved one hand up the hill to his right. "They took her thataway. We'll get on their trail when you've had time to breathe your pony."

Tony nodded, paused to roll and light a *cigarito.* He inhaled deeply. "What of the Señorita Castameto?" he asked next.

Dilliard explained in brief sentences, concluding, "She insists on waiting while I do something about Teresa. She's right, of course, only I was sort of surprised."

Dilliard was surprised a second time when Tony accepted the news of Mariposa's action as a matter of course. "Was she ver' frighten'?" the Mexican asked next.

"Mad more than anythin'; then when she saw the outlaws hold up the carriage, she come around some and talked a mite. Didn't overwhelm me or anythin' like that, though. Kind of uppity, I figure her. . . . Say, Tony, she seems to feel that you and Teresa are her father's servants."

Tony took that quietly, too. "But, of course, Señor Branch."

"Dam'd if I make you out. *Servants!* Hell, Tony, this is a free country. Maybe you're right, the way things used to be, but now California is a part of, is owned by, the United States Government. Old Castameto can't expect to control your actions. All that sort of thing is changed."

Tony smiled lazily. "Other changes may come—but not that. I am of the *patrón*'s people—always Don Salvadore has known I would someday return to the Rancho Sicamoro. *Socorro*! Am I not his most grand *vaquero*?" The Mexican's white teeth flashed humorously, "It is like thees, Señor Branch, if I do not return—*pouf!* The Rancho Sicamoro she go all in the pieces. Don Salvadore cannot get along without Antonio Aguilar."

"Oh, it's like that, eh?" Dilliard said dryly. "My gosh! It's a wonder to me Castameto hasn't had a search warrant issued, so's he could locate you and be saved from ruin."

"That would not surprise me," Tony said solemnly. "Look, I will make the explain—once I am work for the *patrón*, I am like of his family. Always he looks out for my well-being.

Always, when I am ready to bring my Teresa to the *rancho*, I'm know there is a small house will be furnish' us. Had I return' alone, then I would be furnish' a bed and food in a big quarters weeth the othair *vaqueros* who hav' not yet found their woman. But so long as I care to stay, I will be take care of, and my children will be take care of, and their children will be take care of—"

"Well, that's fine," Dilliard cut in, the situation seeming strange to him. "Maybe Castameto is friendly thataway, but I wouldn't say his daughter inherited some of her father's traits. Anyway, she was mighty high-and-toity with me."

Tony looked pained. "Ah, you don' understand, Señor Branch. Look! To her you are only a gringo, a so-common *vaquero*. There are hondreds of you—but of Señorita Castameto there is but one. She is grateful, yes, for what you hav' done, but, remembair, she has of the blood of kings in her veins—what you call heem?—blue-blood, no?"

Dilliard nodded, sighed resentfully. "I reckon it's all you say, *amigo*. Me, I'll have to learn to adjust my sights. My lead's throwing too high, looks like."

Tony smiled slyly. "Maybe, Señor Branch, you take the aim in too much of a hurry—no?"

Dilliard grinned back. "Or maybe I'd better quit shooting at that target, altogether."

"About that, we shall see later."

"True enough, Tony. Let's decide what we're to do about Teresa."

Tony reined his horse around beside Dilliard's. Spurs were touched to the beasts' ribs and they started off. The two men ascended the hillside in the direction taken by the outlaws.

Reaching the brow of the hill, Dilliard and Tony slowed their mounts to a walk. Here, the trail was easy to read, the hoof-chopped earth plainly pointing the way taken by Teresa and her abductors. Tony's shrewd brown eyes flashed along the ground.

"Pro'bly of two dozen hombres—no?"

Dilliard nodded. "Twenty or twenty-five. I didn't count 'em. Can't see why so many was needed for their butcherin' work and to carry off Teresa. . . . We won't have an easy time of it, *amigo*."

"It looks," Tony grinned ruefully, "like we have our work all cut an' slice—no?"

"If you're hintin' we got a job cut out for us," Dilliard said grimly, "you spilled a whole mouthful, Tony."

"Spill the mouthful?" Tony looked puzzled.

"You spoke the truth," Dilliard explained.

Tony shrugged, slowly nodded as he absorbed the phrase. "Spill the mouthful. It is a good saying. . . . Well, shall we make the proceed, and get this cut-an'-slice job over quick like the possible?"

They spoke to the horses, again moved on at a faster clip.

All that afternoon, Dilliard and Tony followed the trail of the bandits, across a series of rolling hills and along tiny washes and canyons. Ever they mounted higher as they climbed the far reaches of the Santa Ana Mountains. At times they crossed hillsides ablaze with the riotous colors of wildflowers. Descending the opposite side of the same hills, the way, more often than not, was spiny with cacti and cholla. Now and then quail or wild doves flushed up from beneath the horses' hoofs. Once a deer was startled into action from the wet banks of a small *cañada.*

The sun had long since swung to the west, its rounded edge touching the distant San Joaquin Hills near the blue Pacific. The air grew chill as a brisk breeze from the coast lifted into being.

Tony asked, "You think those scoundrelly ones will travel all night?"

Dilliard shook his head. "I figure they'll be stopping right soon. We ought to slow down a mite so we won't overrun 'em. That might prove disastrous."

The two men had just dipped down through a park of huge live oaks. Ahead, lay a narrow blind canyon. Momentarily, the evening breeze died down. Dilliard's nostrils twitched at the sudden scent of wood smoke.

"Camp ahead," he announced briefly, drawing

in his horse. Tony halted beside him. They dismounted, tethering the two animals to the lower limbs of a big white oak.

Dilliard took the lead, and the two went cautiously forward on foot, carefully picking their way through the brush. Splashing across a tiny, narrow stream of water, they rounded a bend in the canyon. Dilliard stopped, stepped suddenly back, one hand behind him to halt Tony. They dropped silently to earth, a wide screen of mesquite sheltering them from view.

Through the leafy branches, Dilliard and Tony made an unobscured examination of the outlaws' camp. A fire burned. An odor of burning wood and cooking food was in the air. From a nearby tree hung a side of beef, doubtless from a stray Sicamoro animal picked up on the way.

Nearly two dozen men sprawled about the camp which had been made at the foot of a brush-covered slope in the end of the canyon. Here and there, from beneath the brush, jutted great slabs of yellow sandstone. To the right, a short distance from the bandits' camp, the outlaws' horses were tethered on a rope stretched between two tall trees.

Tony looked anxiously for Teresa, finally saw the girl seated on a blanket beyond the fire. She was still resplendent in Mariposa's finery, though the veil had been withdrawn by this time. The girl seemed cool and collected.

Even while Dilliard and Tony watched, one of the outlaws left the fire and approached Teresa bearing food and something in a tin cup. Dilliard watched him place bits of food in the girl's mouth and judged that her feet and hands were securely bound.

"Anyway," Tony muttered nervously, "they ain' do her none of harm."

Dilliard nodded, satisfied. He was suddenly aware that night had fallen. To his ears came the faint crackle of the outlaws' fire. The camp gradually quieted down, though there was some ribald singing and drinking from flasks for a time. The *Americano* bandits were failing to display their better sides—if such existed—to their Mexican captive.

Cramped from his long position, Dilliard finally edged back, drawing Tony beside him. For more than two hours the two men sat conversing in whispers in the darkness. The camp was quiet by this time, the fire nearly out. Now and then a vagrant blaze flared up a moment to pick out highlights on the blanket-rolled cocoons grouped horizontally about the smoldering embers. One of the bandits tossed a blanket around Teresa's shoulders and sat down not far from the girl.

Dilliard whispered to Tony; then, with the stealth of a Comanche, moved off through the gloom. Tony settled back to wait for the Texan's return. Fifteen minutes passed. Twenty.

A half hour drifted by. Tony stirred impatiently, anxiously, peered through the lacy limbs of the sheltering mesquite. He could see no more than before. The camp didn't appear to have changed in any manner.

Insects of the night made their myriad noises. Somewhere in the trees, off to the left, a night-bird went suddenly insane, and just as abruptly stopped its piercing notes. Again, quiet fell. Tony commenced to grow nervous. Still no sign of Dilliard. Another quarter hour passed. Overhead, the sky was sprinkled with stars. The moon hadn't yet come up.

The faintest of rustling sounds caught the Mexican's ears, then Branch Dilliard's lean form was sky-lighted momentarily, faintly, an instant between the mesquites. Tony's surprise took the form of an effective Spanish oath uttered in an explosive whisper.

Dilliard hissed a low-voiced, *"Shhh!"* Behind him he led a saddled pony.

The Mexican squirmed around in the gloom to get a better look.

Dilliard was laughing silently as he dropped down beside Tony. "Sure was skeery thievin' this bronc in the darkness. Gettin' the saddle, and then riggin' up, was the hardest part, though. But those coyotes never made a move; they're dead to the world I—"

"Teresa?" Tony tried to control his tones.

"She's all right," the Texan replied. "One feller's guarding her, but he's been dozing most of the time. He's got a bottle at his side; hitting that plumb often is helpin' a heap. Ten minutes more and I figure he'll be in shape to sleep it off until noon. . . . Teresa's tied tight. I got near enough to—"

"*Diantre*!" Tony's voice sounded choked. "You hav' spik to her?"

Dilliard shook his head, then remembering Tony couldn't see him in the gloom, responded, "Nope, I didn't dare try that. . . . Listen, *amigo*, you know that rope the outlaws' horses are fastened to?"

"You mean the rope that reach' from the two trees?"

"That's it. I untied both ends. There isn't a thing in the world to stop those horses, should they get a notion to run."

Tony rocked with soft laughter. "Señor Branch, you are one *diablo* for theenk out ideas. I'm theenk those *caballos* get the excuse to run pret' soon—no?"

"That's my thoughts on the matter." The Texan went on, "We'll drift back and bring up our own horses. When we leave here, we don't want to waste any time. Maybe we'll be lucky, maybe we won't, but it's best to prepare for everything."

Tethering the horse Dilliard had taken from the outlaw camp, the two walked noiselessly back, then returned in a short time with their own ponies. Tying the three horses loosely, Tony and Dilliard held a brief, whispered consultation, then separated, following different paths toward the camp.

In a moment they had blended with the darkness. Again silence fell.

9
THE GAUNTLET OF FIRE

The mountain horizon to the east was now edged with an aura of silver. Another ten minutes would bring the rising moon into view. Back in the hills a coyote yip-yipped with startling sharpness. One by one, and in twos and threes, other coyotes took up the cry. The sounds rolled across the hills, gathering form and volume, then abruptly died away.

By this time, Dilliard had worked his way around the rim of the camp and was hidden in the brush, just a few yards back of Teresa. Reluctantly, he left his screening shelter of leaves and branches, wiggled slowly forward on his stomach.

Inch by silent inch, he approached the half-reclining form of the girl, moving across dead leaves and gravelly earth with all the stealth of an Indian. The Texan felt sure Teresa wasn't asleep, even though she made no move. A few feet away, on a second blanket, one of the outlaws, acting as the girl's guard, was sprawled on his back, eyes closed. All around the almost dead embers of the campfire, men were stretched in various attitudes.

Dilliard moved even more cautiously as he

drew nearer to Teresa. He glanced again at the Mexican girl's guard and saw that the man dozed fitfully. Then, Dilliard put out one hand, lightly touched Teresa's back.

At the Texan's touch, Teresa started ever so slightly, then held tense for what came next. She felt fingers fumbling at the tough, rawhide thongs that bound her wrists behind her. Cautiously she came to a sitting position, turned her head slightly to glance at her guard.

The movement was slight, but the guard came awake instantly. Dilliard dropped flat behind the girl, hoping he wouldn't be seen in the semi-gloom before the rising of the moon. The guard said something to Teresa about getting to sleep. Teresa replied quietly that sleep was impossible for her. The guard growled something that had to do with "damn greasers," rose and placed a dead oak limb on the cooling ashes of the fire. A few sparks stirred, flew quickly upward and disappeared.

The guard returned to his blankets, drank deeply from a flask at his side, and stretched out again. Dilliard shrank close to earth, swearing mentally, every nerve fiber tense with the strain of waiting. Minutes dragged past on leaden feet. Abruptly, a deep, contented snore left the guard's parted lips. Dilliard waited to see if the sound would awaken its owner, but after a moment the snoring continued.

The tip of the moon appeared. Again that wild coyote song burst forth and rolled harshly across the hilltops. Momentarily a thought for the girl he had left waiting intruded on Dilliard's thoughts, but he felt she was safe; his mind came back to the business at hand. Twisting easily to one side he fished out his clasp knife, opened one blade, again moved near to the Mexican girl.

Luckily the dead oak limb the guard had placed on the fire didn't catch fire. Dilliard renewed his efforts on Teresa's bonds. In an instant the girl's hands were free. She sat straighter, leaned over to fumble with the knots at her ankles.

Suddenly, the guard sat up, stared blearily at the scene, only half believing what his sleep-sodden senses were telling him. He opened his mouth to shout a warning, but already Dilliard had crossed to his rear and brought down the heavy barrel of his six-shooter on the guard's unprotected head. The man went limp and slumped, unconscious, back to his blankets.

But Dilliard's activities weren't to escape unnoticed: another outlaw, a few yards away, sat up, then opened his mouth in a wild yell of warning. Dilliard stooped, severed the rawhide at Teresa's ankles with one swift stroke, jerked the girl upright.

The camp was stirring into life now. Two outlaws were already on their feet, groping for guns. Dilliard's six-shooter roared, as he seized Teresa and swept her back with him into the brush.

Across the camp sounded a wild, high-pitched yell that startled the outlaws' horses into panic. The gunfire had made the beasts nervous; that yell completed the business. There came shrill, excited sounds from the horses. They reared, snorting madly, twisting free, down-slashing hoofs ripping brush and turf. Then, they were away in a mad stampede that swept them up the hillside, over rocks and through trees and bushes.

Dilliard was still backing away from the camp, pulling Teresa with him. The camp was a bedlam of yelling men, wild shots and curses. Someone was striving frantically to fan the campfire to life, hoping the flames would pick out the escaping prisoner and whoever had come to her assistance. So far, the outlaws had no way of knowing how large a party had come to attempt the rescue.

Brush and small dead limbs were piled on the smoking log and smoldering embers. There came a sudden flare of light as flames gathered headway and rushed up, throwing the scene into bold relief. By this time, Branch and Teresa were half-hidden in the growth that surrounded the camp. The bandits were rushing wildly about, searching for their prey.

Dilliard whispered swift directions to the girl who was too cramped from her bonds for swift movement. At that moment, Tony came plunging up. Dilliard swore gratefully, turned the girl over to the Mexican. Tony and Teresa disappeared in the mesquite, heading in the direction of the place where Dilliard and the Mexican had left their horses.

Dilliard darted off at a tangent, firing his gun as he ran, to draw the outlaws away from Tony and the girl. Whining bullets cut the leaves around the Texan. He emptied his cartridge gun, then the cap-and-ball, circled the camp, away from Tony and the waiting horses.

The camp was a nest of hot gunfire. Three forms rolled on the earth, in agony. A fourth was down, braced on one hand, the other hand a-flame with smoke and hot lead. Dilliard's gun jerked sidewise, exploded in a burst of orange flame. The body of another outlaw suddenly jack-knifed, pitched forward and lay still. Dilliard sprinted on, bullets humming around his running form, but, miraculously, without finding his body.

The Texan was breathing hard now. Swerving to one side he crashed violently into a tree trunk, staggered, then righted himself. He paused, panting, in the shelter of the tree, one hand groping in a pocket for fresh cartridges. Empty shells were plugged out of his cylinder, fresh loads shoved into the empty chambers. There was no time now to reload his depleted cap-and-ball pistol; that was thrust into the waistband of his trousers.

For the moment the bandits had lost sight of Dilliard. He waited, behind the tree trunk, looking over the scene. Dilliard chuckled grimly. "We sure stirred up a hornet's nest looks like," he muttered. Across the camp, hidden in the brush, were Tony and Teresa with the horses. But to reach them now meant that Dilliard would have to run a veritable gauntlet of flaming guns. To go around would require too much time, and every minute counted. At any instant, Tony and Teresa might be located.

"It's now or never," Dilliard told himself, stepping suddenly from behind the tree. By this time the moon was above the hills, bathing the outlaw camp with white light. One of the outlaws spotted the Texan almost immediately. His gun roared.

Something hot burned along the Texan's right ribs as he leaped into full view. He saw swift forms outlined in the moonlight, their hands throwing orange lances of savage fire.

Dilliard muttered, "Straight into it is the shortest distance between two points."

He was already running, his Colt-gun jerking in his right hand. An evil face loomed before him; gunpowder flared wickedly close at hand. Hands clutched at his arms and legs. He shook them off, plunged on, his gun roaring or swinging sharply against bearded faces. A muscular hand gripped his shoulder. Dilliard swung his gun, caught a quick picture of a wide-open mouth, staring eyes. Seemingly from far off, a pain-wrenched cry reached his ears. He jerked loose only to stumble and go sprawling across a form that had just dropped at his feet.

In an instant the Texan was up, throwing off his would-be captors. Quite suddenly he realized his gun was again empty, the hammer falling futilely on empty shells. The wild yells were falling farther to his rear now. It dawned on Dilliard, quite abruptly, that he was at last clear of the camp, running swiftly through the trees and brush.

For a moment he lost all sense of direction. There was a crimson blur before his eyes. The taste of bitter salt was on his parched lips. His right side was queerly numb, carrying a vague sensation of paralysis. The Texan staggered on, spurs tangling in low brush, feet tripping over each other. Sweat blinded his vision against the moonlight pouring through the branches.

As in a dream, Dilliard suddenly saw the figures of Tony and Teresa looming before him. The girl was already mounted.

Tony's words were tense with anguish: "For the love of the *Señor Dios*, hurry!"

Dilliard laughed, a trifle foolishly, his words not quite steady, "Get slopin'! I'll hold 'em off. Tell the Señorita Castameto I didn't really intend to spank her. Go on, drift!"

"It is not necessary that you hold them off," Tony implored. "They have run to catch their horses. It will be sometime before they are successful. More time will be lost in the saddling. If we leave now, they'll never catch—"

"Antonio!" Teresa spoke quick, terse Spanish. "It is you who waste time." She gave quick, snapping orders.

"*Por Dios*!" Tony cried. "You are correct, my Teresa!"

The Texan felt himself half lifted to saddle, then caught a rush of wind against his face, heard the steady drumming of horses' pounding hoofs. He tried to speak, but his lips were dry, his tongue thick.

Tony was riding close, one hand supporting the swaying Texan. There were certain difficult moments of intense concentration before Dilliard got the hang of staying in his saddle. Teresa rode ahead, leading the way, finding the best footing and the more open paths through the trees.

Loose branches slapped viciously at the Texan's face and body, but he didn't feel any pain. Once Tony's anxious voice reached him in a moment of lucidity.

"Sure, sure, I'm all right," Dilliard replied impatiently. "Keep going. I ain't hurt none."

One leg and his right side felt wet and warm and sticky. There were moments when Dilliard passed completely out of the picture, but always he contrived to keep up. He lost all conception of passing time and felt somehow cheated when he noticed, during one of his clearer moments, that the moon had already crossed the sky and was swinging to the west. It seemed not five minutes since he had left the outlaws' camp. What had happened in the meantime?

A sort of nightmare, that ride, a queer business of rattling around in the saddle and losing his stirrups from time to time, and much foolish-sounding laughter which Dilliard was always surprised to find issuing from his own parched mouth. Then he would feel embarrassed and fight to keep clear-headed and sane, but always he drifted back to a semi-conscious delirium in which recent past events assumed exaggerated importance and caused Tony and Teresa to glance queerly at one another.

Dilliard returned to sanity from one of these sessions with the realization that the horses had come to a halt. It was still dark, but a fourth person had joined the party, a slim white figure with cornsilk hair and bare feet. Mariposa.

Tony had been giving details in low-voiced Spanish. Dilliard caught certain words that had to do with his own condition. He felt himself lifted from the saddle. For the moment his head cleared. He felt buoyant; there was a lack of any sensation when his feet touched the earth.

He swayed drunkenly on fast-weakening legs

before the *señorita*, insisted on making a low, mocking bow, trying for certain sarcasms that concerned "the very high-toned Señorita Castameto." He bowed low from the waist—and kept going until his long form was sprawled awkwardly on the earth.

Mariposa's anguished protests didn't filter through to his dim consciousness. Tony was straightening his form on a patch of grass. Teresa hovered near. Dilliard's shirt was torn away. There was a sound of ripping cotton as bandages were manufactured.

A dagger of sheer torture shot through Dilliard's body. He heard Mariposa's words: "I don't believe it is serious."

The old laugh formed on Dilliard's white lips. He mumbled thickly, "You're right—it ain't serious. It's the silver flame in the dusk that really hurts most."

Something of this reached the girl's ears, made her wince. The last thought Dilliard caught for a long time was that of Mariposa giving orders, the Mexican pair obeying with efficient silence. After minutes of this, the Texan was again lifted to saddle, his rope was employed to lash his limp form securely in the seat. The horses moved on again.

There were certain savage joltings during the remainder of the journey that brought Dilliard close to the surface at times, but it was near dawn before he came entirely to the top for a few minutes. Even then, it didn't mean a great deal to him—candles guttering in the early morning breeze, much excited conversation in Spanish, shadowy forms running here and there. Dilliard gained an impression of big trees and buildings. Lights shone on his white face. Then, as he was being lifted from the saddle, he passed out again.

He regained consciousness to find himself stretched on a bed in a large room. Someone was doing something to his side; he caught the sound made by water being squeezed from a cloth. Dilliard wondered whether that really was a dagger being drawn sharply across his ribs. He gritted his teeth against the pain.

After a few moments he opened one eye, met the searching gaze of a pair of keen black ones set on either side of a hawk-beak nose and, beneath it, a firm, straight-lipped mouth. A shock of wavy, iron-gray hair rose above the eyes.

"I'll bet a plugged peso," and Dilliard's voice was none too steady, "that you're Ol' Salvadore Castameto. Well, we brought her home—*patrón.* It's Teresa and Tony that gets any medals you hand out though. They're gamey, that pair. Me, I sort of fumbled my part. I reckon my sights need adjustin'. My lead throws too high. The—the Señorita Castameto can tell you how that went."

Dilliard's eyes closed again. There were many excited and puzzled exclamations in Spanish on the heels of the Texan's light-headed speech. Dilliard listened, eyes shut, too tired to take a hand. That damn' dagger was being raked along his ribs again. Now and then he caught a word or two of Mariposa's story and many references to the "*gringo vaquero*."

Later, a steel-sharp voice cut in, speaking in Spanish, "Now, to you, foolish one. So, you have returned once more."

And Tony's humble reply, "*Sí, mi patrón.*"

"And this time do you remain, with no more of your imbecilic notions?"

"*Sí, mi patrón.*"

Tony's meek mien brought a chuckle to Dilliard's pain-twisted lips. "*Sí, mi patrón,*" Dilliard muttered, without opening his eyes. "Yes, my protector, my father, my guardian. Tony, you jug-headed pack-mule! Ain't this a free country? What's become of the 'so gran' *vaquero*' who nearly wrecked the *Rancho Sicamoro* when he quit his job? Don't tell me you're the same hombre that helped me battle—"

The Texan's words changed suddenly to an explosive "Damn!" They were using that razor-edged dagger on his left leg now. Dilliard caught sharp orders in Mariposa's voice. The cleansing of the wound proceeded more deftly from that point. Castameto was telling Mariposa to leave the room. Mariposa was refusing. Some further argument ensued, before the voices died down and Castameto returned to his discussion with Tony:

"You are content, this time, my so gay *caballero—*" and Castameto's tones were sarcasm-edged, "—to remain with us on the *rancho*?"

"*Sí, mi patrón.*" Tony sounded very subdued.

"So! It is good—perhaps. And you have brought your woman with you."

"*Sí, Señor Patrón,*" Teresa and Tony together this time.

Castameto growled good-naturedly, "That, at least, Antonio, shows you have arrived at some sound sense in your so-thick head. The girl has a good face. With luck, she may yet make something worthwhile of your useless hide, bear you many small *niños.* Is it, perhaps, that one is already on the way?"

Tony gulped and looked uncertainly at Teresa; Teresa replied, low-voiced, "No, *patrón.*"

Castameto nodded sagely. "For the present, that is good. Later, no doubt . . . Now, listen closely, both of you. I will give you comfortable quarters. Come Sunday, the *padre* is expected to stop here on his journey from Capistrano to *El Pueblo de Nuestra Señora de Los Angeles.* He will do that which is necessary. Later, a fiesta may be arranged to celebrate your marriage, if the *Americano*'s condition warrants."

"*Gracias, mi patrón.*" A sort of duet from Tony and Teresa.

A light-headed snicker escaped Dilliard's lips. One eye cocked owlishly open. Somehow, the Texan lacked strength to prevent his next words: "Certainly the *Americano*'s condition will warrant attending your fiesta—providing the yellow rose of Monterey also attends—no, *mi patrón*?"

"*Que dice el*?" Puzzled, questioning Spanish from old Castameto who didn't understand English. "What does he say?"

Dilliard was suddenly weary. "It doesn't matter," he mumbled thickly, closing his eyes.

Once more, the black velvet curtain of unconsciousness fell, enveloping the Texan in its thick folds. . . .

10
CROSS-PURPOSES

Many, many days passed, with Branch Dilliard slowly regaining his strength, this being to the credit, largely, of an old Mexican brought in haste from the settlement of San Juan Capistrano, some miles to the south, where the ancient herb doctor was wont to use his knowledge of healing plants and roots. The main trouble with Dilliard was loss of blood. A rib had been cracked and a thigh bone slightly furrowed. Both bullets had passed cleanly through flesh; there'd been no extractions of lead necessary; infection hadn't set in. And then came the day when the Texan was allowed to rise from his bed and dress, though more than a week followed before he'd regained his full strength.

Teresa played a definite part in the recovery, proving herself a skillful nurse, although, during the period when Dilliard was still delirious, certain matters had been attended to by Mariposa herself, who had insisted that it was her duty to have a hand in the healing of the *Americano*. Once he had regained full consciousness, however, the *señorita* had remained absent from the room that had been turned over to the Texan. It was a high-ceilinged room with a heavy oaken bedstead, on the head of which was carved the coat-of-arms of a noble Spanish line. The windows were recessed in thick walls and equipped with wrought-iron grills of graceful design. The floor of the room was spread with wild animal skins.

Though Mariposa had remained away, Castameto had come in daily, during Dilliard's convalescence, to inquire about the Texan's condition. There was something fine about old Salvadore, a touch of the patrician around the chiseled lips and hawk-beak nose. He was proud, dignified, courteous; his even-toned speech revealed, once or twice, a haughtiness that was entirely natural and clearly revealed where Mariposa had inherited her blue-blooded reserve.

Castameto's dark eyes looked through and into a man, ever on the alert to search out a weakness. Of this last there hadn't been any discoveries where Branch Dilliard was concerned; the *patrón* hadn't been able to uncover anything but straight man. But, always, in their daily conversations, Dilliard had sensed a courteous but persistent probing, as though old Castameto was experiencing difficulty in fitting the *Americano* into the proper pigeon-hole to which he consigned all gringos.

The fact of the matter was that Dilliard hadn't realized his failure to reveal the sort of traits Castameto had grown to expect from all *Americanos* in those early California days. Gradually, reluctantly, Castameto came to accept the Texan as different, though always with certain reservations. And then one day, when Dilliard was feeling himself again, came Castameto's invitation to inspect the big ranch house and surrounding grounds.

The inspection of the place brought a series of revelations to Dilliard. It was constructed of rock and straw-and-adobe bricks, built in the form of a hollow square. Huge timbers, cut in the mountains and hauled down by oxen, gave the house strength and solidity. The roof was covered with tiles from the ovens of Mission San Juan Capistrano, which was situated some miles to the south of the Ranch of the Sycamores.

Inside the hollow square of rooms was a gardened patio, open to the blue, California sky. A rock-walled well stood in the center of the patio, surrounded by flowering plants whose seeds and roots had been brought in by the early Spanish settlers. Above the well, a huge sycamore raised protecting branches that spread almost to the eaves of the rooms on all sides. A roofed gallery, or *corredor*, open to the garden and, with a two-foot-high railing, bordered the inner square all around.

The rooms seemed endless to Dilliard—bedrooms, a large main room with a fireplace at either end. The roof of the kitchen was like a huge inverted funnel where the smoke, from the fire below, escaped to the outer air, and the walls, in addition to a bristling array of pots and pans and kettles, were strung with lines of vari-colored corn and scarlet chili peppers. One room, the *baño*, was equipped with a small sunken plunge for bathers. The main room walls were plastered with adobe mixed with goats' milk to provide a smooth, durable finish.

It was a comfortable house of old paintings, heavy furniture of dark wood upholstered in worn red leather. Indian rugs and goatskins were spread in profusion about the floors. All the dishes for the dining room had been imported from Mexico City and were the best to be had.

The Rancho Sicamoro was situated at the upper end of Borrego Canyon in a grove of sycamore trees. To the east and south and north were the Santa Ana Mountains. To the west, a wide, fertile valley that stretched many miles to the San Joaquin Hills that ranged along the Pacific Coast, a valley dotted with cattle. There were also horses, sheep and goats on Castameto's holdings.

The house proper held quarters for Castameto's ranch boss, or *mayordomo*. Apart from the house were other buildings—corrals, shelters for the *vaqueros*, comfortable huts for married employees, in one of which Teresa and Tony were now domiciled. There was a blacksmith shop, stables, sheds, a kitchen and eating house for the *vaqueros*. There was even a small *carcel*, or jail, which had stood empty for many years.

Dilliard's eyes opened wide at all this; the *patrón* seemed to be fathering a veritable village. Indians and Mexicans and the children of both saluted Castameto respectfully as he and Dilliard walked about on their tour of inspection.

The two had halted near a corral in which were a large number of blooded horses, the sight of which warmed the Texan's heart. Dilliard rolled a cigarette, leaned against the bars of the corral, his gray eyes taking in the moving scene of activity all around.

Castameto chuckled gravely and said, "Well, of what do you think?"

Dilliard shook his head. "I'm beyond thought," he replied in Spanish. "You have a small town here. Everything is clean and run with efficiency. How do you do it?"

Castameto shook his head. "We have always done it—I and my father before me. Our people are loyal. They realize that we work for their best interests." He sighed, added, "No, it is not a question of how I do it, Señor Branch, but of how I am to continue doing it."

Dilliard frowned, "You mean what?"

Castameto shook his head. "Of that, I may speak more fully later. But this is no time for speaking of trouble. We must all be gay, happy. Tomorrow, we hold the fiesta to celebrate the marriage of Antonio to his beloved Teresa."

Dilliard went to bed that night mentally comparing the Rancho Sicamoro with outfits he had known in Texas. He sighed deeply. The old dons certainly knew how to do things in bang-up fashion. No wonder they resented the coming of Americans and American ways, their ever hustling activity, their eternal scratching for gold and land.

The Texan's thoughts turned to Mariposa: for two days now he hadn't caught sight of the girl. She was somewhere about the house, he knew, but he was too proud to inquire after her whereabouts, too proud to risk further snubbings. Oh, well, it didn't matter. He'd be moving on soon, now, returning to his native Texas. The following day would bring the fiesta to honor Tony's and Teresa's marriage. Tony had wanted him to stay for that. Dilliard shrugged his shoulders; another day wouldn't matter. The day after the fiesta he could saddle up and—and Dilliard fell asleep on that thought.

But fiesta day had passed all too quickly to suit Dilliard. Contrary to expectations, he had enjoyed the celebration thoroughly. There had been music by a Mexican orchestra of stringed instruments; fandangos, horse racing and chicken pulling. In a huge pit filled with white-hot embers a beef animal had been barbecued the while a tasty, spicy sauce had been basted over the smoking meat; wine and *aguardiente* had been opened.

The Texan had entered several of the events—mainly the horse racing and roping, and he hadn't always won. And when he laughed and congratulated the winners, the flashing white teeth of the *vaqueros* greeted him warmly and they took the Texas gringo to their hearts.

Mounted on one of Castameto's horses he had won one race, lost the next by a nose to a wiry Mexican mounted on a pony as wiry as its rider. It was just before the start of the third heat that Dilliard saw Mariposa for the first time that day. The girl was standing, surrounded by a group of her women, face flushed with excitement.

For a moment her eyes met Dilliard's. A hot, choking sensation filled the Texan's throat. Impulsively, Mariposa had flung to him a yellow rose she held in her hand. Dilliard's left hand had darted out, snatched the blossom from the air, thrust it inside his shirt. His heart beat madly. Again he tried to reach her gaze, but the girl was looking in another direction. Back of his daughter stood Castameto, a slight frown creasing his dark features.

And in that moment, the signal to *go* was called. The other horses got under way immediately. With an abrupt start, Dilliard came back to his surroundings. A cloud of dust enveloped him from flashing hoofs. Plunging in his spurs, he darted off. One by one he drew abreast of, passed, the riders who had preceded him. Now only one rider held the lead. Tony was two lengths ahead, riding madly. He glanced back, saw Dilliard at his rear, grinned widely.

The horses thundered on, around the course, but try as he might, Dilliard's pony couldn't gain an inch. The air was a bedlam of drumming hoofs and excited cries. Dilliard's horse was straining to the utmost but couldn't overtake the flashing mount that carried Tony. Rather, he had lost a couple of feet.

Again, Tony glanced back. The horses were nearing the finish now. Victory for Tony seemed certain. And then, just as they neared the yelling crowd grouped near the finish, Tony swerved his pony queerly to one side, the beast stumbled and went down, horse and man crashing to the dust. Before he could pull in, Dilliard flashed past the finishing line a winner!

Dilliard pulled his horse to a quick halt and without pausing for the plaudits awaiting the winner, swung back to meet Tony. The Mexican was already back in the saddle, grinning widely. Horse and man were unhurt. Other contestants flew past.

Dilliard reached from his saddle for Tony's hand, pressed it hard. "You dang jug-head," he chuckled, "it don't go down."

"Me, I'm theenk I'm go down ver' hard," Tony replied innocently. "An' my *caballo* as well."

"Chuck it," Dilliard said, "you know what I mean. Tony, that was your race. You made that horse fall on purpose. I'm askin' why."

"It was that gopher hole the horse steps into—"

Dilliard laughed scornfully. "There ain't a hole in this course, Tony. No more bluffin'. I want an answer."

Tony shrugged lithe shoulders. "All right, if you must hav' the truth. In the events today, I'm theenk you win more often if you have your own horse. You have been at disadvantage. Besides, your wounds—"

"You can chuck that, too. My wounds have healed. I'm strong as ever. I'll be ready to leave tomorrow—"

"Señor Branch!" Tony was suddenly serious. "Maybe, I'm think to make you ver' happy to win, then maybe you not be in soch hurry to leave here. I'm ver' much regret to see you leave—"

"I don't see anything more to stay for, Tony."

"I'm think maybe you are wrong. That is why I'm stumble-down my horse so you win. I saw certain things. The throwing of a yellow rose. It was not right that the bearer of that rose should lose—"

"Tony!" Dilliard said eagerly. "Do you think she meant—?"

Tony eyed Dilliard scornfully. "In many things you are the top man, Señor Branch, but in the matters of love it is you who are the head of the jug—no?"

"Tony! I can't believe it—"

"Hah!" Tony's breath was expelled violently, disgustedly. "You have a head like a scorched *frijole*! Do you think the *señorita* threw that rose for the—what you call heem?—the exercise of the arm?"

There was no time to say more. A crowd of cheering men had raced down the track to surround the two. They were lifted from their horses, carried off to partake of the barbecued meat and wine. Tony was grinning like a good-natured gargoyle; Dilliard's face was a bronzed study of perplexity.

In a group, a short distance away, Mariposa stood with her father. Don Salvadore's features were grave as he talked to his daughter. Dilliard waited until the girl had turned in his direction, caught her eyes. His hand held the yellow rose she had thrown.

Mariposa's face flushed hotly, her head rose slightly. There was no answering smile for the Texan. Dilliard felt his face crimsoning. He had been wrong then, in his sudden feeling of exaltation. Tony's surmises had been wrong. Hell! This rose was probably thrown to anyone who could catch it. He had been lucky—or was it unlucky?

Deliberately, in full view of the girl, Dilliard

tossed the yellow rose into the barbecue pit and turned his back. He didn't see the look of pain that dimmed her eyes, as she continued listening, obediently, to her father's words.

The sun was swinging to the west now. Tony and Teresa found Dilliard, carried him off to watch the dancing and hear the music. The two were completely lost in the joy of the moment and in themselves. Dilliard envied the pair, while he watched the Mexicans at play. All of them, all of these men and women were like children in their innocent enjoyment of the *patrón*'s liberal benevolence.

Dilliard swore softly under his breath. "They're like a bunch of overgrown kids," he muttered. "No thought nor care for tomorrow. Enjoy it all today. That's their motto, I reckon. No wonder the *Americanos* are stealing them blind, grabbing their lands and cattle from end to end of California."

It grew darker, torches and bonfires leaped into being. The music and dancing continued. Men and women returned to the barbecue pit to partake of steaming meat and chili.

Night came suddenly, sprinkling the dark sky with bright starlight. Tony and Teresa were dancing. Mariposa and her father were no longer in sight. Dilliard felt alone and depressed. Well, tomorrow would see him on his way back to Texas.

He turned toward the house, pushed through an iron-grated passage that brought him into the peaceful, silent patio. Lights shone from one or two rooms surrounding the patio. It was peaceful here, quiet. The music of the fandangos outside the wall reached the Texan's ear faintly. He walked to the center of the patio, paused a moment beneath the spreading limbs of the sycamore, to drink thirstily of the clear cold water from the well. The path stretching across the patio to the railed gallery leading to the rooms of the house was bordered with yellow poppies. The scent of jasmine was delicately sweet in Dilliard's nostrils, the air about the patio perfumed with its evening fragrance.

Dilliard reached the railed *corredor* and started to step across to the main room of the house. The slightest of movements in the shadow to his left brought him around. He saw Mariposa, lovely in frothy white and with a jet comb high in the coiled masses of pale gold.

The Texan laughed softly, "And I was giving that jasmine all the credit. Wrong, after all, wasn't I?"

"You—you mean about my rose?" the girl asked.

"About that, too—I reckon."

The girl's words came hard. "You—you burned my rose. I saw you—"

"I'm thinking I burned more than your rose in

that moment. A heap of hopes went up in those flames."

"I—I don't understand you."

"It doesn't matter—but I think you do, Señorita Castameto."

The girl came closer, close enough for Dilliard to see her features dimly in the faint starlight that penetrated beneath the roof of the *corredor.* She said quietly, "Is it necessary—the very hateful way in which you utter that 'Señorita Castameto'? Do you hate me so much?"

"Hate you!" Dilliard closed his eyes a moment, waiting for a certain unbearable pain to pass. When he opened them he forced his voice to be cold, hard: "You objected to 'Mary.' "

The girl replied low-voiced, trying to make him comprehend, "I didn't understand that day—I think there were things neither of us understood. But we seem always to be working at cross-purposes—"

"They're not of my making."

"Are you so sure of that point, Señor Branch Dilliard? I can see my ways are strange to you. At the same time, your ways, as well, are different. I can't comprehend why you are as you are."

"Do you think we ever will understand each other?" Dilliard asked tensely. His heart went out of him until he had heard her reply:

"I don't say we won't. I'm learning, learning fast, that all gringos are not alike."

The music, outside the patio, was weaving mysteries in Branch Dilliard's brain. He took one step toward Mariposa, then halted, stubbornly reluctant to go further. Something relative to his "sights needin' adjusting" came to him. He steeled himself against repeating a certain error.

Suddenly Dilliard bowed and stood aside. "We all make mistakes, *señorita*," he said carelessly. "*Buenos noches.* I'm figuring to see your father for a few minutes before I turn in."

"I know. He's waiting for you in the *sala.* He told me you plan to leave tomorrow morning."

"I'm figuring that way."

The girl started to speak, changed her mind, asked, almost to herself, "I wonder why you ever came to California?"

Dilliard laughed easily. "Nothing much to that. I crossed a herd over the Colorado three years back. I only stayed a week after delivering the cows, but that week was enough; I got a bite of California that stuck in my craw. Couldn't get rid of it. I returned a month ago to find out if there was anythin' to it."

"And have you learned?"

Dilliard's laugh wasn't quite so easy this time. "I've learned to wonder if I ever will get it out of my craw."

Mariposa didn't fumble the meaning back of that. "Would it do any good," she asked lightly, "to suggest that you stay until you're certain?"

Dilliard's voice shook a trifle, "You're asking that?"

"My father would like to know you better—"

"Anyone else?" tensely.

"I think—I think Tony and Teresa would miss you."

Dilliard swore softly to himself. Again, memory of a certain mistake in his "lead throwin' " prevented him from speaking the thought in his mind, insisting that the girl drop all evasion.

From inside the house came inquiring words from old Salvadore Castameto, "Are you out there, Señor Dilliard?"

"*Sí*, Señor Castameto. I'll be right in."

Dilliard turned back to find the girl had vanished. He caught a brief glimpse of a white, lacy dress disappearing, wraith-like, through a doorway farther down the *corredor.* His mind in a turmoil, Dilliard swung back to the doorway, saying, "I'm coming, Señor Castameto."

11

UNWELCOME VISITORS

As Dilliard entered the big room, Castameto came up out of a high-backed chair, before the fireplace of the *sala*, to greet him. A similar chair stood nearby, facing the flames, and between the two chairs was a small tiled table. Burning logs of oak spread a pleasant glow through the long room. A servant entered, bearing wine, thin glasses and a long, narrow cedar box of *cigarros*. Castameto spoke a few words to the servant. The wine was poured and gleamed like topaz in its fragile containers.

There was but little conversation at first. Dilliard settled himself in the comfortable depths of his high-backed chair to enjoy the wine and fragrant tobacco. After a few minutes the servant passed to their rear and withdrew. Music from the fiesta still faintly penetrated the silences of the room.

Dilliard said at last, "The fiesta was a huge success." He spoke in Spanish, the *patrón* neither speaking, nor understanding, the English tongue. "I enjoyed myself hugely at the celebration."

"Probably it is the last ever to be given on the Rancho Sicamoro," Castameto said. He corrected himself hastily, "That is, by a Castameto."

Dilliard evinced a certain surprise at this and said as much.

The Spaniard's reply was evasive: "There is little need to dwell on my troubles. Cattle are nearly finished in California. The drought of '64 wiped out most of the large *ranchos*. Many large holdings have been lost to—" he paused, then, "—to newcomers to this land. Many of the invaders have entered into agriculture, knowing it is useless to run beef stock. Many of my friends have lost their places and returned to Mexico and Spain, leaving only hate in this California where they were raised and where their fathers were raised."

Dilliard said, a trifle uncomfortably, "Anyway, you've still retained your place."

"So far, what you say is true. I have been fortunate—to some extent. A goodly half of my cattle have been disposed of. By paring expenses to the bone, and with the aid of sheep, I have managed to hold the old place together."

Dilliard predicted, "Cattle prices will return to normal one of these days. You've held on—"

"Never in my day," Castameto cut in. "Stock prices are down. Only a miracle will restore them." The iron-gray head drooped a bit sadly, lifted again. "You may find it extremely difficult to believe I have seen a herd of fifty thousand cattle sold for less than a *peso* a head. That took place at Santa Barbara, not so many years back. I witnessed the sight of ten thousand more head being driven over the bluffs into the sea that the pasturage might be conserved for sheep."

Dilliard said, shocked, "Good God!"

"It is true, Señor Branch. The dry years have ruined the cattle raisers. Cattle must have food. When the rains fail us, the grass doesn't come. The past ten years have been a continual struggle—some years worse than others, of course. Five summers ago, when all was parched and brown and the ribs of the cattle stretched tight their hides, we drove to the Mojave Desert for our grazing."

"The Mojave Desert!" Dilliard exclaimed incredulously. "Grazing—in a desert?"

Castameto smiled sadly. "All around us cattle were dying, dropping to earth, finished. Flies, like black clouds, droned over the range. All of my neighbors were wiped out. Day by day, I watched my herds dwindle, powerless to do anything. Then, I happened to think of the Mojave River which flows through the desert."

"And you got water in the desert?"

"It was grass the cattle required. There was enough of water to get by on, at the water holes and at small streams. But there was no grass. Everyone said I was crazy, that there wouldn't be enough water in the Mojave River—"

"But there was enough, eh?"

Castameto smiled. "The river had dried up, but I'd been fortunate enough to think of something else. Beneath that cracked surface of the river bed, deep down, a certain moisture had been preserved—enough at least to grow edible brush and sparse grass. It meant making daily drives for the grazing, then a return from the desert to the nearest water." Castameto ended abruptly, "That year I saved many cattle I had expected to lose."

Dilliard whistled softly. "I want to meet the man who claims the *Americanos* have all the enterprise. Why, you played a hundred to one shot—and won!"

"Won only temporarily. I brought my herd through that season. That winter, rain was more plentiful." Castameto sighed, "Yes, sometimes I have ideas. Even now, were conditions different, I could profit with my stock. But the *Americanos* increase daily with their land projects and agriculture. Most of the large holdings have been broken up within the past few years and resold to grangers. The movement hasn't spread to Southern California completely yet, but with travel increasing by rail across the continent, the end isn't far off."

"It may take longer than you think."

Castameto sorrowfully shook his head. "Why, look you, already there is talk of the Southern Pacific laying rails to *El Pueblo de Los Angeles*, southward from Yerba Buena." The old man still clung persistently to San Francisco's earlier name. "What think you such a railroad will mean to this part of the country, in particular to the old *ranchos*?"

The answer to that one was clear in Dilliard's mind, but he sidestepped the issue, changing the subject slightly, "Speaking of railroads across the continent, I've wondered why you had the Señorita Castameto travel by ship from New England, rather than by the steam-cars. Much time could have been saved."

Castameto drew thoughtfully on his *cigarro*, then explained grimly, "The ships sailing on either side of the isthmus are owned by friends—wealthy Spanish folk. The railroads are operated by gringos—your pardon, *señor—Americanos*. I am not entirely persuaded to—" Castameto broke off, his tones softening, asking, "Besides, what need to save time? By any route, Mariposa could not have arrived in time for the funeral of her brother. Anyway, that part must be now put away, forgotten if possible. Only today I told Mariposa she must put off mourning. The fiesta furnished a good excuse, Señor Dilliard, it all comes to one point: I wanted Mariposa here for my last days."

"May they be many years' distant," Dilliard said courteously, sipping the topaz wine.

Castameto glanced shrewdly at the Texan. "Almost," the old man said, "I am sometimes persuaded you are a Spaniard at heart. You have the language as good as mine; in addition, you know the correct phrases to use at the proper times. And then, when I am almost convinced, I hear you speak strange words in that barbaric *Americano* tongue whose syllables come so fast to my ears, and I know that there can never be any common ground upon which Spaniard and Anglo may meet."

Dilliard laughed softly, shrugging his shoulders, "*Quien sabe*?"

"True. Who knows? But I do not think so."

Silence fell between the two. The flames in the fireplace crackled and roared. Castameto refilled the wine glasses. Finally he said grimly, "So far as concerns my last days being many years' distant, I thank you for the thought, but I see plainly you haven't knowledge of recent local history—but enough of that. Let us talk of yourself. I want to say that I regret sincerely that you are departing tomorrow." The old man's smile broadened, "Do you know, I never thought to see the day when I would speak such words to an *Americano*. But *you* are different, Señor Dilliard."

Dilliard thanked him, adding, "There's a heap more of us, Don Salvadore."

"Doubtless," dryly, as though the subject were open to considerable argument. "It occurs to me again that I have never sufficiently thanked you for what you have done."

"That's unnecessary," Dilliard said. "I will

admit though to a curiosity regarding the abduction. I've always felt there was more to that than just the matter of ransom—"

"Which, thanks to you, was never paid—"

"Don't forget Tony and Teresa."

"Those good ones, too, I shall never forget. . . . Oh, yes, I would have paid a ransom had it been necessary. The man named Corill who accompanied the carriage when the Mexican girl was abducted—it was he who brought me the news, stating he had been informed the Señorita Mariposa would be returned safely in exchange for a certain sum of gold. That scoundrel. Then he departed, so villainously confident, saying he would return for the money."

"I heard something of the kind. Good for him he didn't return."

The servant entered again, leaned toward Castameto to speak. Dilliard caught from the low-voiced tones two names: "Drake Scabbard—Bart Fustian," but no more. Glancing at Castameto, the Texan saw that the old man had gone white and drawn. After a moment, Castameto nodded reluctantly to the servant, saying, "Allow them to come in."

The servant disappeared. Castameto turned to Dilliard. "Visitors from El Vaca," he stated, drawing himself up rigidly.

"I'll leave you alone." Dilliard rose.

"Wait!" Castameto pressed Dilliard back in

the chair. "Don't go. I hope to dispose of them shortly. They are very unwelcome visitors."

"Just as you say." Dilliard sank back in the high-backed chair, his eyes asking questions of the leaping flames in the fireplace. He wondered what Drake Scabbard wanted—and the man named Fustian who accompanied Scabbard. There'd been a breath of death in old Castameto's tones when he had asked Dilliard not to go. Something serious was afoot, no doubt on that score.

Castameto rounded the chairs, walked to the center of the room to await his callers. There came a few moments of silence, then loud voices at an outer doorway. The servant entered, leading Scabbard and the other man—so Dilliard judged. From the spot at which he was seated, he couldn't see the rest of the room, nor could anyone else see the Texan.

Castameto's voice was stiffly courteous, "Señor Scabbard, Señor Fustian. Can I do anything for you?" Then to the servant, "No, it is not necessary to remain. You may go."

Dilliard caught the departing servant's footfalls, then a loud, roaring voice in execrable Spanish, "Evenin', Castameto. We just figured to drop in and see why we weren't invited to this fiesta you're holding."

"The fiesta was for friends." Castameto's words were like chilled steel.

"You must remember, Bart," came Scabbard's cold tones, "that Señor Castameto has no particular love for us gringos right now. He's a trifle mistaken in his ideas, of course. Isn't that so, Señor Castameto?" Scabbard's Spanish was passably good.

Castameto replied, "I'm not so sure that I am mistaken, Señor Scabbard."

Scabbard's insulting laugh brought a ruffling of the hair at the back of Dilliard's neck.

In English, Bart Fustian said, "I heard there was an American stayin' here now."

Scabbard replied in the same language, "Forget it, Bart. Castameto's alone here now. That's all we care about. Don't forget we got important business ahead."

Castameto couldn't understand this last exchange. He remained standing stiffly before the two, near the doorway, while the conversation in their own tongue was taking place between Scabbard and Fustian.

Dilliard's chair was placed with its high back to the room. The top of the chair reached well above Dilliard's head. Neither of the two *Americanos* near the outer doorway could see the Texan; they didn't even suspect there was a fourth man in the room.

Dilliard heard Fustian say in English, "Sure looks like the old buzzard is alone, all right, Drake."

"We're playing in luck." Scabbard added in Spanish, "The rest of your household is outside, enjoying the fiesta, I suppose."

Castameto replied, "The fiesta is nearly finished, *señor.* I was about to go to my bed, shortly. If you have business to talk over, let us get on with it."

Moving cautiously, Dilliard peered around the edge of his high-backed chair, took in the two figures facing Castameto. Bart Fustian was a bulky-shouldered individual with closely-set eyes beneath his droop-brim felt sombrero. A gun hung at his right hip. He wore black trousers tucked into knee boots. Drake Scabbard looked about as he had when Dilliard had talked to him in the *cantina* in Santa Lozana.

Somehow, the whole set-up didn't look good to the Texan. He settled noiselessly back in his chair, waiting to see what further conversation would bring out. Scabbard was urging certain prompt actions on the old man, which Castameto protested against.

Scabbard was saying, ". . . and I insist that's the only way you'll have a chance, Castameto. It means the scaffold, surely, if you don't let me handle the business in my own way. I want to be your friend. I've done my best to show you I'm friendly. I'll admit, right now, things don't look any too secure, but you leave things to me and they'll all come out right in the end."

"And I say 'no,' " Castameto replied quietly, dignified dislike in his tones. "That is all. I bid you a very good evening, *señores*."

Bart Fustian laughed raucously. In English, "Drake, I told you it wouldn't work. He's throwin' us out. It's a show-down. No time like the present. I'll be ready when you say the word. That paper can be fixed up later."

"Better edge around behind the old fool," Scabbard answered. His voice was even, cool-toned. In Spanish, he said to Castameto, "It's good evening then, Señor Castameto. I'm sorry you won't reconsider. It would be safest."

"No!" Anger tinged Castameto's single word of refusal.

Scabbard yawned, said wearily to Fustian, "I reckon you might as well let him have it, Bart. He's damned stubborn. We can put a gun in his hand—"

Dilliard lost the next few words. He heard three quick footsteps, then came quickly, quietly, up from the depths of the high-backed chair. He wasn't noticed at first. Scabbard stood near the door, Judas eyes smiling coldly in Castameto's face. Behind Castameto and a trifle to one side, Bart Fustian was just in the act of raising his long-barreled cap-and-ball pistol!

12

POWDER SMOKE!

A sudden, loud warning was ripped from Dilliard's throat. Castameto spun around, his face white. Scabbard cursed, said, "Cripes a'mighty! Dilliard!"

Fustian lowered his gun, turned swiftly. There came a clattering of chairs and tables as Dilliard charged swiftly along the room. He was unarmed; the safest way was to get in close.

Fustian swore, raised his gun toward the Texan. Scabbard shouted something just before Dilliard closed in. Fustian's gun crashed loudly in the room. Dilliard felt burning powder scorch his left cheek.

There was a moment of black desperation as Dilliard grappled with Fustian. The man was too big, too powerful, to be handled easily. Their locked bodies swayed about the room, struck violently against a heavy oaken table.

"Get him, Drake, dammit, get him!" Fustian panted.

Scabbard cursed and yelled advice to Fustian that had to do with holding Dilliard quiet. But the two men were moving too fast for Scabbard to take careful aim. Castameto was facing Scabbard, his eyes hard on the derringer in Scabbard's right fist, alert to knock the gun to one side should Scabbard start to shoot.

Dilliard jerked partially free. His right fist thudded twice into Fustian's middle. Fustian grunted and gave pace before the Texan's savage onslaught. Dilliard's fingers were groping for Fustian's gun hand now; grimly he concentrated on that muscular right arm.

Fustian's curses were coming through set lips, as he struggled to throw off the relentless Texan. But Dilliard clung like a leech, his left hand locked about Fustian's gun-wrist, his right seeking a hold at Fustian's throat.

Fustian roared like a maddened bull. The roar ceased suddenly, as he almost went to his knees. He flung his huge form to one side, carrying Dilliard with him. Dilliard hung on like grim death, digging his fingers into Fustian's throat. His hold tightened.

Fustian commenced to give ground. Dilliard dug his head into the huge chest, panting, sobbing for breath. He tightened his grip on Fustian's right wrist. For an instant Fustian steeled his muscles to resist, then his wrist commenced slowly to bend back.

Suddenly, he uttered a cry of pain. The gun dropped from his outstretched hand. Dilliard stepped quickly back, the old fighting grin twisting his lips. Fustian's face was crimson with rage. Snarling, he came in with a rush which Dilliard sidestepped.

As he lunged past, Dilliard struck out with all of the strength at his command. Fustian stumbled, tried to save himself from falling. Dilliard spun around, hit him a second time—and a third. For one brief instant Fustian swayed erect, then he pitched forward. Dilliard saw his head strike the corner of a table before he crashed down across a goatskin rug and lay silent.

The Texan whirled to face Drake Scabbard, then stopped short to discover servants and several *vaqueros* crowding in from the patio. Mariposa pushed through the knot of men, looking very white. Her slim form was covered from throat to toes in a long yellow shawl of silk. Drake Scabbard stood at one side, the derringer still clutched in his hand. His thin lips were twisted in a sneer of resentment.

Castameto was speaking stern, cutting words. After a time, Dilliard caught Scabbard's words of attempted explanation:

". . . you're mistaken, Castameto. You should have told us there was another man in the room. Doubtless when Dilliard rushed out, Bart was startled into drawing his gun—"

"Fustian's gun was out before I got into it, Scabbard," Dilliard panted hotly.

"You're trying to make trouble, Dilliard?" Scabbard snapped.

"I stopped some," the Texan jerked out. "If your intentions were peaceful, what's your gun doing out?"

Scabbard laughed insolently. "I didn't recognize you, at first. I didn't know what was up. I was ready to protect myself. There was no reason for you to jump Fustian that way. It could all have ended peacefully."

Dilliard said, "That's a lie and you know it. If I hadn't moved fast, you'd have murdered Señor Castameto."

"Murdered him?" scornfully. "You're crazy, Dilliard."

"I'm not crazy enough to put any faith in anything you say. I heard your conversation with Fustian, when you first come in. You planned to kill—"

"Oh, cripes! You're crazier'n a hoot-owl, Dilliard," Scabbard said wearily.

The room was ringed with wide-eyed *vaqueros*. Mariposa had retired to the fireplace and stood, anxiously, watching the men.

Castameto said, "Señor Dilliard, you have met this man before?"

Dilliard nodded, "Talked to him a spell in Santa Lozana—the night before the attempted abduction of your daughter."

"So?" Castameto nodded sagely. "No doubt he was in Santa Lozana to arrange that abduction—"

"That's a lie!" Scabbard scowled. He half-raised the derringer in his hand.

Dilliard reached forward, caught Scabbard's wrist. "If you want to keep that gun, put it away *pronto*, hombre."

"Oh, all right." Scabbard shrugged his shoulders. Dilliard released Scabbard's arm. The gun disappeared in a pocket of the man's long-tailed coat. Fustian's gun still lay on the floor, not far from the body of its unconscious owner. One of the *vaqueros* stepped forward and placed it on a table.

Dilliard said, "I suppose you don't know anything about that abduction, eh, Scabbard?"

"Not a thing," Scabbard said flatly. "Of course, I heard an attempt of that sort had taken place. I didn't pay any attention to it, though."

"Where'd you hear that?" Dilliard asked.

"I don't remember. Rumors get around. I told you I didn't pay any particular attention." Suddenly anger got the better of Scabbard's usually cautious reason. "I'm asking what you know about it, Dilliard."

The Texan laughed softly. "Couldn't resist your curiosity, eh, Scabbard? Sure, I know quite a bit about it. I overheard two coyotes named Bisbee and Corill planning that job. I had a hand in the rescue, if you want to know. To cut it short, Scabbard, if you were the one that planned that job—and I think you were, though I don't yet know why—I'm the man who spilled your beans! Is that what you're itchin' to know?"

Scabbard's face had gone white. He said nervously, "You're talking in riddles. I don't give a hang who engineered that job, nor do I care. I know I had nothing to do with it. Why should I want to carry off the old man's daughter? What your part was, matters not the slightest to me."

"Your bluff don't go down, Scabbard."

"I'm not bluffing, Texas man. I don't care whether you believe me or not. If you think you can make something of it, why not appeal to the law?"

"That's up to Don Salvadore. Maybe he will." Dilliard turned to the old Spaniard, rapidly translated the talk that had taken place. When he had finished, Castameto slowly shook his head.

"Not yet, Señor Dilliard. The nearest law-officer is at El Vaca. Drake Scabbard controls El Vaca. Everything would be against us."

Scabbard laughed triumphantly. "You see, Texas man. You couldn't even get started, if you tried to buck me."

"I'm not so sure of that," Dilliard snapped. "There's other law-officers. El Vaca can't hold all the law."

"It holds enough to control the country hereabouts," Scabbard chuckled coldly. "Cripes, Dilliard, can't you realize what you're up against? Look here, you and I started off on the wrong foot in Santa Lozana. I intimated it wouldn't be healthy for you to come to El Vaca. I remember we had words. Well, maybe you were mistaken in me. I'm willing to admit I might have made a mistake in judging you. I'll reopen my offer. Come to El Vaca. I'll make it worth your while—"

Dilliard laughed softly. "Is that your way of trying to prevent me from putting the law on your tail, Scabbard?"

Scabbard said carelessly, "Sure, if you want to put it that way."

"You got a nerve, Scabbard—" Dilliard was amazed at the scoundrel's effrontery, "—admittin' that much here."

Scabbard smiled coldly. "Certainly, I've got nerve. That's how I run El Vaca. For that matter, I've admitted nothing. It's your word against mine. I could swear you were a liar, and who could prove differently?"

Dilliard said dryly, "You and I aren't the only ones in this room."

Scabbard's reply held contempt, "These people don't matter, Texas man. Don't you understand that white men run this country now?"

Dilliard grinned suddenly. "Do you know, Scabbard, I got a notion to show you these folks *do* count. I sort of owe it to my blood to stop you—and stop you in a hurry."

"Don't be a fool, Dilliard. You'd make very little headway. I don't hold grudges. Let's be friends. You come to El Vaca tomorrow. I pay good money for keen minds—"

"And for killer's bullets, I'm taking it," Dilliard said coldly.

Scabbard's black eyebrows raised slightly. "You're missing my point, Texas man. What I'm trying to make you understand is, it's more profitable to work for Drake Scabbard than against him—and not half so dangerous."

"Is that a threat?"

Scabbard shrugged his shoulders. "Suit yourself. I'm giving you your last chance. Come to El Vaca and—"

"Nope!" Branch shook his head. "I like it here. And I don't like raw deals."

"You prefer these greasers?" sneeringly.

"To *Americano* scum," Dilliard nodded.

Scabbard's dead-white features momentarily crimsoned with anger, then he controlled his anger and turned away, forcing a cold laugh. "You've had your chance, feller. Don't blame me for what happens."

"I'd advise you not to let anything happen," Dilliard said warningly.

Scabbard had no reply for that. He glanced down at the floor where Bart Fustian was commencing to stir into life, then, turning coolly to Castameto, asked for help. Castameto called two of the *vaqueros* to carry Fustian outside and place him on his horse.

Scabbard paused a moment before leaving, his eyes baleful on Dilliard's. "You're a stranger around here, Texas," he said in chilly accents. "You better learn right now that men in this country don't buck Drake Scabbard. Take my advice and get back to Texas as fast as you can. Otherwise, you won't be able to get back."

"That," Dilliard nodded, "is pretty plain. I'm warned now. Well, even a rattler warns before striking." He paused, adding, "And I'm plumb sure you're no different than a rattler."

"We're both poison," Scabbard agreed lightly, and stepped outside, flinging back, "to those that buck us."

Of the people left in the room, only Mariposa, and Tony, who stood to one side, understood the import of the words that had passed between Dilliard and the Texan. To the girl and the *vaquero*, Scabbard's threats seemed to seal Dilliard's death warrant.

Tony was worried, started forward to speak to Dilliard as the sounds of Scabbard's and Fustian's horses were heard moving outside the house. The two *vaqueros* returned. In the patio a clamoring of voices filled the air.

Castameto spoke shortly, "You men can leave now. Go out, silence your women. Tell them all is well, and that once more we owe much to the Señor Dilliard."

The *vaqueros* and servants started toward

the door, Tony flinging tragic glances toward Dilliard. Outside, the hoofbeats were dying away. In a few moments, except for Mariposa, Castameto and the Texan, the big room was once more empty of humanity.

Mariposa came close to Dilliard, so close that he caught the faint fragrance that always seemed to hover about the girl. All the color was drained from her face, her dark eyes wide with fear.

"You—you understand what Scabbard's words mean?" she asked tremulously.

"I reckon," Dilliard nodded.

"Are you sure you understand completely? That it will mean death to stay here now?"

Dilliard replied quietly, "I understood completely. But I'm not so sure Scabbard will be able to carry out his threats."

"Señor Branch!" A half sob tightened the girl's throat. "I was wrong to suggest that you delay your departure, very wrong. I think it will be best for you to leave in the morning, as early as possible."

A whimsical smile twisted Dilliard's lips. "It's too late now," he said softly. "You see, this California country's got a call to it. I'm plumb curious to see more."

"No, no!" Mariposa's hand caught at his sleeve.

Castameto had been watching the two. "Mariposa," he cut in quietly, "at this hour you should be in your room."

The girl's eyes held, pleading, to Dilliard's a moment longer, before they dropped under the burning intensity of his gaze. Then she turned and passed slowly from the room.

Castameto crossed the floor in quick strides, hand outstretched in nearly complete acceptance of the gringo.

"Friend—good friend," he said simply.

13
GRINGO RENEGADE

"It is difficult for a stranger," Don Salvadore was saying, "to realize the fiend that dwells in Drake Scabbard's black heart."

"I felt the hate of the man," Dilliard nodded, "just before he left this room. It was like a hot foul breath, seeping into everything it touched. I don't underestimate him. I know he'll hit low when necessary."

The two men had returned to their chairs before the fireplace. Fresh logs had been stacked on the flames. The big house was wrapped in the silence that comes with the second hour after midnight. Candles in their wrought iron standards burned with a slow, steady flame. The farther end of the long room was in dim shadow. Dilliard's eyes were weaving pictures in the leaping flames, pictures that had to do with a slim white figure in a shawl of yellow silk. The firelight gleamed in the topaz wine Dilliard held, bringing a warm glow of liquid light to the center of the fragile glass.

Castameto was speaking again. Dilliard reluctantly gave over his thoughts, jerked himself to attention to hear the words. "Once," Castameto was saying bitterly, "I considered Drake Scabbard a friend—so far as there can ever be friendship between a Spaniard and a gringo. It has made me suspicious. Perhaps you'll be good enough to realize my feelings—"

"But, Don Salvadore—"

"Wait, *amigo*. I have already admitted that you are different. You've proved yourself. Scabbard never did. It's not many years back. I tried to meet the new order, saw that conditions were changing. It was for that I consented to allow Mariposa to be educated at one of your eastern schools, though since I have regretted my decision. But I thought I was doing my best to conform to changing standards. I wanted to be a good neighbor to the *Americanos* who were coming—"

"That is the best way."

"I'm not so sure. I tried to adapt myself, did my best to treat with Drake Scabbard on equal grounds."

"I judge Scabbard has considerable power."

"Power! *Poder de Dios*! I tell you, Señor Branch, Drake Scabbard is a king in El Vaca."

"What sort of a town is El Vaca? I have never been there."

"It is Scabbard's stronghold. He built it himself, such as it is. It lies less than ten miles from here, as the crow flies, just beyond the line of my holdings. There he has built himself wealth, but few genuine friends. Money buys his companions. The man is a devil, quick to employ gunfire at the slightest offense. He is surrounded by hired killers."

"But what of the law? Is there no law there?"

Castameto scowled. "Law!" disgustedly. "Gringo law! There is a deputy-sheriff and a *juez de paz*—justice of the peace. Both are miserable rascals, and both were appointed with the influence of Scabbard's gold. The early residents of this country have no say in the administering of the law. Mexicans and Spaniards seek justice in vain. We are given slight, or no consideration by Scabbard's hirelings. Any wonder I have only hate for *los gringos*?"

"There is more to your own story, of course?"

"True. It commences with Ramon's death—Mariposa's brother—a matter of nine months back. Ramon never had the steadiness of his sister. Where Mariposa is reasoning, intelligent, Ramon was wild, stubborn—but a lovable son for all that, with a thorough understanding of his inheritance and what was expected of him. In the young there is always the crop of wild oats to be sown. Can you understand a boy of that kind?"

Dilliard nodded. " 'One can break a wild horse but not tame him until his spirit has run its course,' " he quoted.

"Exactly," Castameto said gratefully. "You understand." The old man sighed. "So it was with Ramon. He was but a boy, but gaming and wining were in his blood. I thought to give him his head, as one trains a spirited colt, let him run free, until the time came when such pleasures had exhausted his interest. All might have been different, had his mother lived, but I was rearing Ramon in the only way I knew. If I failed, it was only through ignorance."

"You have not failed with Mariposa," Dilliard pointed out.

Castameto frowned slightly. "Of that I am not yet sure. Of late, she shows a tendency to follow her own inclinations, with no thought of my commands. But always, in the end, she has obeyed. As yet, nothing serious has arisen. When it does—well, I trust she'll remember her breeding."

Dilliard wondered what difference had passed between the two, wondered if it referred to himself. He remained silent, waiting for Don Salvadore to continue.

Castameto went on, "But to Ramon . . . There was a girl in El Vaca whom Ramon and other young men were in the habit of visiting. This I had forbidden when it came to my ears, but Ramon was headstrong, disregarded my words. One night a quarrel ensued between Ramon and a young *gringo*, one Lucas Reardon. The quarrel had to do with the girl's favors. This girl was—well, her type doesn't matter. Perhaps you have guessed. Anyway, she was the sort that glories in fights over herself. A short time later, Lucas Reardon shot Ramon between the shoulder blades, when Ramon was leaving this girl's house."

"That sounds like murder."

"It was sheer murder! This Lucas Reardon fancied himself as a gunhand. He had always boasted of his prowess in accurate and swift shooting. Well, I appealed to the law at El Vaca. As I have mentioned, Drake Scabbard controls the law in that town. Scabbard promised to arrange for the arrest of Lucas Reardon, but two weeks dragged past with Reardon still at large and bragging of his killing. I appealed a second time to Scabbard. Scabbard put me off, saying it would be bad policy to prosecute an *Americano*. After all, an *Americano* had killed a greaser. So ran sentiment in El Vaca. Why bother to punish anyone? Ramon Castameto was only a greaser."

The bitter irony in the old man's voice was making Dilliard ashamed of his own race.

Castameto continued. "As I was leaving Scabbard's office, I came face to face with Lucas Reardon on the single dirty street of El Vaca, and he laughed openly at my distress." The old man paused, apologetically spreading his hands. "Perhaps all of my hot blood hadn't descended to Ramon. It may have been wrong, though I'm not sure that it was. I challenged Lucas Reardon to meet me in fair fight. He accepted my challenge as a joke, swearing he would shoot me down before I could put finger to trigger. Finally, after considerable jeering at my expense, he consented to meet me. We used guns, at fifteen paces, on that dirty street in El Vaca, with a crowd of *gringos* cheering Reardon on, and no man of my own race daring to lift his voice."

"You hit Reardon?"

"I killed him," Castameto said coldly. "Oh, he was faster than I. He shot twice. I pulled trigger but once. But my hand was the steadier of the two. Reardon dropped, wounded. The doctor who attended him pronounced he would live, but that night Reardon's wound opened and he bled to death with no one near to save him."

"To me, that seems good. He had it coming."

"Perhaps," Castameto admitted grudgingly. "The duel had cooled my blood. I was glad I had only wounded Lucas Reardon. I do not like the thought of taking a man's life. But then he died in the night. . . . Now, look you, Señor Branch, a great outcry was raised! There was talk of a lynching. Ah! The situation had changed: *a greaser had dared murder an* Americano*!*"

"I still insist Reardon had it coming."

"That was not the question," Castameto said bitterly. "I was arrested, taken to the jail. Bail was set at fifty thousand dollars—"

"Whew!" Dilliard whistled softly. "That's a lot."

"True. The *Americano* law called for less, but the justice of the peace established that figure and I had no recourse. After all, what is *Americano* law when applied to a greaser? Drake Scabbard, in friendly guise, offered aid. As I have told you, there is no longer money in cattle. I had not the necessary fifty thousand dollars. Scabbard loaned me the necessary sum."

"With your right eye as security?"

"Ah, the security! I was forced to turn over to Drake Scabbard the land grant awarded my family by the Spanish King. In addition, I was made to deed Rancho Sicamoro to Scabbard. You see," sarcastically, "I didn't understand the honorable *Americano* ways as I do now. And besides I had thought of Scabbard as a friend."

"Do I understand," Dilliard said indignantly, "that Drake Scabbard now owns this *rancho*?"

"Papers were drawn up. Scabbard can call upon me for the money at any time with only two weeks' notice. If, at the end of two weeks, I do not return the money loaned me, Scabbard retains the deed and my land grant."

"Has the deed been registered by Scabbard?"

"Not as yet, for a wonder. He is so confident of securing my property."

Dilliard's eyes narrowed. "I suspect the attempted abduction of Señorita Mariposa had something to do with all this."

"Doubtless you are correct. Had the plan been

successful, the abductors could have demanded, as ransom, the amount of my bail money. I should have been forced to surrender it, return to jail, in order to gain her freedom. Once I was in jail, Drake Scabbard could have run affairs to suit his own ends."

"You suspect Scabbard of engineering the abduction, of course."

"And so do you, Señor Branch." Castameto smiled thinly. "Proof, we both know, is lacking, so we cannot punish him for it."

Dilliard frowned. "But why should Scabbard be so eager to place you in jail?"

"To prevent my raising the money to repay his loan. You see, there is a slim chance that I may get some money from another source. For the present Scabbard does not want that loan repaid. He has his eyes on greater gain."

"You say he already has great wealth."

"Never so much as he desires. Let me explain. There is much talk of the Santa Fenicia Railroad building through this state. The proposed rail line would run directly through my property—almost straight down from the town of Santa Ana to Capistrano."

"I'm commencing to see light."

"As any intelligent man would. You see the price Scabbard could demand of the railroad people were he to own, outright, the Rancho Sicamoro? I, of course, shall refuse to sell a right-of-way to the railroad people if they continue with their plans, and if it is within my power to do so, but Scabbard—"

"Scabbard is playing for high stakes. This all sounds not so good, Don Salvadore."

"I am facing that fact, and more," the old man stated grimly. "A few days before you arrived here, Scabbard came with a request that in order to hold my loan, I must deed over to him all of my cattle and horses and sheep—"

"In addition to the land and buildings?"

"You find it incredible, but it is so."

"The dirty, hoggish, thievin' son!"

Castameto didn't understand the American slang, but he caught the import of the words. He bowed, saying, "I evaded answering right then. I wanted time to think, plan, see if there were any other way. Tonight, he came—he and Fustian—to demand his answer, claiming he must have greater security on such a loan. I told him 'no,' as you heard. And so now he insists on the return of his fifty thousand dollars in the two weeks' time as stipulated by the paper that was drawn up."

"It looks as though you were caught in a trap," Dilliard frowned. "I can't see why he would have had Fustian kill you tonight."

"Ah, my death would have simplified matters. Scabbard could have gained much quicker control of the things he wants, had Fustian succeeded in murdering me. They could have put a gun in my hand, claimed it had been necessary to fire in self-defense. They thought I was alone, with no one near. With me dead and Scabbard holding the deed and grant to my property, they could have forged other necessary papers to carry through their plans. In an *Americano* court of law, any protest that Mariposa might make would be futile. Do you see now?"

"I see," Dilliard growled, "that we must stop Scabbard, or Scabbard will be running this whole country. But—how to do it? There's the rub!"

"Wait! You haven't heard all yet. There is more. A short time back I arranged to sell a herd of cattle to raise the money to repay Scabbard."

"You haven't been idle then—"

"No credit is due to my industry." Castameto frowned, "I still do not quite understand. Had the offer to buy not come from an old friend, Don Alvaro Serrano, I should have mistrusted it."

"Where is this Don Alvaro Serrano?"

"In San Diego. Years ago he had a small *rancho*, not very far from my holdings. The drought ruined him, so he sold his property and left for San Diego. Suddenly, out of a clear sky came his letter asking if I would be willing to sell him cattle. The price he offered took my breath away. Look you, Señor Branch, it is fully two dollars higher than the standard now paid in California. I do not understand it."

"Cows bring almost twice that in Texas at present—some parts of Texas—though it's good, that I admit."

"These days in California," Castameto said earnestly, "it is unheard of. Think, I have seen cattle sell for less than a *peso* the head and not so many years back. I cannot think what Don Alvaro is up to, but he assured me the money could and would be paid. Perhaps it is that he has taken land near San Diego and plans to raise beef—it may be wealthy relatives have died and left him money. He had relatives in Barcelona, in Spain. Still, if he planned to raise beef, why should he stipulate only sleek beeves in the shipment he wanted—"

"Shipment?" Dilliard frowned. "Ship where, how?"

"Merely a figure of speech. The cattle must be gathered and driven to San Diego for delivery. Scabbard will do everything in his power to prevent our making that drive—"

"How did Scabbard get wind of it? Did you tell him?"

Castameto shook his head. "On the contrary. I've tried to keep the business secret, but evidently the word leaked out. It may be news crept up from San Diego. . . . But no matter. You know now why Scabbard is demanding the deed to my stock. He'll do his utmost to prevent my closing the sale. And time presses. Even were I successful, I'd still have to come to trial for the death of Lucas Reardon, but at least I could save Rancho Sicamoro for Mariposa."

The old man's face was gray with worry. "Ah, *poder de Dios*! If there were but one among the *Americanos* whom I could trust, one who would understand the situation."

"There is, Don Salvadore," Dilliard said warmly.

Castameto smiled wearily. "I understand what you mean, Señor Branch. Your heart is good. But I referred to an *Americano* with influence in the courts of law."

"Look here," Dilliard said earnestly, "get it through your head that I want a hand in lickin' this Scabbard coyote. I ain't got any influence, but perhaps there's another way. We can dope it all out. Your luck's due for a switch-over. With half a chance I figure we can beat him yet—"

Dilliard paused suddenly, laughing at the look of perplexity in Castameto's dark eyes. It occurred to him abruptly that, carried away by his enthusiasm, he'd been speaking in English. Swiftly he repeated the words in Spanish.

Castameto's eyes widened. "But—but you leave in the morning. Your plans are made."

Dilliard laughed. "Haven't you already seen how fast we gringos can change our plans? Even so, now that I understand things, do you think I'd go away, leaving you to fight a situation of this kind, when I might just as well stay and lend a hand?"

"You'd join with me?" Castameto said slowly, as though he couldn't believe his ears. "Be one of us—against the *Americanos*?" Unbelief, incredulity was evident in every word.

"To the last ditch. Sure. Why not?"

"But—but, Señor Branch. You—you are of the gringo race—" Voice failed the old Spaniard for a moment, then, his words coming in a hot rush, "You wouldn't dare! You'd be fighting men of your own blood—"

"Wouldn't dare?" Dilliard's easy laugh filled the room. "I'm eager to try it. Men of my own blood, perhaps, but not my kind of men—"

"You'll bring down on your head the combined hate of the *Americanos*—"

"I doubt that—"

"They'll call you a renegade!"

"Do you think it matters what a certain type cares to call me?" Dilliard asked. "Any name Scabbard and his scum puts on me, matters not in the least. I'll be glad to be termed a renegade, if only for the reason that it will set me apart from Scabbard and his snakes."

Sudden hope lighted the Spaniard's eyes. He was on his feet now, right hand reaching for Dilliard's. Their palms met in a warm, hard clasp.

Castameto's voice shook a little. "It will be something," he said earnestly, "to have one of their blood on my side, helping to fight my fight. Perhaps—perhaps—"

His voice faltered. To cover his confusion he reached for wine, poured two brimming glasses, passed one to Dilliard with a hand that trembled. Raising his glass high, "*Salud*, *señor*!" the Spaniard offered.

The Texan was on his feet, glass even with Castameto's. He said clearly, "*Salud*! And to the damnation of Drake Scabbard, *mi patrón*!"

That last brought moisture to Castameto's eyes. Dilliard laughed softly to himself, "For once, I reckon my sights don't need adjusting."

Castameto caught the sound, but not the meaning. Dilliard shook his head, "It doesn't matter. We'll talk more now. I want to understand this situation thoroughly, before I plunge in."

Fresh wood was piled on the flames, *cigarros* lighted. Dilliard asked question after shrewd question, demanding to know more about the men who worked on the Rancho Sicamoro, how large a fighting force could be raised. He put forth certain suggestions to which Castameto protested violently. The talk went on and on. Gray dawn was commencing to sift through the windows and the oak logs had burned to thin ashes before the conversation had ceased.

14
CASTAMETO REBELS

The following morning Castameto stood, frowning anxiously, near one of the corrals back of the house, watching Dilliard saddle up. It was before eight o'clock. The *rancho* was stirring to activity. At another corral, a knot of *vaqueros* had come in from the range for a change of horseflesh. Several Indians employed mesquite branches to sweep the grounds about the outer wall of the ranch house. Smoke curled from chimneys here and there. A heavy, hide-laden *carreta*, with huge wheels of solid wood, and drawn by a span of big work cattle, the yoke placed across their foreheads, rumbled past on its way to a storehouse.

Dilliard placed one booted foot against his pony's ribs, pulled his cinch tight. He straightened up, mopped his perspiring features with a bandanna. It was hot, the sun bearing down from a sky of cloudless blue.

Dilliard grinned, "Going to be plumb warmish, today." He repeated the thought in Spanish.

"*Madre de Dios*!" Castameto protested. "You are bound for El Vaca and you think only of the weather."

"Well," the Texan grinned, "it may be hot there too."

"Exactly what I fear. Señor Branch, I ask once more, please give up this mad idea. It will bring you naught, but ill-fortune I fear. Why do you have to see Scabbard?"

Dilliard smiled patiently. "Don Salvadore, we went over that last night. I still think there's a chance of making Scabbard listen to reason. I don't want to overlook anything that may avert bloodshed. We haven't time for fighting, if a fight can be avoided."

"But, the danger—riding into the lion's den—"

"You flatter Scabbard," Dilliard laughed. "He's no lion—only a coyote wearing a lion's skin. I think I can bluff him out of any thoughts he may have regarding me, while I'm in El Vaca. After I leave—"

"If you are allowed to leave—"

"—I can look out for myself," Dilliard continued, apparently not noticing the interruption. "I'll tell you frankly, I think my trip will prove useless, but I've got to try anyway. You must pay that money in two weeks. I suppose the cattle are gathered, ready to start—"

About that, Castameto was uncertain. He shrugged his shoulders. "Such matters I leave to my *mayordomo*, Manuel Estudillo, a very good man—"

Dilliard swore suddenly. He looked unbelievingly at Castameto. "Don Salvadore, do you mean to tell me you don't know whether or not the cattle are gathered?"

"I have told Manuel to gather them. Gave him proper instructions, and explained that the work must be put through—"

"Did you tell him there was unusual need for haste, that your life and the life of the Rancho Sicamoro depended on—"

"Señor Branch, I am not in the habit of taking my people into my confidence. It is enough if I tell them—"

"Oh, my God!" Dilliard burst out wearily. In quick Spanish he went on, "Your men will work harder if they realize the urgency of the matter. Another thing, when the cattle are delivered to Don Alvaro Serrano, will he have ready the cash on hand to pay—?"

"Señor Branch," Castameto interposed stiffly, "Don Alvaro is an honorable man. I did not go into such details. It is not the custom. If Don Alvaro says he will pay such-and-such, I know he will pay—"

"But when?" Dilliard struggled to hold his patience. "Look here, Don Salvadore, keep in mind that you're fighting the gringos now. What the custom is doesn't matter. You've got to forget that. I don't doubt that Don Alvaro is an honorable man and that he will pay, but remember this—you've got to deliver five thousand cattle to San Diego, get your money and return with it to El Vaca. Money—cash! Do you understand? There'll be no time for a draft to go through some bank, necessitating maybe a couple of months. Scabbard will use any pretext to avoid receiving payment. You've got to be able to put the cash in his hand!"

"I—I think," Castameto commenced uneasily, "that all will go well—"

"You *think!* This is no time for thoughts when we are dealing in certainties. You'll pardon me, Don Salvadore, when I tell you you've got to employ some of this Yankee energy you detest so much. Scabbard will win if you don't. There's been too much of this 'put it off until tomorrow' attitude—too much *mañana*—"

"Señor Dilliard! Stop!" Castameto drew himself erect, dark eyes snapping angrily. "I am not in the habit of being criticized. Perhaps it will be best if you let me handle my own affairs. You have my thanks for what you have done, but—"

This was no time for courteous fencing. Impatiently, Dilliard unloosed a tirade of sarcastic Spanish: "*Diantre*! Must you ride always the horse of great stature when I am trying to help you? Dignity is no longer a virtue when rats gnaw at its silken cloak! It is a time for action and not for dwelling on past glories. *Madre de Dios*! Why do you insist on closing your eyes when gringos come raiding your lands?"

Could he have understood them, the same words coming in English would have resulted only in Castameto receiving them as an insult. In his own tongue they were far more impressive. Dilliard continued, "Look around you! By your own admission, the gringos have taken the lands of your neighbors. Is it to be said that one of your intelligence is too old to change his ways that he may meet the *Americanos* in their own type of fighting? Are you already beaten at the mere threat of *Americano* invasion?"

"But, Señor Dilliard—" Castameto commenced weakly.

"Can't you realize the time for dreaming has passed? You've got to act! You've got to act with the speed and strength of an eagle. You must display the brains and the power of—of a Castameto! Otherwise, Scabbard will be victorious."

"*Socorro*!" Castameto swore, snapped to sudden activity. "You are right, Señor Branch! I must adapt myself to the new conditions. Forgive me for—"

Dilliard smiled suddenly, "*No es importe.* It's not important. My feelings weren't hurt. I've just been trying to make it clear that we've got to move fast."

"I see that you are right." The old man was suddenly bewildered, "But—but what shall I do? You still feel it necessary to see Scabbard—"

"More than ever necessary," Dilliard said earnestly. "I want to put him off, if possible. Your job will be to see your *mayordomo.* Learn how many cattle are gathered and ready for the trail."

"Yes, Señor Branch, I can do that. I, myself, shall see to it."

"Good!" Dilliard swung up to the saddle, wheeled his horse. "I'll see you later in the day."

"God grant your words come true," Castameto said worriedly. "I do not like it."

He stood watching while Dilliard directed the horse around the house and disappeared beyond the first rise of land. Then, Castameto wiped the perspiration from his brow. "*Valgame Dios*!" he muttered. "I feel as though I had been caught up in a great wind. Such energy as that *Americano* displays! It wearies me. But he must be correct." Suddenly he raised his voice, calling to a young Mexican who was passing, "Narcisso! Move quickly!"

The youngster came on the run. "*Sí, mi patrón*?"

"Saddle for me, at once, a horse."

"*Sí.* A particular *caballo*? Or matters it not?"

"It matters not. Except that it must have the spirit and dash of three devils, a mountain torrent, a—a—" Castameto paused, groping for a suitable simile, and finished triumphantly, "—the spirit and dash of the *Americano*, the Señor Branch!"

"It shall be done, at once."

"See that you speak truth. No *mañana*, understand? I want the horse today—not tomorrow. I go to superintend the round-up."

Narcisso's jaw dropped. He was aghast. "You—you, in person, *mi patrón*?"

Castameto scowled. "What is so strange in that? Am I so ancient that I cannot attend to the handling of my own cattle?"

"No, no, *mi patrón*!" hastily.

Don Salvadore was placated. He said gruffly, "All right then. See to the horse at once," and strode off toward the house to change his clothing. Just before passing through the archway in the wall that surrounded the patio, Castameto paused, turned back to look. Narcisso was still standing as Castameto had left him, eyes wide with amazement, mouth hanging open, staring after the *patrón*.

Don Salvadore's face darkened up like a thunder cloud. He shouted angrily, "Narcisso! Would you crave to have the skin flayed from your miserable frame? No? Then move your worthless carcass with dispatch! I want that horse saddled today—understand. Not tomorrow, not next week. Today! Move quickly lest I decide that your listless soul shall perish on an ant-hill!"

A twinkle came into the old Spaniard's eyes as he watched the Mexican youngster dash frantically to the building where saddles were stored. Don Salvadore strode on, into the patio, scowling. "What has come over this place I do not understand. My people grow lazy! Were it not for the energy of two men—the Señor Branch and myself—the Rancho Sicamoro would fall to ruins with no hand raised to preserve it. *Cascaras*! What a state of affairs!"

15
EL VACA

Leaving the house at his rear, Dilliard loped his pony along Borrego Canyon for the first mile and a half. Then he turned toward the southwest, heading up into the slopes of a group of small hills. For a time he followed a long ridge, covered with chaparral and mesquite, before descending into a small canyon through which flowed a shallow branch of Aliso Norte Creek.

Eventually, the canyon opened up, the creek branched off to the south. Ahead was open range, covered with tall grass, wild mustard and a scattering of greasewood. Here the horse was forced to retard its progress through the tall growth. Another half hour slipped past before Dilliard sighted the roofs of El Vaca; twenty minutes more brought him into the town.

El Vaca consisted of a single, dusty, crooked street, bordered along either side by adobe huts and frame shacks. There were two saloons, a general store, a dirty-looking wine shop, two restaurants with fly-specked windows; a sign above the doorway of one building proclaimed the offices of a deputy-sheriff and justice of the peace. The town seemed more *Americano* than

Spanish or Mexican, though most of the men on the street were Mexicans and Indians, the majority of the latter having their hair done up in a sticky mixture of wet clay, held in place with colored rags.

Dilliard chuckled at this last, "Must be the season for getting rid of the animal life," he mused.

Hitch-rails ran along either side of the street. Dilliard didn't see anyone he knew. No one appeared to pay him any attention. A passing Mexican, upon Dilliard's request, pointed out the way to Scabbard's house. Scabbard's place proved to be just around the next bend in the street. It was a slope-roofed frame structure, erected in the shadow of a big live oak tree. Near the front, at one side, rose the highest clump of prickly-pear cactus Dilliard had ever seen.

A low-railinged porch ran across the front of the building. Two windows and a door were to be seen beyond the railing, the latter standing open. Dilliard reined his pony over to a hitch-rail jutting from near the clump of prickly-pear and running at right angles to the street. Behind the prickly-pear, and on the porch, he could hear men's voices.

The voices sounded somewhat familiar. Dilliard dismounted, flipped his reins over the tie-rail, shifted his holstered forty-five a trifle nearer to the front. Then he crossed to the single step that stood at the entrance to the porch, his head turning toward the voices behind the prickly-pear.

There came two loud oaths. A chair that had been leaning against the front wall of the building came crashing down on all four legs.

Dilliard laughed and said genially, "Hello, hombres. Haven't I encountered you some place before?"

Clem Corill and Wirt Bisbee were just rising from their chairs. Bisbee's right shoulder was swathed in dirty bandages; his face was ashen white behind the matted red whiskers. Corill's dark features were contorted with rage, but for the moment he was too surprised to speak.

Dilliard laughed again. "How'd you leave things in Santa Lozana, Bisbee? Hope your shoulder is getting along all right."

Bisbee muttered a curse and dropped his eyes. Corill snarled something unintelligible, started to draw his gun, then stopped short upon noticing that Dilliard's right hand was already wrapped about the butt of his own weapon.

"Damn you, Dilliard!" Corill sputtered. "I'll—"

"You'll not do a thing," Dilliard snapped. "I come here lookin' for your boss. Is he in there?" nodding toward the open doorway.

"Dilliard!" exclaimed a voice from inside. There were quick footsteps, and Drake Scabbard appeared in the doorway. For a moment he stopped short, apparently astonished at seeing Dilliard in El Vaca. Then he recovered himself, said coldly, "Thought I warned you to stay out of El Vaca."

"Seems like you did," Dilliard replied easily, "now that you mention it, Scabbard."

Corill commenced, "Drake, shall I—?"

Dilliard's narrowed eyes turned momentarily in Corill's direction. "No," Dilliard cut in coldly, "don't shoot me in the back, Corill. It might work out to Scabbard's disadvantage. Besides, I got business to talk over with him. There's something he should hear before he goes orderin' any executions."

"Leave be, Clem," Scabbard ordered shortly. His eyes narrowed momentarily, and he added, "You might go round up a few of the boys, Clem, and give 'em a look at this Texas hombre that's set to ride rough-shod over Drake Scabbard. The damn fool doesn't seem to realize just what he's up against."

"Sure, call 'em in," Dilliard grinned. "The more the merrier."

The sneer left Scabbard's face; he glanced suspiciously along the street in both directions, wondering what, if anything, this Texas man had up his sleeve. Dilliard was too cocky, too confident, to make Scabbard entirely easy in his mind.

Clem Corill stepped down from the porch and

made off in the direction of the nearest saloon. Wirt Bisbee, looking rather relieved, dropped down in his chair again, his pig-eyes glaring at Dilliard.

Scabbard turned back to the Texan. "You changed your mind about going to work for me?"

"I didn't say so."

"What in hell do you want?"

"Maybe I can give you some good advice."

Scabbard considered the Texan's words, then said, "I'm not sure whether I want any advice from you."

Dilliard shrugged his shoulders. "Suit yourself," carelessly. "I'm just talking for your own good. However, if you aren't interested . . ." He left the words unfinished and made as if to step from the porch.

"Wait a minute!" Scabbard snapped. "At any rate, you're not leaving yet. Come on in, I'll listen to you. You better make my time worthwhile, though."

He turned and entered the building, Dilliard at his heels. The room was scantily furnished: an iron safe stood in one corner, its door tightly closed; there were several stiff-backed wooden chairs ranged along the walls. A couple of yards from the safe was a board table on top of which were several papers, pen and ink, and a couple of ledgers. In the left-hand wall was a closed door, evidently leading to Scabbard's bedroom. In the rear wall, a door led to the outside.

Inside the room, Scabbard turned to face Dilliard. "What's your business?" he demanded.

Dilliard crossed the room, picked up a chair, set it near the table. "You better sit down, Scabbard," he advised coolly. "We might have quite a talk."

Scabbard hesitated, then shrugged his shoulders, rounded the table and sat down facing the Texan. "Get started," he said shortly.

Dilliard laughed. "You in a hurry?"

Scabbard nodded coldly. "Yes, I am. There isn't any telling just how long you're going to be able to talk. You're the one that should be in a hurry."

"You're frank about it, anyway," Dilliard smiled. "All right, here's the proposition: Scabbard, you're holding a deed and the Spanish Grant to the Rancho Sicamoro."

"There isn't any secret about that. I'm holding 'em as security on a loan of fifty thousand dollars. There's nothing illegal there."

"Perhaps not—according to the law you run in this town, but, Scabbard, you fooled an old man who trusted you, deceived him. But, that's according to your lights. Now, you're demanding the return of that fifty thousand, knowing that Don Salvadore will have to return to a jail cell."

"Not necessarily. I'll extend his loan if he'll deed over to me his stock. That's legal too."

"No doubt. But you know damn well he has

to have that stock to raise the money to pay you back."

"Suppose I do?" Scabbard queried angrily. "That's his lookout, not mine. He got himself in this fix."

Dilliard nodded. "I thought you'd look at it that way, Scabbard. You're fixin' to grab the Rancho Sicamoro for yourself."

"Well," Scabbard laughed harshly, "supposing I am? What of it? It's a nice property. If these damn greasers can't hold on to their land, that's their fault."

"I suppose you'll deny staging that attempted kidnapping, so you could get a hold on Don Salvadore?"

Scabbard hesitated, then replied coldly, "No, I won't deny it, Dilliard."

"You got plenty nerve," Dilliard said contemptuously.

"Probably," Scabbard agreed. "I'll admit anything else you want to know. What of it? It'll never get into court. If it did, and you swore I admitted these things, I'd swear you were a liar. It'd be your word against mine, and in this country my word carries a heap more weight."

"You're a cold-blooded skunk!" Dilliard snapped.

Scabbard's lips tightened. "Look here, Dilliard, what did you come here for? Let's get down to cases."

"Scabbard, I'm asking you to give Castameto a chance. If you'll give him a little time, he'll raise that money and pay you back. Any decent white man would do that much. You won't lose a cent. If Castameto has to go to the gallows for killing young Lucas Reardon, he'll go like a man, but he won't have to, if you'll do your part—"

"Hell! Don't talk like a damn fool, Dilliard. Castameto's only a greaser . . ." He broke off suddenly, "Say, what you so interested in his affairs for?"

"I want to see justice done."

"Hmm! Justice, eh?" Scabbard laughed scornfully, took out and lighted a slim black cigar, then laughed again. "You know, Texas man, I just had an idea."

"Yes? So far I haven't liked your ideas."

"This may change your mind. It just occurred to me that you're the one that's had the wool pulled over his eyes."

"How so?"

"We-ell, it's like this," Scabbard said with affected geniality, "Castameto figures he might get some place if he had a white man on his side. Mebbe, under the conditions, the proud old fool is willing to put up with you at his place for a spell—"

"Under what conditions?" Dilliard was puzzled.

Scabbard eyed Dilliard slyly. "Y'know, I wouldn't be surprised if you'd been hit sort of hard by Castameto's daughter. The old man, seeing how things stand, uses her to draw you on. You've been bilked, Texas man. I ain't surprised though. She's a good-lookin' wench, though I never did go for those white-and-gold hussies—"

Scabbard stopped suddenly. Dilliard hadn't said a word. He'd just drawn his Colt-gun and laid it softly on the table, the muzzle pointing toward Scabbard's body.

"What—what's the idea?" Scabbard stammered.

The Texan's voice was quiet, steady, eventoned, "Let's start farther back, Scabbard. You were saying something about swearing I was a liar, if this matter ever come to court."

Scabbard swallowed hard, then becoming angry, snapped, "You fool, what else do you expect? I'm playing for high stakes. I can't afford to be cheated by a cow hand from Texas."

Dilliard smiled, replaced the gun in his holster. "That's better," he stated softly.

Scabbard's face flamed. "We've had just about enough of this shilly-shallying. You said something about having some good advice for me. Get talking, fast!"

Dilliard nodded. "I come to see if you wouldn't give Castameto a chance. I should have known better. Now, here's the good advice, Scabbard. Go slow, or you won't go anyplace. You've got things your own way here, while you're bucking poor Mexicans and Spaniards, but there's plenty decent *Americanos* in this country; they're not going to stand very long for you and your kind. I'm going to enjoy gathering the right men to see that justice is done. Is that plain enough for you? Change your dirty ways, or they'll be changed for you. That's my advice. Take it to heart!"

The eyes of the two men locked, held for half a minute.

Dilliard started to rise. "That's all. I'll be drifting."

"Sit down!" Scabbard's voice was cold, menacing. "Look around you, Dilliard. Figuring to drift, eh? Just where in hell you figuring to drift to?"

Sardonic laughter sounded at Dilliard's rear. The Texan turned to gaze at a dozen or so men who had filed silently into the room and who stood with their backs to the doorway, their eyes hard on this gringo renegade. They formed an evil-looking group with their tattered sombreros, unshaven countenances and dirty clothing. All carried six-shooters, except one old rascally individual who toted a rifle and a wicked hunting knife at his belt. They were fit companions for Bisbee and Corill who headed them. Bart Fustian glowered at one side, his head swathed in bandages, the lower part of his face swollen and bruised to an extent that prevented speech.

"How do you like my pets?" Scabbard was

saying mockingly. "Dilliard, these men are loyal; they realize it pays well to work for Drake Scabbard. They'll do anything I tell 'em to—and they won't even ask why. Do you get what I'm hinting at?"

Dilliard nodded, laughed easily. "Nice clean looking group of boys. They've got such wholesome, honest faces. Pro'bly spend their time studying wild flowers, don't they? I'll bet they're as sweet a crew as ever plugged a stage driver in the back."

The insolent remarks brought a number of oaths and threatening looks. Dilliard singled out the villainous old fellow with the rifle. "Who's that crow-bait? Don't tell me he's fooled you into believing he's Dan'l Boone or Kit Carson. They're dead, you know."

The old "crow-bait" was a dirty-looking individual with ragged gray whiskers, stained with tobacco juice, and one squinting eye. He had a wiry frame, and wore a coon-skin cap, a fringed buckskin suit and worn moccasins, instead of the usual knee-boots common to the country. Cradled under one arm was a Spencer repeating rifle.

The owner of the rifle gave vent to a vile epithet together with a long brown stream of tobacco juice. "Tell the galoot who I am, Drake," he squealed, in injured tones.

"Dilliard," Scabbard said pleasantly, "you've heard of old Cat-Eye Fremont, haven't you?"

"Can't say I have," the Texan denied.

"I'm surprised at your ignorance, Dilliard. Old Cat-Eye is just about the finest rifle shot in all the length and breadth of California."

Dilliard grinned suddenly, "Well, you tell Cat-Eye for me, Scabbard, that if he doesn't keep his rifle any cleaner than his ugly face, his barrel will get fouled and he'll find himself in trouble—"

"Jumpin' catamounts!" Cat-Eye yelled indignantly, "if ye can show me a cleaner barr'l than what I got here—"

"Shut up, Cat-Eye," Scabbard snarled suddenly, losing his temper. Cat-Eye "shut up" as did the rest of the gang. Scabbard turned back to Dilliard, saying savagely, "So you figured you'd drift, eh? Just where you goin' to drift to, Texas man? You fool! Did you think you could come to El Vaca and get out again, unless I gave the word. And I'm not giving the word, see? You've overplayed your hand and in one minute you're due—"

"Take it easy, Scabbard," Dilliard interposed carelessly, "you'll be havin' a stroke of apoplexy if you aren't careful. Scabbard, did I ever mention that I had influential friends at the capitol—?"

"You mean in Sacramento?" Scabbard asked quickly.

"Got a few in San Diego, too," Dilliard laughed.

"Who are they?" Scabbard's voice was eager.

"That doesn't matter. You know, Scabbard, before I left for El Vaca, I had a rider sent in both directions to tell those friends I was headin' for El Vaca to talk to a skunk named Drake Scabbard. Of course, if anythin' was to happen to me, it would happen, but, Scabbard, think of the questions you might have to answer. Man, you might find yourself in a tight fix."

Scabbard looked uneasy. He remembered now that Dilliard had seemed to display a great deal of confidence. He looked steadily at Dilliard. Dilliard laughed contemptuously.

"Dammit!" Scabbard scowled. "You're running a bluff."

The Texan's grin was insolent. "Scabbard, I sure am," he admitted truthfully. "Why don't you call it? Go on, I dare you to call it."

The very frankness of Dilliard's manner deceived Scabbard. He was uncertain what to do. He couldn't find anything to say.

Again, Dilliard laughed contemptuously, rose from his chair. "Yep, I'm ready to drift," he stated. "S'long, Scabbard. See you on the gallows sometime."

Scabbard turned white with anger but didn't dare halt the Texan on his progress toward the doorway. Dilliard eyed the unbroken front of scowling faces barring the doorway. "Out of the way, scum," he said coldly.

The scum, awaiting the signal from Scabbard that didn't come, suddenly parted. Laughing coolly, Dilliard passed through to the outside, crossed the porch, reached his horse and mounted it, expecting any minute to hear gunfire break out at his rear. He gave a long sigh of relief as he turned the pony and loped swiftly out of El Vaca.

As his hoofbeats died away, Scabbard and his henchmen gave way to a fit of cursing.

"Dammit, Drake!" Corill growled, "Why didn't you give the word? We'd have finished him *pronto*."

"Give the word!" Scabbard snarled. "You fools! Didn't you hear what he said?"

"Aw," Bisbee blustered, "that was all bluff—"

"Yes," Scabbard cut in, speaking slowly, "I think it was. But there's just a small chance that he was talking straight. If he was, it wouldn't do to have the authorities coming here. El Vaca wouldn't stand an investigation right now. I've got to get more money before we can stand anythin' like that. Once I've got what I want we'll tell the whole state to go to hell. Nope, it wouldn't do to kill Dilliard in my town—"

"By Cripes!" Corill questioned, "You aimin' to let him get away?"

"Away from El Vaca—yes," Scabbard said coldly. "Far enough away so a killing can't be hung on us. . . . Cat-Eye!"

Cat-Eye Fremont stepped up to the table. "You got work for me, boss?"

Scabbard nodded jerkily. "You're not only the best rifle shot in California, but the best trailer as well. Get on Dilliard's trail. Once he's out of town he'll be takin' it easy. You won't have any trouble catchin' up. Once you sight him, put that Spencer to work. Understand?"

"He won't do no driftin' within my range," Cat-Eye boasted.

"Make that statement stick, Cat-Eye, and there's gold waiting for you on your return. Otherwise—don't return."

"Oh, hell, thet feller will be easy—"

"Drop that attitude right now, Cat-Eye," Scabbard said sternly. "If he gets wind you're following him, he'll try to outfox you."

"He won't outfox this Injun," Cat-Eye affirmed.

"Good! Get going, now." Cat-Eye started for the door. When nearly there, Scabbard called to him. The old scoundrel turned and waited. "I just happened to think, Cat-Eye," Scabbard said cruelly, "that I need a new pen-wiper for helping me keep my accounts."

"Is that so?" Cat-Eye queried blankly.

Scabbard nodded. "That's so. Bring me his scalp, Cat-Eye!"

16
TWISTING TRAILS

One mile out of town, Dilliard reined the rangy, chestnut gelding to a walk and glanced back toward El Vaca. No pursuing rider was in sight, but that fact didn't deceive the Texan.

"Scabbard won't give up a chance to rub me out this easy," Dilliard mused. "If I'm not mistaken in the man, he's delegatin' somebody right now to finish me off. Reckon I'd better go easy until I learn who it is. Scabbard wouldn't want me killed in, or near, El Vaca, but if my dead body was to be found out on the range some place, that coyote could disclaim all knowledge of the affair."

Dilliard touched a spur to his pony and the animal moved into a faster gait, breasting through the wild mustard and tall grass. Before long the southern branch of the Aliso Norte was reached.

Dilliard chuckled, "Here's where I have some fun with whoever gets sent on my trail."

Reining the pony into the shallow depths of the creek, Dilliard followed its winding course upstream for a quarter mile, before again riding out of the water *on the same side on which he'd entered.*

"There, mister," he grinned at his supposed tracker, "you can waste some time looking for the spot at which I crossed the river. If that move don't fool you, you're a better man than I think."

The canyon walls on either side of the stream were now growing higher as Dilliard advanced. For a mile and a half he followed the southern bank, before a second time sending his pony into the water. This time he crossed over on a long diagonal. Even at its deepest point the water wasn't much above the pony's hocks.

Emerging from the Aliso Norte near a natural break in the canyon wall, Dilliard turned the pony's head toward the long hogback he'd traversed a few hours before. But now he rode directly west. In a short time the hogback commenced to slope toward the canyon, and before long Dilliard had reached a point above the spot at which he had first pushed his pony into the stream. Here he dismounted and, screened from the creek by a high shelter of mahogany bush, sat down to wait.

It wasn't long before his vigilance was rewarded: a horseman rounded a bend in the canyon, riding slowly and scrutinizing the earth for hoofprints as he progressed. As the rider came nearer, Dilliard, looking down on him from above, recognized old Cat-Eye Fremont.

Dilliard considered. "Cat-Eye, eh? I sort of expected Scabbard to send one of his other coyotes, instead of old Cat-Eye. I wonder what the idea is. Let me see . . . Scabbard said Cat-Eye was the best rifle shot in this country. Hmmm! That means, I reckon, that Scabbard wants me killed from a distance. Must be he don't figure his six-shooter men as being so good—not good enough, anyway. Yep, that's pro'bly it. Cat-Eye knows this country; he'll figure to reach a point where he can command any trail I take, then let me have a slug from his rifle, from a distance. Yep, that's it. In that way, there won't be any betrayin' 'sign' left near my body, to be traced back to El Vaca. Scabbard's tricky, I got to admit that much."

Cat-Eye Fremont was reining his pony into the water now, following on Dilliard's trail. Dilliard watched, chuckling to himself, when Cat-Eye rode out of the water and again commenced looking for the hoofprints he'd been following. Slowly, back and forth at the water's edge, Cat-Eye rode, looking for "sign" that wasn't there.

Dilliard saw the old fellow remove his coonskin cap and scratch his head in perplexity, then turn his pony back into the water again and scan the opposite shore.

Dilliard laughed softly. "I sure got that old coyote baffled! Hoofprints led into the water but they didn't come out again. I'll bet a plugged *peso* that he follows the stream, just like I did, until he finds those prints comin' out on the same side where they went in. Then he *will* wonder what I'm up to—No, by gosh!"

Dilliard sobered suddenly, as Cat-Eye suddenly wheeled his pony back to the north shore of the creek, emerged, and sent the pony along at a brisk trot.

Slowly, an involuntary feeling of admiration for Cat-Eye's mental processes crept over Dilliard. "Dam'd if he isn't a cagey old coot, at that," Dilliard admitted ruefully. "I didn't fool him at all. I reckon Cat-Eye knows something about reading 'sign' himself. He pro'bly doesn't figure just why he can't find my prints on this side of the stream, but he does know that I'm heading for the Rancho Sicamoro, and that's where he's heading to. He knows this country better than I do. Maybe that break in the canyon wall is the only one for miles, and he knows I'll have to take it to get back to the ranch. Branch Dilliard, you aren't as wise as you thought you were, and if you don't move fast, old Cat-Eye is going to cut you off."

Whirling, Dilliard ran back to his pony, leaped into the saddle, plunged in his spurs and headed back toward the break in the canyon wall. Now, as he rode swiftly along the hogback, he was formulating new plans for "stopping" Cat-Eye Fremont. He hadn't much time in which to work, either, if he were to reach that opening from the river before Cat-Eye did.

As a matter of fact, Cat-Eye wasn't more than twenty minutes behind Dilliard in reaching the same point. Following the northern bank of the stream, Cat-Eye finally came to hoofprints left by Dilliard's pony when it left the shallow water.

"Knew dang well," Cat-Eye mused, "that he'd have to come out here. Can't see why in time he followed the stream so far, though."

The old fellow was entirely unaware of Dilliard's unsuccessful maneuvers on the opposite shore, and Dilliard had accomplished nothing in his attempted deception, except loss of time.

The hoofprints were plain to follow now; Cat-Eye's gray horse moved along at a good gait until it reached higher ground. Here the hoofprints were lost once more: a *bajada* of flat broken rock sloping gently from a low hill, presented a hard, uneven surface upon which passing hoofs left very little or no "sign" to follow. It was at this point Dilliard had turned to gain the spot from which he had first caught sight of Cat-Eye Fremont, and only twenty minutes previously, Dilliard had spurred his swift-running horse across the cluttered, rock-strewn terrain to disappear around the first shelter of protecting hill that presented itself.

Cat-Eye didn't waste time looking for sign now: "Dang it!" he grunted irritably, "a hawss don't leave no tracks on that stuff. Reckon I might as well head for softer ground, then cast around until I pick up his trail."

He took out a much-soiled chunk of "eatin'

terbaccy," sunk his broken fangs into the brown weed and tore off a "chaw." Then, once more, he got down to business, searching on the relatively softer earth, beyond the *bajada* of broken rock, for Dilliard's trail, little realizing that, by this time, the Texan had gained the crest of a low hill and, screened behind a wide spreading *madroña* tree, was gleefully watching every move made by his pursuer.

Crossing the *bajada* in the direction leading toward the Rancho Sicamoro, Cat-Eye was considerably surprised that he didn't at once spy the hoofprints of Dilliard's horse. He cursed a little, then commenced to ride in wide circles, his shrewd eyes ever intent on the surrounding earth. Suddenly he found the "sign" for which he sought.

"Damn odd," he grunted, frowning. "From this here, it looks like Dilliard was headin' up inter th' mountings, 'stead of goin' to Castameto's place. Wonder what's his idee?"

But without losing time over that question, Cat-Eye took up the trail.

And then the chase commenced! It was a regular hare-and-hounds game that Dilliard was playing, with himself in the role of the hare and the wily Cat-Eye sticking like a leech to the trail.

Up hill and down, Dilliard led the chase, without at any time nearing the Ranch of the Sycamores. He doubled back on his trail, cut down into deep ravines, mounted to high altitudes, but without being able to elude his persistent pursuer.

From time to time, from behind a sheltering screen of brush Dilliard caught brief glances of old Cat-Eye. “Danged if that old codger isn’t a hound on a trail,” Dilliard muttered appreciatively. “I’ve used every trick I can think of, but I can’t shake him off.”

Never once had it occurred to Dilliard to ambush and destroy the old fellow, despite the fact he knew that Cat-Eye was following the trail with only one end in view: the wiping out of the *Americano* who’d had the utmost temerity to buck Drake Scabbard.

The sun swung to the west. Still the chase continued. This was all familiar ground to Cat-Eye Fremont. Three times he had waited at points on the shelves along certain ravines, feeling sure, from the course Dilliard was taking, that he must appear, before long, on the opposite side of the ravine, where he’d provide an open target for a slug from the Spencer rifle. But, somehow, the Texan and his chestnut horse had failed to put in the expected appearance and Cat-Eye had been once more forced to take up the trail.

“Damn his hide!” Cat-Eye swore. Cat-Eye was growing weary. It was a long time since his old frame had been forced to undergo such riding and scrambling along mountain slopes. “I don’t see what’s got inter Dilliard. Why don’t he act sensible an' go home? What's he climbin' around these here mountings for all afternoon? Must be he's lookin' for strays, though I don't see no sense ridin' around these here hills. If I didn't know different I'd think somebody had tipped him off to Scabbard's orders and that he knowed I was a-follerin' him."

Gradually, as the afternoon waned, the chase swung around to the vicinity of the Rancho Sicamoro. "Well, he's gittin' toward home at last," Cat-Eye grumbled. " 'Bout time—"

The old fellow paused suddenly. From the matted underbrush to his right a rabbit had darted into sight. Cat-Eye gave one soft, quick whistle and jerked his horse to a stop. The rabbit halted, raising on rear haunches to locate the whistle. Cat-Eye's right hand swept to the belt at his waist, came up holding his long keen hunting knife. His wrist flicked back, then out. The knife was a streak of blue light through the air, ending in a frightened squeal in the jackrabbit's body.

Cat-Eye grunted with satisfaction as he dismounted, retrieved the bleeding carcass and tied it to his saddle. "Looks like I might have to make camp tonight, with all this chasin' over the hills. I don't aim to sleep on an empty belly."

He started his horse, eyes intent on the seemingly endless string of hoofprints that led the way before him. Fifteen minutes passed. The prints were leading to lower ground now.

"Yep, Dilliard's headin' home at last, dang his ornery hide. He'd orter be 'shamed of hisself leadin' an ol' man like me across these hills all afternoon, 'thout oncet givin' me a clean look 'tween my Spencer sights. I'm gettin' too old fer sech traipsin' 'round. I jest reckon I'll take me a short cut over towards Castameto's diggin's. He'll have to come into plain sight when he nears home. I can be holed up, neat, in some brush, and throw my lead the minnit he heaves inter sight. By Cripes! Thet's whut I'll do."

Wheeling his horse, Cat-Eye swung off at a tangent through the brush. The sun was low now. Half an hour later, Cat-Eye was entrenched behind a mesquite thicket, high on a hilly slope. Below him was spread out the Ranch of the Sycamores, and, to reach the ranch, Dilliard would have to pass Cat-Eye's line of vision—the line of vision being trained between the sights of a straight-shooting Spencer rifle. Impatiently, Cat-Eye waited for Dilliard to put in an appearance.

"Dang his ornery hide," Cat-Eye wailed, "he's wasted so much time foolin' around these hills, that it's goin' to be night before he gets here. It'll be too dad-blamed dark to see him. Curse my luck!"

Which was exactly what Dilliard had figured on. He had timed the chase well, and, under cover of darkness, would be able to reach the ranch without being seen by Cat-Eye.

The sun was below the horizon now. Twilight lingered but a few minutes, then darkness closed down like a great velvet curtain in which twinkled the first of myriad stars.

Cat-Eye sighed deeply, groaned when he straightened his ancient limbs. "By Gawd," he swore, "I'll git him tomorrer, anyway. Nothin' ter do ternight, but camp out and wait."

Getting his horse, Cat-Eye moved farther up the hill, then stopped again and dismounted in a thick clump of chaparral and mahogany bush. Here he built a small fire that was screened by thick brush from the sight of those in the *rancho* below, and tenderly lowering his aching limbs to the earth, spread his blankets and commenced skinning the dead rabbit. . . .

Five hundred yards higher on the slope, Dilliard chuckled as he caught a tiny glimmer of firelight below him. He'd been waiting for that for some time.

"Now that I know where Cat-Eye's located," the Texan grinned in the darkness, "I reckon I'll get down to my own supper. I can take care of Cat-Eye later."

Slipping noiselessly through the brush, Dilliard went to his waiting horse a few rods away, climbed into the saddle, and with the stealth of a Comanche, swung down the slope in a wide circle that carried him to the Rancho Sicamoro.

17
THE GRINGO RIDES SOUTH

Dilliard turned his pony into the corral and, slinging his saddle to shoulder, started for the small shelter nearby, where saddles were left overnight. Overhead the stars shone brightly. Near the shelter, a cigarette glowed momentarily, then was cast to the earth. A slim form took shape in the darkness, then Dilliard caught Tony's words:

"*Por Dios*! Señor Branch, you return alive!"

Dilliard laughed softly. "Looks that way, *amigo*."

"Almos' I'm sweat' blood when I'm hear you ride to El Vaca. I'm theenk I nevair again set my eyes on your body. Only that the *patrón* forbid' I would, long since, ride to see what happen. But Don Salvadore order' that we should wait yet a small time, then we should ride in force—but, what hav' happen?"

"I'll tell you later, Tony. I want to see Don Salvadore as soon as possible—"

"But you saw Scabbard?"

"I saw Scabbard. Tried to persuade him against the course he's following, but he couldn't see it my way—"

"*Socorro*! And you live to tell the tale—"

"I made a bluff. Scabbard didn't dare try anything in El Vaca."

"Señor Branch! I am surprise' Scabbard did not send one to follow your trail and kill—"

"Scabbard did. Tony, did you ever hear of an old codger called Cat-Eye Fremont?"

"*Sí, sí*!" Tony said quickly. "Once or twice this Cat-Eyes he comes to Santa Lozana when I'm live there. It is said he can shoot out the eye of a scorpion, at a mile's distance, with hees rifle. Yes, I know of him. A dirty old devil if one ever lived. You killed him?"

Branch related briefly the story of the chase he'd led Cat-Eye Fremont that day, chuckling as he talked. When he had finished, Tony shook his head dubiously, saying, "You should have put a bullet through hees ribs when you had the chance, Señor Branch. Thees is not so good. Today, you have make of him the monkey, but always tomorrow comes, and thees Cat-Eye will be on the alert to shoot—"

"I've thought of that, too," Dilliard said quietly.

"What, then, do you intend?"

"We'll talk about it later," Dilliard said. "Right now I want to see Don Salvadore as soon as possible, learn how many cows are rounded up ready for the drive."

Tony vented an exclamation of dismay. "That

I can tell you. Of only five hondred head are gathered—"

"Five hundred head!" Dilliard swore bitterly under his breath. "Cripes! What have the men been doing?"

"Rounding up the stray animals from the leftovers of past years. There was branding to be done—"

Dilliard swore again. "They should know you can't bring a cow along a drive in good condition when it's been fresh branded. What's Don Salvadore thinking of?"

"Perhaps it is not entirely the *patrón*'s fault. Manuel Estudillo, the *mayordomo*, did not realize the reason for hurrying. Today, the *patrón*, himself, rode out to oversee the business. *Diantre*! He was a whirlwind, a storm, a cyclone. He drove the men like a fiend from hell—"

"But, five hundred head." Dilliard shook his head gravely. "That's not so good—"

"All day," Tony said dryly, "the *patrón* have been impressing that fac' on the minds of us."

Dilliard nodded shortly. "All right, I'll talk to Don Salvadore, Tony. I'll be back in a short spell. Meet me out here. We'll have to decide something about Cat-Eye Fremont, too."

"*Sí*, Señor Branch."

Dilliard strode on toward the house, crossed the passageway into the patio and thence arrived before the door of the main room of the dwelling.

His quick knock brought an invitation to enter. Dilliard stepped into the *sala* to find Castameto pacing the floor restlessly before the fireplace at one end of the room. Sudden relief flooded into the old Spaniard's eyes.

"It is really you! You are back, Don Branch!"

"Back safely, despite your worries."

"You saw Scabbard?"

Dilliard nodded, related briefly what had taken place, but made no mention of being followed by Cat-Eye Fremont.

"Thank the *buen Dios*!" Castameto said fervently. "At least you are safe, even though your journey was less successful than you had hoped. Come, we shall eat. I would not have the meal served before. As to Scabbard—his attitude is no more than I expected."

He called to an Indian servant, who entered and received certain instructions, then led the way to the dining room. Mariposa entered within a few minutes, dressed in some soft gray material. Dilliard's heart skipped a few beats at sight of the girl, but he managed to hold his voice steady and greeted her quietly.

Throughout the meal, Mariposa took but small part in the conversation, and when wine and *cigarros* were brought, she asked to be excused and took her departure. Castameto frowned slightly upon noticing the way in which Dilliard's eyes followed the girl from the room. But the old

Spaniard said nothing. Instead he changed the subject, saying somewhat apologetically, "*Señor*, I learned today, to my regret, that only five hundred head of cattle have been gathered for the drive."

"I saw Tony Aguilar, outside. He told me. You'll have to hasten the work, Don Salvadore."

"You speak the truth. Today I took charge in person. I think things will move faster."

"Let it be hoped so," Dilliard replied courteously, though at heart he was storming with impatience. "By the way, Don Salvadore, have you a map of any kind showing the country through which the drive will pass—"

"Manuel Estudillo knows the way—every foot of it. You need have no worries—"

"I wasn't thinking of that. I sort of plan to make the ride to San Diego, myself, first, to look over the ground. I'll return before the drive starts."

Castameto appeared puzzled but rose and left the room. Within a few minutes, he returned bearing a small map drawn on parchment, which he spread on the table before Dilliard.

"The original of this was made many years ago, around 1850, but there have been few changes, and those I have noted on this copy. You see—" and Castameto's finger traced along the map, "—the drive will follow the Camino Real—the King's Highway—as it is called. Here, at this point, is Capistrano. That, the drive should reach the first day. At this point is Las Flores—a small settlement. Then, comes Agua Harionda, next Encinetos. By the time you have arrived at Soledad, you are nearing San Diego."

Dilliard indicated several small crosses in ink, placed along the trail, at fairly regular intervals. "What are these?"

"I have friends at those points. Some have *ranchos*—a few only *rancherias*—small settlements of their own people."

"Good!" Dilliard said promptly. "Exactly what I'm looking for. Don Salvadore, could you let me have a letter to those friends, requesting them to furnish me with fresh horses along the way?"

"Of course, but I do not see why—" The old Spaniard paused in perplexity.

Dilliard explained. "As I said, I want to go to San Diego. It's too long a trip for one horse to make in a hurry. I want to get there and back as soon as possible."

"You shall have your letter," Castameto promised, though it was plain to the Texan that Castameto felt that the ride to San Diego was just a waste of time. "I'll write it at once."

Dilliard requested a few further details regarding Castameto's friends, then, when the letter was written and in his pocket, took his departure as quickly as possible.

Castameto held him at the door. "When do you expect to start, Señor Branch?"

Dilliard shrugged carelessly, "I don't know exactly. Probably tomorrow morning sometime. *Buenas noches*!"

"*Buenas noches*!"

Dilliard passed from the room leaving a much-puzzled Spanish gentleman wondering—but too courteous to ask—why the gringo should want to make what appeared to be a long, useless ride to San Diego.

Dilliard crossed the patio. Beyond the outer wall of the house he found Tony awaiting him, smoking in the darkness.

"I have giv' your *caballo* the oats and the rubdown," Tony said.

"Thanks. That's fine. Fits right in with my plans."

"What are the plans?"

"Listen, Tony, I'm headin' south—to San Diego. I have a letter from the *patrón* to certain of his friends along the way, where I can get fresh horses. I figure to get there and back in less time than it takes to talk about, almost."

"But I do not understan' why this journey is necessary."

"All right, I'll tell you. But don't spill it to the *patrón*. Tony, we may be able to get the cattle delivered, in time, and we may not. Even if we do, Don Salvadore doesn't know whether or not the purchase money will be ready for him. The hell of it is, he's too damn polite to ask. He was plumb shocked when I brought up the money question. Any way you look at it, this is no time for politeness—"

"That much I'm admit—"

"I'm glad I got somebody on my side," Dilliard said with grim humor. "Here's the proposition. I'm aimin' to ride to San Diego and talk to this Don Alvaro Serrano personally. I'm going to try and make Serrano see our side of the situation, and see if he won't have the money—cash—ready for us when we deliver the cattle."

"That is all right, I suppose," Tony commenced dubiously, "but I do not think Don Salvadore would like it—"

"I know damn well he wouldn't," Dilliard grinned, "but once it's done, it's done. Don Salvadore can take it out of my hide later, if he likes. Right now, I'm aimin' to do anythin' in my power to beat Scabbard. If I can only persuade Serrano to have the money ready for us—well, we'll have a slight chance. But, remember, not a word to Don Salvadore. I'll tell him myself when I get back."

"And I will catch his boot in the seat of my pants, if the *patrón* learns I have known all the time."

"That," Dilliard chuckled, "is your hard luck, Tony—"

He broke off at Tony's sudden exclamation of dismay.

Dilliard said, “Now, what’s up?”

“Cat-Eye Fremont! I’m almos’ forget heem—”

“What about Cat-Eye?”

“He will follow you and shoot—”

Dilliard laughed. “Tony, you and I are going to take care of Fremont before I leave. I can’t afford to have that hombre on my trail any longer.”

“But how—?”

“Say—” Dilliard commenced to laugh, struck with a new idea, “—didn’t I see the barrel of an old muzzle-loadin’ rifle, with the stock busted off, in that junk shed the other day?”

Tony shrugged his shoulders. “That may be so. Everything else may be found there—saddles that are worn out, old kettles, rusty knives—”

“I’m aimin’ to take a look. You saddle your horse. Saddle up for me too, will you?”

“Gladly, Don Branch.”

The two parted, Tony heading toward the corrals, Dilliard striding across to one of the sheds where all discarded equipment was stored for no good reason that anyone could think of.

In a short time the Texan returned, bearing in one hand a length of old gun-barrel. Tony was waiting with the horses. He looked puzzled, but to his questioning Dilliard returned only laughing chuckles to the effect that Cat-Eye Fremont was going to be made to “look plumb foolish.”

Mounted, the two men swung away from the

ranch buildings and headed up into the slopes of Borrego Canyon, Dilliard leading the way and swinging gradually in a wide arc that carried them close to the point at which Dilliard had seen Cat-Eye making camp.

Finally, behind a thick clump of chaparral, Dilliard gave the signal to halt. The two men crept forward on foot, moving noiselessly through the brush, until, a hundred yards below them, Tony suddenly spotted the dim embers of a small campfire.

"Now, you kill him—yes?" Tony asked.

Dilliard laughed noiselessly. "No," he replied. "I couldn't kill an old codger like that. I'm goin' to do somethin' worse—I'm goin' to make him plumb ridiculous. He's a pretty wise ol' coot at that, when it comes to a matter of trailin' and readin' 'sign.' Look, it's up to you to get his horse, while I'm gettin' his rifle."

"I am willing, but how—?"

"Here's the plan . . ." Dilliard's voice dropped to a dim whisper. For several moments the two men conversed, then they parted to take different directions to reach Cat-Eye's camp.

Dilliard crept silently down the slope, his lean form slipping through the growth, under the starlight, with the cunning of a Comanche Indian. It took him fully fifteen minutes to cover the hundred yards necessary to reach Cat-Eye's camp, but in time he found himself crouching behind a mesquite bush, directly behind the camp's sleeping owner.

Cat-Eye was rolled in blankets, snoring loudly, his face to the sky, his head resting on his saddle. Beyond his feet, the small campfire had almost burned out, but now and then a flickering flame picked out high-lights on an empty whisky flask thrown among the ashes. The flask was one of the reasons, together with Cat-Eye's extreme weariness, for the man's sound slumber.

By his side, lay the Spencer rifle, one hand resting loosely across the barrel. A few yards beyond the fire, Cat-Eye had picketed his horse.

It was the horse upon which Dilliard's eyes were fastened, while he waited in the brush, one hand clutching the length of useless muzzle-loading rifle-barrel. Suddenly, in the dim light, Dilliard saw a hand stretch out to the horse's picket, pull the picket from the earth where Cat-Eye had driven it. Then, the rope tautened, the horse's head turned obediently and followed off through the brush beyond the fire. In a few seconds the horse had disappeared and with scarcely a sound beyond that which it would ordinarily have made, anyway, during the course of the night.

Dilliard laughed softly, musing, "Nice work, Tony. Now comes the ticklish part."

The Texan waited another five minutes until all sounds of the horse's passing had died away, then he commenced to edge toward the sleeping Cat-Eye. Inch by inch, he moved nearer and nearer, until at last he crouched, silently, by the side of the snoring man.

Holding the length of rifle-barrel in one hand, Dilliard plucked a long blade of grass and drew it softly across the knuckles of the protecting hand resting on Cat-Eye's Spencer rifle.

Back and forth moved the blade of grass. The skin on Cat-Eye's hand commenced to twitch as Dilliard kept up the tickling action. Abruptly, Cat-Eye ceased snoring, grunted something unintelligible. Once more, Dilliard drew the blade of grass tantalizingly across Cat-Eye's knuckles.

Without opening his eyes, or becoming thoroughly awake, Cat-Eye jerked his hand away from the Spencer and with the fingers of the other hand commenced to scratch vigorously the spot the grass had touched.

Like a flash, Dilliard lifted the Spencer rifle from the earth, and in its place substituted the useless length of barrel from the broken muzzle-loader, and it was on this useless length of barrel that Cat-Eye, a few seconds later, dropped his guarding hand. Once the hand had touched that length of gun-barrel, Cat-Eye again relaxed, with a drowsy, muttered something that had to do with damning all bugs that go crawling around at night.

Dilliard didn't move a muscle until Cat-Eye

had commenced snoring once more, then the Texan, bearing the Spencer rifle, commenced to edge his way back into the brush.

Twenty minutes later he reached the spot at which he and Tony had left their horses. Tony was waiting anxiously in the saddle, one hand gripping the rope of Cat-Eye's horse.

"You did it all right?" he whispered tensely.

Dilliard laughed silently, holding the Spencer rifle aloft. "So long as that old coot can feel a gun-barrel beneath his hand, he'll sleep until dawn—"

"But how did you do it?"

"Let's get moving, I'll talk on the way."

The horses moved quickly down the slope. Both men were laughing by the time they had come within half a mile of the Rancho Sicamoro.

Finally, Dilliard said, "You drift on home, Tony. Here, take Cat-Eye's rifle. If he's got nerve enough to come and ask for it and his horse, let him have 'em. Man, he'll sure feel foolish about sun-up time."

"But where do you go?"

"I might as well get started south. I told Don Salvadore I aimed to start in the morning. It's after midnight now. I'll be seein' you soon's I get back, Tony. Take care of yourself. And if you can speed up that gatherin', I'll sure appreciate it."

"Me, I'm do my best," Tony said seriously.

"None of us can do more." The two men shook hands. Dilliard said, "*Adiós, amigo*."

"*Adiós. Vaya con Dios*."

Dilliard turned his pony, spurred it into swift action. Horse and man faded into the darkness, but Tony didn't resume his homeward journey until the drumming hoofbeats had blended into the silence of the starry night.

"*Diantre*!" the Mexican murmured admiringly. "What a man!"

18
CAT-EYE'S FATAL SLIP

Cat-Eye Fremont awoke slowly to find the sun already tipping above the eastern horizon in wide streaks of flaming crimson. He opened one eye, cocked it at the turquoise sky directly above, then opened the other. His ancient bones ached as he stretched his spare frame between blankets. His left hand, according to an old, established habit, still rested on the gun-barrel at his side.

A wide yawn stretched Cat-Eye's jaws and he was about to settle back in blankets for another half hour's dozing, when something warned him that all was not quite well; none of the usual morning sounds were being produced from the point at which Cat-Eye's horse should have been picketed. Cat-Eye lifted his head, then abruptly came to a sitting position. Something *was* wrong—radically wrong! The horse was nowhere in sight!

"Dang thet pesky animile!" Cat-Eye snarled. "He's done pulled his peg and strayed off. I figgered I druv thet peg plumb solid, too. Now, I 'spects I'll hev to tromp these yere mountings half th' mornin', catchin' up thet pesky critter. An' I shed orter be drawin' a bead on thet Dilliard feller. Oh, damn my luck!"

Flinging back his blankets, Cat-Eye rose, his left hand closing on the rifle-barrel at his side. At once, something else appeared to be wrong. That Spencer gun didn't appear to have no heft this mornin'. . . .

Cat-Eye gave vent to a sudden startled yell as his eyes fell on the useless rifle-barrel clutched in his left hand. It was a yell that contained no small depth of agony as well as anger. Thick, hot rage welled in his throat as he gazed at the discarded rifle-barrel. Then his rage erupted violently in a torrent of rich profanity. For several minutes the atmosphere was colored a vivid purple hue while Cat-Eye unleashed a soul-stirring flow of foul invective.

Gradually, from sheer lack of breath, his voice dropped to a more level tone. "Why, th' slab-sided, aig-stealin', pig-hearted sons-of-packmules!" he wailed. "Th' thievin', billy-be-damned, hide-lickin', carcass-stinkin' coyoty sneaks! Somebody's done come here while I slept an' stole my rifle! An' my hawss! A man can't trust nobody these days, goldern 'em! Cheatin' a deservin' ol' feller like me outten his right to make a decent livin'. And this! This—!"

Cat-Eye glowered balefully at the useless rifle-barrel, then, overcome by a second violent rush of baffled rage, he lifted the offending length of steel tube high in the air, whirled it above his head and, releasing his grip, sent it crashing, as far as strength permitted, into the brush surrounding his camp.

Even that failed to lessen his anger appreciably. He cursed, hurled savage, jaw-cracking oaths. He tramped furiously up and down beside his rumpled blankets. No need now to waste time looking for his horse. Cat-Eye was well aware that it hadn't strayed off of its own volition. Once the old man glanced down the slope toward the distant buildings of the Rancho Sicamoro. All appeared peaceful there. It was due to those at the *rancho* that Cat-Eye found himself in this predicament. Cat-Eye clenched his fist and shook it savagely in the direction of the ranch buildings, then resumed his futile raging about the camp.

No horse. No gun. It suddenly occurred to Cat-Eye that he was without breakfast as well. And he suddenly became hungry for his morning meal and coffee. That brought on a fresh fit of cursing. Gradually he quieted down as his breath ran short. A slow wave of crimson crept up through his matted gray whiskers.

"How in the devil am I to go back to El Vaca and tell whut's happened? I'll never hear th' last of this! Th' boys'll laugh their heads off. I been ridyculed, thet's whut, ridyculed! Somebody ain't got no proper respect for old age! Damn 'em for measly scuts!"

He dropped disconsolately down on his blankets, struck viciously at his unoffending saddle.

"They'd proberly lifted my rig, too, if I hadn't had my head on it. I sure been made out to look a fool. Curse sech dirty, thievin' varmints!"

Again, he rose and commenced to scan the underbrush surrounding the camp, looking for "sign" of the villains who had perpetrated such an outrageous business. "Sign" was plentiful in the growth to the rear of the camp: a foot-print here, a bruised leaf there; twigs pressed to one side where a man had passed through. It was all plain to Cat-Eye's shrewd gaze.

In time he came to the point where Tony had waited for Dilliard with the three horses. Here he scanned the earth eagerly. Suddenly, an agonized exclamation left his lips as he recognized certain hoofprints he'd followed the previous day.

"It was thet damn Dilliard!" he groaned. "There was another feller with him, but Dilliard was here. It must have been him what stole my Spencer. But how did he do it? S'help me I'll get another gun and he won't escape me today."

Cat-Eye little dreamed that, by this time, Branch Dilliard was far to the south, riding hard, on the trail that led to San Diego. The old man returned disconsolately to his camp, sat down on his blankets to ponder the situation, and cursed feebly the machinations of that Dilliard varmint. Cat-Eye suddenly felt old and weary and defeated.

Suddenly he stiffened, remembering now the

chase Dilliard had led him the previous day. “By Gawd!” Cat-Eye exclaimed, “Thet slimy galoot wanted to tire me out, so’s I’d sleep sound last night and give him a chance to steal me blind. Thet was it. He knowed—all th’ time—thet I was a-trackin’ him! Plumb foxy, he was. But how did he know? I’ll swear I didn’t make one slip.” An anguished groan parted the old fellow’s whiskered lips: “I been outsmarted!”

And in the next instant: “No, by Gawd, I wa’n’t the one thet was outsmarted. Scabbard’s the one. That damn Dilliard just had a hunch Scabbard would send a man trailin’ him. He’s a fox, thet Texas man, at thet, to outsmart Scabbard. An’ he come here while I slept and done this!”

Slowly, in spite of himself, a feeling of respect and admiration for Dilliard seeped into Cat-Eye’s brain. “Yep, by crackey! Dilliard knowed all the time I was gunnin’ fer him. He outfoxed both me’n Scabbard.” Cat-Eye’s face paled suddenly. “By Gawd! Dilliard could have killed me when he was here, and I’d never knowed it. Think o’ thet!” The thought made his heart beat faster for a minute, then, “I almos’ wish he had, s’help me! The boys’ll sartain laugh fit to die when I tell whut happened.”

Moodily, Cat-Eye pondered that thought. Finally, “I reckon I better not tell ’em. Nor Scabbard, nuther. Scabbard might get mad. I’ll have to fix up some sort of a yarn to explain things, though. Then I'll get another gun and come back here and wait for Mister Smart-Aleck Dilliard, and once I draw a bead on him I'll l'arn him a lesson thet'll show him it don't pay to steal off'n a man old enough to be his father. Yep, I'll get another gun and—Cripes! I plumb forgot. Oh, hell and tarnation! I got to walk all th' way back to El Vaca. It'll be late afternoon 'fore I gets in. Damn thet Dilliard hombre!"

Sadly, Cat-Eye rolled his blankets, tied them to his saddle, then boosted the burden on to one shoulder. His moccasined feet made wide strides down the slope, as he swung in a big arc toward the southwest, in order to avoid being seen by anyone at the Rancho Sicamoro. Now, Cat-Eye's one thought was to contrive a convincing story for Scabbard's ears, to explain the failure, get another gun and horse and return for a second try.

Gradually as he left the miles to his rear, Cat-Eye's wiry frame commenced to tire. The saddle and blankets proved—or so it seemed—to grow heavier with each passing minute. The first two miles dropped behind in good time, but, from that point on, Cat-Eye indulged himself in long rests.

The sun swung high, crossed meridian, and started on its downward journey. Cat-Eye staggered on, resting more frequently now. He was covered with dust, sore, weary and angry, but some indomitable spirit in the old man kept him pushing on.

It was dark when Cat-Eye limped the last mile into El Vaca. Leaving his saddle and blankets at the first saloon he passed, Cat-Eye refused to stop for conversation, but went directly to Scabbard's place. The building was dark, the door locked. Cat-Eye left and went to the nearest restaurant. Scabbard wasn't there, either. Cat-Eye pushed his aching feet into the saloon next door. Corill, Fustian, Bisbee and several other of Scabbard's henchmen stood at the bar.

Corill spotted Cat-Eye first. He whistled softly in surprise. "You back, Cat-Eye! What's happened to you? You look all drawed out."

"Had a mite of tough luck," Cat-Eye admitted reluctantly. "I'll tell you about it as soon's I've seen Scabbard. Where is he?"

Fustian put in, "Drake left for Santa Lozana couple hours back. He's been wonderin' where you were. He wasn't in very good humor 'bout you stayin' away so long. Didn't make him feel no better at the thought of stayin' in Santa Lozana all night, neither. You know how Drake hates to part with money for a hotel bed, when he's got a bed in El Vaca—"

"Won't he be back tonight?" Cat-Eye asked.

Bisbee shook his head. "He's got to be in Santa Lozana first thing in the morning. Business. He's foreclosin' on that Morales property, y'know.

Reckon he's bled all the interest out of that greaser's hide by this time and figures him ripe for foreclosure. That's a right nice property, too, I understand."

The men gathered closer to Cat-Eye. Corill lowered his voice, "Cat-Eye, how about that piece of business Drake sent you on?"

"I run into some tough luck," Cat-Eye explained glibly. "When I left here yesterday I didn't have no trouble follerin' Dilliard's trail. Well, for some reason he rode up inter th' mountings. I was follerin' along on a narrow shelf of rock. Th' footin' wasn't very good. My hawss shied at a rattler, a-sunnin' hisself, and slipped over th' edge. I dang nigh went with him, but slipped outten my saddle jest in th' nick of time—"

"Kill the horse?" Fustian asked.

Cat-Eye glanced scornfully at the speaker. "My Cripes! It must've been nigh a thousand feet to the bottom of the ravine below. Sartain, it killed him. Worst of the matter was, my Spencer gun was on the saddle, and thet's gone too. I tried to find a way to get down to thet ravine, but it's jest walled up, all around. So hawss and gun is gone."

"How about the rattlesnake?" one of the other men wanted to know.

"I killed thet pesky critter with my knife," Cat-Eye said smoothly. "Thar we was, me'n thet reptile a-facin' each other on thet shelf of rock. I pulls my knife and thrun it hard, with thet snake a-hissin' an' wavin' his fangs at me. Th' next instant, his head was cut clean off—"

Someone laughed scornfully. Cat-Eye glowered at the speaker and drew his knife. "Ye don't believe I can throw thet straight? Cripes A'mighty, feller, look at th' bloodstains on this yere blade."

Dried bloodstains there were on the steel, all right, but Cat-Eye neglected to state the blood was that of the rabbit he'd killed the previous day. His knife-throwing prowess was known and usually respected, so the story went down all right.

Only Corill appeared a trifle suspicious. "Hell's bells! That was yesterday. Where you been ever since?"

Cat-Eye had a reply ready for that question too. "I been hidin' out near the Rancho Sicamoro, hopin' to get a chance to use my knife on Dilliard but he didn't come nowhere in reach—"

"Did you see him?" Corill persisted.

Cat-Eye nodded. "Yeah, several times. I was hid-out in the brush, but he never come nigh enough to get within throwin' distance. Then I figgered to steal a hawss to get back on, but all night long they had a coupla *vaqueros* guardin' th' corrals. This mornin' I give up an' started for El Vaca. Boys, I'm hungry. I'm goin' to get me some chow—"

"Gosh, Cat-Eye," another man put in, "you sure

must have worked fast when you saw your horse goin' off'n that shelf."

"Fast!" Cat-Eye said scornfully, warming to his subject. "Man, you never seed sech fast movements! Thar I was, on th' hawss's back. Quick as a flash I throwed my body to one side. Th' shift in weight helped the hawss's balance for a jiffy. Then I flung clear of the saddle, my hands jist catchin' thet shelf of rock. Boys, I sure thought I was a goner, but I clumb back and fit thet snake, while my poor hawss went crashin' to his death below. That's what I call fast thinkin'!"

"Sure is fast," the other man nodded gravely. "I don't see how you ever got time to loosen your cinch and get your saddle—"

"My—my saddle?" Cat-Eye said weakly.

"Sure. I was in that saloon at the edge of town when you come in carryin' your saddle and blankets and left them there, sayin' you'd come back for 'em later."

Cat-Eye paled. Carried away by the yarn he'd fabricated, he'd entirely forgotten the saddle left at the saloon. For a minute he was speechless.

Corill snapped, "Is that right, Cat-Eye?"

Cat-Eye gulped miserably, then was struck with a sudden inspiration: "Sure, it's part correct," he admitted brazenly. "Only it wa'n't *my* saddle and blankets. Y'see, I picked up thet rig an' blankets at the Rancho Sicamoro, last night, when I was scoutin' around, tryin' to steal me a pony. Th' corrals was close guarded, but I found an empty shed thar, an' inside was the saddle and blankets. I took 'em with me, hopin' to get a hawss—"

Corill's eyes bored into Cat-Eye's. "I think," and Corill was trying a bluff he couldn't back up, "I'd know your saddle if I got a look at it." His voice was cold, hard, slow.

"Ye might an' ye might not," Cat-Eye snapped defiantly.

"You'll have trouble makin' that yarn stick with Drake."

"Thet's my look-out."

"Damn right it is. You better come clean with us, Cat-Eye."

Cat-Eye said indignantly, "T'hell with th' lot of ye. Drake will believe me. I'm goin' out to get my supper." He turned aggrievedly toward the doorway. Corill called after him:

"Think up another yarn, Cat-Eye. One that'll hold water."

"T'hell with the lot of ye!" Cat-Eye snarled again. "I'll see Drake th' instant he gets back. He's got sense. He'll understand." And with that, Cat-Eye fled from certain jeering remarks and went morosely to get his supper.

19

LAW OF THE FUGITIVE

But Scabbard failed to return the following day. Cat-Eye spent a full twenty-four hours lamenting the slip he'd made regarding his saddle. The night passed, a very sleepless night for Cat-Eye Fremont. The morning of the second day, along toward noon, Drake Scabbard pushed a foam-flecked pony into El Vaca, tossed the reins over the hitch-rail before his house and strode across the porch to his doorway. His face was like a thundercloud as he unlocked the door and stepped into the building.

Corill entered an instant later. "Come out all right, boss?" Corill asked.

Scabbard spun savagely around. "No, it didn't," he snarled. "That damn Morales had a lawyer. I've wasted a lot of time in court. Can you imagine a country where they'll let a greaser have a lawyer?"

"That's a hell of a situation," Corill agreed.

"It's worse than that. This damn lawyer brought up some sort of technicality about me charging more than the legal rate of interest. I argued with the judge, but I couldn't get any place. Morales got an extension. And I had to stay at that goddamn hotel two nights."

Cursing bitterly, Scabbard flung himself into a chair at his table. Corill said, "Cat-Eye's back."

Scabbard perked to attention. "Did he get Dilliard?" he asked eagerly.

Corill shook his head. "There's somethin' funny up, chief. Cat-Eye come walkin' into town, night before last. He gave us a story that's so full of holes you could drive a steer through it. All day yesterday I tried to get at the truth, but that old coot is stubborn. Then this mornin' I tried again, but—"

"What's his story?" Scabbard's face was black with anger.

Corill explained. Scabbard swore and said, "Go tell Cat-Eye I want him in here *pronto*!"

Corill started toward the doorway, but, just at that moment, Cat-Eye was just entering. Cat-Eye said cheerfully, "Good mornin', boss. Hope you had a good trip—"

"Cat-Eye," Scabbard's tones were low and vicious, "I gave you a job to do. You didn't do it. Instead you return with a tall yarn about your horse going off a shelf—"

" 'S'true, s'help me Gawd!" Cat-Eye commenced earnestly. "There I was, fightin' on th' edge to keep from plungin' to sure death and—"

"You're a liar."

"Now, chief, I don't take that kindly—"

"You lie, you old bustard!" Scabbard said angrily. "I told you to get Dilliard, I thought I could depend on you—"

"You can, Drake, you can. Let me have enough money for another horse and gun and I'll show you that Dilliard won't escape me next time—"

Scabbard cursed Cat-Eye in a steady flow of language. "Don't come around here askin' for money, you lousy coyote. I don't pay for failure. Get out!"

"But, chief—"

"Dammit! Get out! Get out of my sight," Scabbard almost screamed. His hand went to the derringer in his pocket. Cat-Eye beat a hasty and undignified retreat.

Scabbard swore bitterly for several minutes, ending, "Well, if I can't get Dilliard one way, I'll get him another. I been thinkin' it over. Day before yesterday when Cat-Eye didn't show up, I was afraid he'd failed. By God! I'll make him pay for that failure—"

"What you aimin' to do about Dilliard?" Corill asked.

"I'll show you. Go find Bart Fustian. Tell him I want him to come here right away."

Corill nodded and left the building.

Meanwhile, Cat-Eye had wandered disconsolately across the street and entered the first saloon he came to. He called for a drink, then saw Bart Fustian standing at the far end of the bar.

Bart said, "Did you see Drake?"

Cat-Eye nodded. "I just come from there."

"I suppose he believed that story."

Cat-Eye didn't say anything.

Fustian laughed. "I'll bet he was plumb peeved."

"Kind of," Cat-Eye admitted reluctantly. "Guess he must have run against some tough luck in Santa Lozana, or somethin'. He was sort of short tempered."

"It's best to keep out of Drake's way when he gets them riled-up spells," Fustian said dryly. "I know how it is. But he'll cool down. He needs men who'll fight for him."

"Exactly the way I figure it," Cat-Eye said hopefully. "Oh, Drake will come around all right. You see. I'll stay out of his sight for a couple of days, then next time he sees me he'll be sweet as apple pie. He can't afford to stay peeved at anybody thet can handle a rifle like I do."

"That's the best policy. Just stay out of his sight for a couple of days. He'll get over his mad. . . . Say, Cat-Eye, when you was over near Castameto's place, you didn't see anythin' of that herd that's bein' rounded up, did you?"

Cat-Eye shook his head. "They're roundin' up farther to the north, I reckon. Wonder if Castameto's got much of a gatherin'."

"I sure hope so," Fustian laughed.

Cat-Eye looked surprised. "*You* hope so? How

come? I figgered Drake planned to block thet move."

"He does. And he will. *We* will. That herd will never make more'n one day's drive."

"No?" Cat-Eye looked puzzled. "This is th' first I've heard about it."

"That's right. You wasn't here when Drake talked it over with us. It was right after you left on Dilliard's trail. Cat-Eye, it's one of the slickest schemes I ever heard of. You see . . ."

Fustian's words dropped to a lower tone. For several minutes he talked earnestly, his story eliciting wicked chuckles from old Cat-Eye. When he had concluded:

"By Gawd!" Cat-Eye exclaimed admiringly. "You got to admit the boss can plan straight. Why, at one blow he'll wipe out that whole outfit."

"You're correct as hell," Fustian grinned evilly. "Say, Cat-Eye, now that you've talked to Drake and he didn't believe your yarn, give me the straight of what really happened."

"I already done thet," Cat-Eye insisted, determined, come what may, not to make the slightest change in the story he had told. He still hoped to convince Scabbard, at a more appropriate time, of the truth of his story.

Corill entered the saloon, started to laugh when he saw Cat-Eye. "The boss sort of stripped the hide off'n you, didn't he, Cat-Eye?"

"Some," Cat-Eye admitted sheepishly.

Corill nodded. "It don't pay to report a failure. You keep out of his sight for a coupla days, Cat-Eye. The less he sees of you, the more likely he is to forget what happened. He'll be needin' you again, probably."

"That's the way I figger it."

Corill turned to Fustian. "Drake wants to see you, Bart."

Fustian looked uneasy. "Now, look here, I didn't have anythin' to do with this business of Cat-Eye's."

Corill swore good-naturedly. "Who in hell said anythin' about Cat-Eye? This is somethin' else."

"What's he want to see me about?"

"You'll have to ask Drake. He didn't take me into his confidence. Somethin' about Dilliard."

Fustian paled a trifle. He put one hand to his jaw which still showed a trace of discoloration. "We-ell," he said lamely, "I ain't in no shape to buck that Texan just yet. I was just thinkin' a spell ago that I was a mite hasty in takin' the bandages off'n my head."

"You tell all that to Drake," Corill said shortly. "Come on. Drake ain't in no mood to be kept waiting."

Reluctantly, Fustian followed Corill from the saloon, crossed the street and entered Scabbard's room. Scabbard looked up, nodded shortly, "Sit down, Bart, I want to talk to you." Fustian uneasily pulled up a chair. Scabbard continued, speaking to Corill now: "Go find Luke Dangler."

"Want the deputy brought here?" Corill asked.

"Soon's possible," Scabbard replied shortly.

Corill departed. Scabbard turned to Bart Fustian: "How you feeling, Bart? Have you recovered from your little brush with Dilliard the other night?"

Fustian gulped, shook his head. "I ain't quite up to snuff yet. I figger mebbe I took the bandages off'n my head too soon. My head aches all the time. My jaw's so sore I can't scarcely eat a bite."

Scabbard laughed coldly and said, "That's fine, Bart. Just what I wanted to hear."

Fustian stared, mumbled, "I don't understand, chief—"

Scabbard went on. "If you can't chew properly, you might starve to death, Bart. Anyway—" ironically, "—you've lost weight. With that head injury, you got to be careful. Get dizzy spells, don't you, now and then?"

Fustian nodded. "They get pretty bad sometimes."

"Probably notice 'em most after you've had a few drinks," Scabbard sneered. "That's all right, though, Bart. You were pretty badly injured in that fight with Dilliard. If I was you I'd stay in blankets for a few days and get your strength back."

"Just as you say, chief. I been thinkin' that myself." Fustian was puzzled—and greatly relieved at not being ordered into another fight with Dilliard. He started to rise, but Scabbard detained him.

Corill crossed the porch, entered the open doorway, followed by Luke Dangler, El Vaca's deputy-sheriff. Dangler was a long-jointed, slouching individual with vacillating eyes and a sandy mustache. He wore knee boots and two cap-and-ball six-shooters at his waist. A tarnished badge of office was pinned to his vest.

"You want to see me, Drake?" Dangler asked.

"Yes. Draw up a chair. I want you to serve a warrant."

"Who on? What's charged?"

"Dilliard. Charge of assault and battery on the person of Bart Fustian."

"Huh?" Fustian's mouth gaped open. Luke Dangler looked a trifle uneasy, and said, "That hombre might be hard to handle."

Corill put in, "Ain't afeared of Dilliard, are you, Luke?"

"Ain't never seen him," Dangler evaded. "Still, he might make trouble."

"I've thought of that," Scabbard said shortly. "Luke, you take Mitch Riker with you when you ride to serve the warrant."

"It ain't all clear—" Dangler commenced.

"I'll make it clear. Poor Bart, here, has been badly injured by Dilliard. Dilliard attacked him without provocation at Castameto's place a few nights ago. We both suspect internal injuries. The attack came without warning, and Bart had no chance to defend himself. He's subject to continual headaches and has dizzy spells. It may be years before he recovers from the results—"

"Haw-haw-haw!" Corill guffawed. "Pore Bart, I'm surprised he's able to take his snifter several times a day. Bart, you should get to a horspital right quick, before you croak on our hands. You don't look like you had th' strength of a kitten—"

"Cut it, Clem," Scabbard ordered shortly. Corill closed his mouth. Fustian glared at Corill and received only a sneering glance in reply.

Scabbard went on, "You see what I want, Luke? Take Bart down to the justice-of-the-peace and help to get that warrant sworn out. Then you and Mitch Riker go serve it. Deputize Mitch. You should be able to find another badge around some place."

"Sure, sure, I'll do it," Luke Dangler nodded. "I hope he don't make trouble. I'll arrest him, but what you aimin' to do when Dilliard gets here? We got to do things legal, Drake?"

"Dilliard isn't going to reach El Vaca," Scabbard announced.

"Huh? What did you say?" Dangler looked his amazement. Corill and Fustian sat listening, mouths wide with surprise.

Scabbard laughed coldly. "We'll be extra legal, Luke. We'll enforce one of the old Mexican laws.

Ever hear of the *Ley Fuga*?—the Law of the Fugitive?"

Dangler paled a little. "You mean . . ."

"Exactly," Scabbard went on smoothly. "It applies to prisoners, under arrest. If they attempt escape, the guards are legally empowered to shoot them down. That law accounts for many a shot in the back."

"My Cripes, Drake," Dangler protested, "supposin' he doesn't attempt to escape?"

"Once you get Dilliard on the road, on his way to El Vaca," Scabbard spaced his words slowly, letting their intent sink in, "a shot in the back is just as effective—whether he tries to escape or not. Is my meaning clear?"

Dangler swallowed hard. "You mean we should say he tried to run away and then—?"

"Your perception is unusually keen, Luke," Scabbard said sarcastically.

"My God, Drake! I don't know's I could do that—"

"I told you to take Mitch Riker," Scabbard said coldly. "Mitch hasn't your compunctions about such things, Luke. He's sensible, Mitch is."

Dangler shook his head. "I don't like it, Drake."

"I do!"

"But, look here, Drake, you can't get away with that. I don't want to be responsible. You can do those things to Mexes and Indians, but Dilliard's a white man. There might be a stink stirred up."

"Nothing can be proved," Scabbard said impatiently. "Dilliard will be dead. You and Riker can swear he tried to escape. Who's going to know any different? It'll all be legal, warrant and everything."

"I still don't like it," Dangler said feebly, not meeting Scabbard's eyes.

Crash! Scabbard's clenched fist resounded on the table top. "Dammit, Luke, I don't care whether you like it or not! Those are my orders. My money put you in office. I expect you to cooperate with me. If not, get out! I don't want any chicken-hearted bustards in my outfit. Either you do as I say, or El Vaca will have a new deputy-sheriff, and that in damned short order! Now, what's it to be? Make up your mind. Quick!"

"All—all right," Dangler surrendered weakly. "Just as you say, Drake. But—but Mitch Riker will have to be the one to—to—"

"Hell," Scabbard snarled. "I told you Mitch would take care of that end. I know Mitch, know what he'll do for a few extra dollars. Don't worry any more about that."

"You're the boss," Dangler gulped. "I'll serve the warrant."

"Good!" Scabbard swung around to face Corill and Fustian, "How about you two, you got any objections to my scheme?"

"It's all right with me," Fustian nodded. "Suits me right down to the ground. I'll swear out the warrant."

Corill said slowly, "I just see one flaw in the idea, Drake."

"Out with it," Scabbard snapped.

"Get me right, I'm not bucking your idea. It's fine. But suppose Dilliard or Castameto happen to smell a rat, get suspicious, and insist on a body-guard of Castameto's *vaqueros* riding to El Vaca with Dilliard and your deputies? What then?"

Scabbard laughed harshly. Tiny malevolent gleams burned in his pale, glassy eyes. "I've thought of that, Clem. If that should happen, and a crew of *vaqueros* insist on accompanying Dilliard here—well, we can say they started a disturbance. Those greasers are hot-headed. It shouldn't be hard to work 'em into a fight."

Corill nodded enthusiastically. "Let 'em come! If our fellers can't wipe out a crew of Mex hombres I'll eat my hat. The scheme's air-tight, Drake. Either way, they stand to lose. And if we can clean out Castameto's gang now—well, it may save doing the job later."

"You get the idea," Scabbard smiled coldly. "All right, Bart, you go with Luke and get that warrant sworn to, then both of you come back here. . . . Clem, go find Mitch Riker. I want to talk to Riker myself, make it clear just what's needed. Hurry up, now. I want this business finished before nightfall, and Dilliard wiped off my books. I've wasted too much time on him as it is. Get going!"

20

AMERICANO METHODS

Dilliard came racing his horse across the level stretch of earth between two series of long, rolling hills. Horse and man were streaked with sweat and dust. More dust floated in low clouds across the slightly undulating plain. Cattle were held at one side. Other cattle were being rounded up and worked down from the hills. *Vaqueros* in high-peaked sombreros, swinging slim, rawhide *riatas* of unusual strength and durability, darted here and there on silver-mounted saddles.

Dust lifted on vagrant breezes swept across the scene. Cattle bawled, horses snorted. Hoofs drummed across the sod, accompanied by the soft *swish-swish* of flying lariats. The atmosphere carried a faint odor of overheated flesh, perspiration and scorched hair and hide. At one side burned a small branding fire to take care of such animals as had escaped being marked in the early spring round-ups of previous years. Mostly, though, the *vaqueros* were searching out the larger, plumper cattle—two-, three- and four-year-olds.

Dilliard's heart warmed to the sight. It was his first opportunity to witness the California *vaquero* at work. As he rode on, his eyes alert for a sight of Don Salvadore, the Texan's gaze also took note of the stock he passed. The animals were sleek and in good condition, though they showed a variety of mixed breeds: yellows, blacks, reds, spotted, black and whites, whites, line-backs; many of the cows showed evidence of the Texas long-horn strain; here and there the marked influence of improved breeding could be seen.

The Texan finally sighted Castameto a short distance beyond the branding fire. The old Spaniard sat his mount like one born to the big, high-horned saddle, calling directions; now and then sitting in moody silence, absent-mindedly fingering the silver buttons on his jacket. He lifted his head, caught sight of Dilliard, raised his fancy, plaited reins in a warm gesture of greeting. Castameto was clothed in well-worn breeches of soft, pliable leather, a short jacket, and a huge, saucer-brimmed sombrero trimmed with silver braid. His spurs were great, shining metal affairs, adorned with jingling steel ornaments.

Dilliard pulled his weary horse to a halt beside Castameto, wiped the perspiration from his forehead. The two men shook hands, their palms meeting firmly in the greeting.

Castameto looked at Dilliard with something of wonder in his dark eyes. "Already you have returned," he said, as though scarcely able to believe his own words.

"And met your man in San Diego," Dilliard nodded, with a laugh. "I certainly—"

"You saw Don Alvaro Serrano?" The Spaniard's eyes widened further. "*Socorro*! But you departed only morning before yesterday."

Dilliard grinned. "And I gave a bunch of horses a beating they'll remember for many a day. Don Salvadore, I was really *riding!* I presented your letter at all your friends' places. They were glad to help you out by loaning me horses, but I reckon they were a bit suspicious of an *Americano.* Anyway, I couldn't have asked for better cooperation: on my way back, horses were relayed along the way, waiting for me—about ten miles apart." The Texan added as an afterthought, "There's some nice horseflesh in this California country—the kind that stands up under a hard pounding."

Castameto still seemed a little dazed. "And—and you say you talked to Don Alvaro?"

"As a matter of fact," Dilliard said carelessly, "he was the reason for my making the ride to San Diego." Catching the puzzled frown commencing to appear on Castameto's forehead, Dilliard pushed on, "I talked to his partner, Jim Hawkins, as well. Don Salvadore, why didn't you tell me Don Alvaro had an *Americano* partner?"

"Don Alvaro? An *Americano* partner! Don Alvaro Serrano! *Por Dios*! What is this you speak of?" Castameto seemed stunned at the news.

Dilliard laughed. "Exactly that, Don Salvadore. A man named Jim Hawkins."

Castameto shook his head at such unbelievable, incredible news. Finally his eyes commenced to twinkle. "It is probably that Don Alvaro, knowing how sensitive I am on the subject of *Americanos*, purposely neglected to mention this Señor Hawkins."

"Perhaps that is it. What is more, this Hawkins is an old friend of mine. I didn't even know he'd come to California. I knew him several years ago when I was rodding the Ladder-B outfit near Bandera, Texas. Then he went away. I heard from him once or twice, then we lost track of each other."

"But—but—Don Alvaro—an *Americano* partner!" Castameto mumbled. "Now, I am prepared to expect anything—earthquakes, gold falling from the heavens, suns that set daily in the east—"

"What did I tell you, Don Salvadore?" Dilliard chuckled. "Did I not say there were other *Americanos* like myself? We're not half bad, when you get to know us. It's this same Hawkins who is putting up the money for the partnership. He furnishes the cash and he counts on Don Alvaro's connections to get good beef."

"The old order changes," Castameto mused.

"It is mighty fortunate for the Rancho Sicamoro that it does," Dilliard replied. "Otherwise, you wouldn't be getting such a good price for your stock. Both Hawkins and Serrano think cattle a good investment in California—though both admit the old days are gone. Still, they're willing to play a long gamble on the market coming back. Folks down in San Diego think Hawkins and Serrano have gone insane, paying such prices for beef cattle. But watch! The *Americanos* are flowing into California by the thousands. Beef will be needed. Hawkins and Don Alvaro figure to supply most of that beef, and they're willing to pay a trifle better than average in the hope of building up reliable sources of supply for the years to come. . . . How goes the round-up?"

Castameto looked serious. "Not as speedily as I could hope for, though my *vaqueros* are working to the limit."

Dilliard nodded, the lines in his face a trifle grim. "I've been afraid things wouldn't move fast enough. . . . Let me see, to get the return of your papers from Scabbard, you must repay his loan a week from this coming Monday. Is that right?"

"That is correct, Señor Dilliard."

"Already, three days of your allotted time have passed—four, counting today. We should count on, at the least, seven days to drive the cattle to San Diego, in order to receive your money and get back to Scabbard. Even that means pushing the cattle hard, every step of the way—"

Castameto raised one protesting hand, as

though unable to bear hearing more. "I have thought all of that out," he said sadly. "Even so, I do not see how the money can get back here in time; besides, we must always consider that Don Alvaro may not pay at once—"

Dilliard smiled. "Whoever brings the money to you can make the same ride I did and get it here on time. Your friends can furnish fresh horses as they did for me—"

"But, Don Branch—" Castameto's tones sounded hopeless, "—I must admit, now, that I do not see how the herd can be delivered. I have wasted too much time. It is not the fault of my *mayordomo*, but of myself. Weeks ago I should have taken charge. Look you, at the very latest, the herd should leave here within two days—"

"Agreed. I figure it will—"

"*Valgate Dios*! I do not see how that is possible. Remember, I must deliver five thousand head. So far we have gathered, and have ready to drive, less than two thousand. There would be more, except that you cannot drive fresh branded cattle. The burns must have time to properly heal. So you see, it is not possible."

Dilliard nodded complacently, then announced in cool tones, "We start, day after tomorrow, with two thousand head."

Castameto looked aghast. "But, Señor Dilliard," he protested, "of what use to deliver only two thousand? Payment for two thousand head will not bring enough money to repay Drake Scabbard. I should still be too late."

Dilliard could restrain his wide grin no longer. He winked one eye. "Just the same, we're going to do it, Don Salvadore." He laughed wholeheartedly at the look of consternation struggling on the Spaniard's features. "Look you, it's a gringo trick, *mi patrón.* Jim Hawkins and Alvaro Serrano will make payment for the whole five thousand head, on delivery of the first two thousand, the remainder to be delivered within thirty days."

"Señor Dilliard! You are *demente*!"

"I'm not as crazy as you think I am."

Castameto's jaw dropped open. "But—but—how—how—you are making—making the jest—" Further words wouldn't come.

Dilliard explained briefly. "My word's good with Jim Hawkins. I've told him what we're fighting here—about Scabbard and everything. Besides, I've got some holdings back in Texas. Jim's willing to take a chance on you, holdings or no holdings, but I felt better offering security."

"*Por Dios*! I cannot let you do this!"

"It's done, *patrón.* Day after tomorrow, at dawn, we start with two thousand cattle in charge of your *mayordomo.* I'll accompany them. We'll take half of your *vaqueros.* The other half will remain here to finish gathering the balance of three thousand head. Have you a man—"

"Don Branch, you—you—how can I thank you—I—" The old Spaniard swallowed hard. Words wouldn't come. His eyes were moist.

Dilliard grinned awkwardly, embarrassed by Castameto's show of emotion. "Aw, shucks!" he said. "Forget it." He repeated the words in Spanish, adding quickly, to prevent another outburst of gratitude, "Have you a capable man to put in charge for the gathering of the remainder of the herd, after we have left?"

Castameto brushed the back of his hand across his eyes, stiffened to attention. "Myself, I shall do it! Of course, there is my *segundo*—a good man—but I shall feel better seeing to such affairs myself—" Castameto broke off to hail his *mayordomo*—ranch boss—just trotting past on a buckskin horse: "Manuel! To my side, at once, if you please!"

Manuel Estudillo, a grizzled, weather-beaten, spare man with a complexion akin to well-worn leather, reined his pony skillfully around and, after greeting Dilliard cordially, waited at respectful attention for orders.

"Manuel," Castameto went on, "Saturday, at dawn, two thousand head leave on the trail for San Diego. The work must be hastened."

"*Sí, mi patrón*!" But Manuel looked dubious, as he reminded Castameto, "Already our *vaqueros* work to their limit."

"True, Manuel. Nevertheless, it must be done."

Estudillo tried to argue the point but wasn't getting anywhere. Castameto explained the arrangements Dilliard had made. The *mayordomo* eyed Dilliard with respect, gratitude, admiration. No doubt regarding his loyalty to Castameto's interests. He'd do what he could to speed up the work. Castameto thanked him courteously.

Dilliard had been watching a couple of *vaqueros* at work. After considerable maneuvering, the pair had managed to edge a small spotted calf to the edge of the herd, and from that point had driven it to the branding fire. Twice the small animal had escaped; time was lost rounding it up again.

Once close to the fire, the two Mexicans got into action: their sweat-streaked panting ponies closed in with a rush; long, rawhide *riatas* hissed through the air. One loop settled about the calf's neck, the other snared the hind hoofs. The horses stopped, backed, pulling the *riatas* taut, stretching the calf between them on the earth. A man on foot approached from the fire and applied a hot iron to the small animal's ribs.

Dilliard nodded slowly; he could appreciate the work with the *riatas*, the superb horsemanship. At the same time he saw that here was the reason for the delay in the gathering of the herd: the men were employing valuable time branding calves when all of their energies should have been devoted to gathering the animals necessary to make up the trail herd.

Dilliard looked around, a slight frown creasing his forehead, to find Castameto and Estudillo watching him, awaiting his comment. The *mayordomo* asked, "Is it that way you do it in your country, *señor*?"

"Something like that," Dilliard evaded. "I think we're a bit easier on the horses, though your *vaqueros* certainly know how to rope and ride."

"In all the world," Manuel Estudillo stated proudly, "you will find no better riders and ropers than our California *vaqueros*! But how do you mean your way is easier on the horses?"

Dilliard explained, "Seems to me you have two men doing the work of one," he smiled. "Besides you waste time, and the strength of your ponies, chasing your animal to the brand fire."

Estudillo was slightly nettled by the Texan's remarks and said again, "There are no better ropers and riders in the world than the *vaqueros* of California." His tones were stubborn.

Here was a distinct challenge Dilliard couldn't allow to go unanswered. His smile broadened. "Is it permitted that I borrow your *riata*, Manuel?" he asked. "My own rope is at the *casa*."

"But surely, *señor* . . ." Manuel replied courteously. He lifted the coiled rawhide from his saddle, extended it to Dilliard.

Dilliard accepted the *riata* and handled it appreciatively. Heretofore he had been accustomed only to a hemp rope, but there was something about the feel of the coils of supple leather that appealed to him.

Tony Aguilar was just riding past. Catching sight of Dilliard examining the *riata*, he called, "Hi, Señor Dilliard, you learn us the lesson in the roping—no?"

Dilliard shook his head, grinned, "Just aimin' to try and show how I do it."

"For you to make the try is to do eet," Tony said confidently. He sat back, waiting for what was to follow.

Castameto said to Dilliard, "Your horse is weary. May I offer my animal, which is fresh? Or you may have your choice of any of the animals over there." He waved one hand in the direction of the waiting, reserve saddle stock, bunched beyond the branding fire.

Dilliard said, "*Gracias*, *mi patrón*, but I'll need my own *caballo*. He is trained to my way. Besides, I'm not trying for a record of speed, but only to show you, in one way, how our work differs from yours."

Estudillo said, with just the faintest trace of sarcasm, "It will be very interesting to see."

"I hope so," Dilliard grinned.

He tied one end of the rawhide *riata* firmly to his saddle-horn, this alone causing the eyes of the *mayordomo* to bulge in surprise. Something of what was taking place permeated the atmosphere. Other *vaqueros* drew nearer, reining in their ponies to watch the gringo work.

Dilliard shook out his loop, getting the feel of the rawhide, then, carrying the loop loosely at his side, touched spurs to his horse and moved quickly across the intervening earth that separated the branding fire from the loosely held herd of cattle a couple of hundred yards' distant.

Straight into the herd, Dilliard pushed his horse, singling out a small red-and-white calf about the size of the one he had seen worked by the two *vaqueros*. The calf lumbered clumsily to one side. Now Dilliard's horse was quick to catch the idea: it closed in, nipping lightly at the flanks of the small animal.

The calf bawled frantically, dodged to one side, only to find itself cut off by the intelligent cow horse. Frightened, the calf broke blindly for the rim of the herd, seeking an escape in the open range. Dilliard's wrist and arm moved like a flick of light. The rawhide loop sailed low and out, settling deftly about the calf's hind legs.

Already the horse had swung toward the brand fire. The loop tightened, spilling the calf off balance. The calf struggled, bawled. Dust clouds raised about its kicking, squirming body as Dilliard trotted his pony across to the fire, dragging the helpless calf at the end of the *riata*. Abruptly, when nearing the blazing embers, Dilliard left the saddle. His horse stiffened to a halt, moving only enough to keep the *riata* tight and prevent the calf from arising.

Moving swiftly, Dilliard ran down the *riata*, seated himself on the calf's head, stretched its forelegs. The horse held steady. Between man and pony the calf was helpless. Dilliard glanced up, laughed. The man handling the branding iron was standing erect, mouth open, gazing at the performance.

"Quick, *amigo*, the iron!" Dilliard called.

The man recovered himself with a jerk, came hurrying up. The brand, a queer Spanish device of a triangle surmounted by a cross, was applied to the accompaniment of bawling calf and the odor of scorching hide. The brand man straightened up. Dilliard loosened the *riata.* The calf rose and lumbered stiffly away, seeking the dubious security of the herd.

Dilliard coiled the rawhide, remounted and rode back to Castameto and the *mayordomo.* A sudden cheer went up from the surrounding *vaqueros.* Tony yelled,

"Eet is nevair too early to catch the dog with new tricks, eh, Señor Dilliard?"

Castameto was smiling gravely as Dilliard approached. Manuel Estudillo looked slightly crestfallen. Dilliard returned the rawhide, smiling.

"It's a nice *riata*, Manuel. Would it be too much if I asked you to make one for me, some day?"

The Mexican flushed with pleasure. The Texan's compliment had taken much of the sting from his heart. "Señor Dilliard," he promised breathlessly, "I shall make for you the finest *riata* in all California! Such handling of stock deserves only the best."

Dilliard smiled, shook his head. "It's not all my part. There's a good deal in the training of the horse," he pointed out. "Usually we have a man on hand, too, to flank our calves. I did it myself merely to demonstrate how it could be done."

"Thus," with a graceful gesture of one hand, Castameto said, "we learn new ways from the *Americanos*. But I wonder, Señor Dilliard, if your method isn't hard on the livestock. To see that calf dragged over the hard earth—well, you understand what I mean?"

Dilliard shrugged his shoulders. "They get over it quickly. I don't think it was harmed much. However, the point is—" changing the subject, "—to get two thousand head of cattle rounded up, ready to take the trail. If we could only postpone the branding of small animals to a later time and concentrate on gathering cattle that will be ready to travel, I believe we'll be ahead in the long run. What do you say, Manuel?"

Estudillo nodded vigorously. "You are more than correct, *señor*. I see that now. I have been wasting precious hours. Now, we shall do as you suggest. The work shall go forward with the greatest haste. By tomorrow night there shall be two thousand head ready to travel. The following morning we start. I, Manuel Estudillo, give my word on that."

"And Manuel," Castameto commented, "has never yet broken his word to anyone."

"Thank you, *mi patrón*." Estudillo bowed, wheeled his pony and dashed away, issuing orders, speeding up the work.

21

DANGLER'S WARRANT

Dilliard watched the retreating form of the *mayordomo*, nodded with satisfaction, then turned back to Castameto. "It looks as though we'd make progress now," Dilliard smiled.

Castameto didn't reply. He was gazing off across the range.

The Texan continued, "There's a couple of hours of daylight left. I think I'll take a hand myself. Every cow counts, and I might as well help out. By tomorrow night—" Dilliard paused suddenly, noting the frown on Castameto's face. "What's up?"

"A man rides this way," Castameto explained, his eyes focused across the slightly undulating plain to the hills, where a narrow canyon cut through from the southwest.

Dilliard turned in his saddle to sight the moving horseman, and a moment later saw a second rider emerge from beyond a mesquite tree. "Two men," he corrected. "Know them?"

"Gring—*Americanos*," Castameto said after a few minutes. "One has the appearance of that law-officer—how do you say it?—deputy-sheriff?—whom Drake Scabbard had appointed in El Vaca. The other man I do not know."

His face was grave as he watched the two riders approach. They came nearer. Finally, Dilliard caught the glint of a badge on the foremost man's vest. Then, a few moments later, he saw that the second man also wore a badge.

"Yes," Castameto frowned, "it is the deputy-sheriff."

The two men trotted up, Dangler slightly in the lead. The rider accompanying him was of stocky build, with a bullet-head and heavy, brutish features. He had a cast in one eye; the other eye was dull; muddy as to color. His unshaven chin was tobacco-dribbled. The only clean thing about the man were the six-shooters he wore at his waist; both guns looked efficient.

Dilliard had already reined around, to face the pair, at Castameto's side. The men drew to a stop a few feet away, the horses' heads almost touching those of Dilliard's and Castameto's.

"Howdy, Castameto," Dangler jerked out. "You know me, Luke Dangler, deputy-sheriff in El Vaca. This is my new assistant deputy, Mitch Riker."

Riker nodded shortly but didn't take his eyes from Dilliard.

Castameto bowed without answering. The words had been spoken in English, doubtless for Dilliard's benefit, though the deputy hadn't as yet addressed the Texan.

Dangler continued, "I'm lookin' for a white

man, one Branch Dilliard. Know anythin'—?"

"Maybe if you'd look my way," Dilliard interposed, "you'd see him, Dangler."

Dangler's eyes slid cornerwise toward the Texan. "You Branch Dilliard?" he demanded.

"Do I have to tell you twice?" Dilliard asked gently, almost too gently. Dangler and Riker should have been warned by the Texan's soft drawling tones.

"I'm Luke Dangler," the deputy stated importantly.

"So you said before," Dilliard smiled. His voice took on a reminiscing note: "I remember about three years back, a horse-thief drifted down from Santa Fe to Santone. We run him out. His name was Dangler, too."

The deputy flushed. "It wasn't me. I never was in San Antonio."

"Ain't that queer, now?" Dilliard drawled. "I could swear you was the same man."

Dangler's flush deepened. Riker cleared his throat impatiently, his eyes still on the Texan, one hand close to a gun.

Dangler found his voice: "Dilliard, that ain't neither here nor there. I ain't no time to waste discussin' similarities. I come for you, Dilliard."

"Yeah?" Dilliard yawned. "Sorry, but I can't go, sort of busy right now."

"Your business can wait. I got a warrant for your arrest!"

Castameto glanced from one to the other, trying to grasp an inkling of the situation. His ear caught the single word "warrant." One hand came up in hot protest. "Beware of a trick, Señor Dilliard!"

"I'm figuring to hold all the tricks myself, *patrón*." Dilliard nodded. Then to Dangler, "What you cravin' to arrest me for?"

"You're accused of assault and battery on one Bart Fustian, on the night of—"

"Never mind the date. I remember. Fustian was figuring to use a gun on Señor Castameto. I busted up that idea. Fact is, I seem to remember Fustian taking a shot at me. Then I had to sort of work him over. I'm glad to hear I did a good job, though when I saw him in El Vaca couple days back, he appeared able to be up and around—"

"That's whatever," Dangler cut in nervously. "I'm figuring to serve this warrant, which is made out proper, accordin' to law."

"Who swore to the warrant?"

"Fustian, of course."

"With Scabbard's help, I suppose."

"Now, look here, Dilliard, I ain't no mind to waste time in this matter. You better come quiet."

"Yeah?" Dilliard laughed softly. "What happens to me if I go back to El Vaca with you?"

"I promise a prompt hearin' before the justice—"

"*You* promise?" Dilliard sneered openly. "Why,

you measly horse-thief, I'm bettin' a plugged *peso* that you can't even draw your breath without Scabbard's say-so."

"You wouldn't talk to Scabbard like this!"

Dilliard chuckled. "I've already talked to him worse than this. Oh, hell!" Dilliard turned half away, saying contemptuously, "Better slope, Dangler—you and your sweet-lookin' pard'. If Scabbard wants me so bad, tell him to come and get me; not to try and hide behind crooked laws of his own making."

"Are you comin' quiet or not?" Dangler demanded angrily.

"Pro'bly not! What then?"

"I reckon we can handle you," Dangler flared. "Me'n Mitch Riker, here. I figured you might get tough. All right, I'm warnin' you: Mitch is a holy-terror with a gun—"

"Yes, and somethin' else," Riker growled, "we've hearn about that new-fangled ca'tridge loadin' pistol of yourn, but I ain't frettin'. I'll stick to the old cap-and-ball pistols. It's the fust shot that counts, and I only need one—"

Dilliard laughed softly. "Figure there'll be some shootin', soon, Riker? In that case, I'm sort of glad I got me a new supply of ca'tridges when I was in San Diego. Yessir, if I'm due to shoot against this holy-terror with a six-shooter, I'm mighty glad I'm prepared—"

"You been to San Diego?" the question popped

involuntarily from Luke Dangler's mouth. Dangler looked startled.

Dilliard nodded. "I sure have. That's somethin' else for you to tell Scabbard. Let him worry a mite what I went there for."

Dangler cast swiftly about in his mind for a reason that could have taken Dilliard to San Diego, and leaped to an incorrect conclusion: "Oh, hell!" he said, recovering some of his composure, "You can't worry Scabbard. Shucks! There ain't hardly no soldiers left at the military barracks in 'Sandy Ague.' Most of 'em was ordered eastward, 'way back in '63. I'll bet you was plumb surprised to find them barracks nigh empty. Why don't you write Pres'dent Grant a letter, tellin' him you need soldiers out here—?"

Dilliard smiled. "Who said anythin' about soldiers? It's all in your own mind, Dangler. Guilty conscience? Or maybe Scabbard has done somethin' that makes him fear troops might be called up into this country. How about it?"

"Aw—aw, shucks!" Dangler said uncomfortably. "We didn't come here to talk, Dilliard. You know what we come for!"

Mitch Riker edged into the conversation again, chest puffing out. "You take my advice, Dilliard, and come quiet."

The Texan favored Riker with a cold glance as though seeing him for the first time, meeting the baleful glare of Riker's good eye. An aura of evil, filth, seemed to emanate from Mitch Riker with his loose, tobacco-stained lips and gorilla-like arms and shoulders. Dilliard eyed the man with extreme distaste, saying, "And you take my advice, Riker, and go take a bath! You've drooled tobacco-juice somethin' scand'lous. That's what comes of not keeping your mouth shut. Open it again and you're li'ble to find yourself in worse trouble—"

"Dammit!" Dangler snarled. "Are you comin' quiet, or ain't you? Watch him, Mitch!"

Riker's hand had already closed about one gun butt. He had angrily opened his mouth to reply to Dilliard's words, but, momentarily, couldn't think of a fitting retort.

"Oh, all right," wearily from Dilliard. "I suppose I should obey the law. Let me see this warrant you're so anxious to serve."

Riker relaxed, removing his hand from gun-butt. Dangler appeared considerably relieved. "I'm glad to see you got sense, Dilliard," Dangler grunted. He reached to an inner pocket of his vest and passed over a folded sheet of paper.

Dilliard unfolded the warrant for his arrest, glanced at it and commenced to read. The whole was in scrawly pen-and-ink writing. As he read, Dilliard's grin broadened.

Suddenly, he looked up: "My gosh, you got this all wrong. I'm not the feller you want."

"What's wrong with that warrant?" Dangler demanded suspiciously.

"Why," Dilliard explained gravely, "accordin' to this warrant, Bart Fustian must be pretty nigh his grave."

"Fustian's a right sick man," Dangler maintained seriously. "And it's all your fault."

"Can't be my fault. Shucks, Dangler, I *couldn't* be responsible for all the things this paper says happened to Fustian. You sure he wasn't in a train wreck some place—?"

"I tell you—!"

"Or mebbe Fustian met up with an earthquake," Dilliard ran on, "or he might have been trampled by a stampede. I'll bet he was tryin' to pick his teeth with a stick of dynamite, or a mountain fell on him, or—"

"You don't sound funny—" Dangler commenced indignantly.

"You do though," Dilliard grinned.

Castameto glanced from man to man not understanding anything that had been said. He saw, however, that the Texan didn't appear greatly worried, even though Dangler looked upset.

"Dammit!" Dangler snapped. "Are you aimin' to come quiet, or what do you intend to do?"

"Watch me," Dilliard laughed, suddenly tearing the warrant down the center.

Dangler's mouth fell open in indignant surprise.

Uneasily, Riker started for a gun, then paused, noting that Dilliard had made no move toward a weapon. Dilliard, meanwhile, was crumpling the two halves of the warrant in either hand.

"Now, look here, young feller," Dangler commenced, "them sort of actions won't help your case a bit. You can't trifle with the law. You best come along quiet, now—"

"I'm not coming quiet and I'm not coming now," Dilliard snapped curtly, "—nor any other time. And if you try to take me, you'll find yourself stirrin' up a nest of hornets. Is that plain you two dog-robbin' horse-thieves? Now make yourselves hard to see, before I run you out!"

It had never occurred to Dangler that Dilliard might refuse to heed the summons. For a moment, he and Riker sat their horses, nonplussed, uncertain what to do next.

Suddenly, Dangler swore and reached for his gun. Riker's hand was already closing about the butt of one of his weapons. The Texan's hands moved with lightning speed, the two crumpled portions of the torn warrant flew through the air, straight at the faces of the two law-officers.

For a brief instant, they were thrown off-guard as they forgot to draw their guns in the attempt to dodge the paper missiles Dilliard had snapped at them. Dilliard was laughing now. His own gun flashed into view. There came a double crash of the heavy forty-five. Small holes appeared, as though by some force of magic, in the crowns of Riker's and Dangler's sombreros.

It was all over as quick as that. The hands of the two law-officers flew high in the air. Dangler's mouth was opening and shutting like that of a fish out of water. The tobacco stains on Riker's lips showed to greater contrast against his pale features. The brute courage of both men had suddenly vanished into thin air.

"Throw your guns on the ground!" Dilliard ordered sternly.

The hands of the two men came down, their eyes wide on the menacing muzzle of Dilliard's Colt gun. Cautiously they extracted their guns from holsters and dropped them to the earth.

Dilliard smiled coldly. "Now turn your ponies and get out," he ordered. "I don't feel like being arrested today. Tell Scabbard that. Tell him if he wants me real bad, to come for me himself. If he sends any more jackals to arrest me, I'll figure he's too yellow to do his own work. Can you remember that, you white-livered scuts?"

"Ye—ye—yes," Dangler's teeth chattered.

"Then get!" the Texan snapped. "And don't come back or Don Salvadore will shoot you for trespassin'. *Vamos pronto*!"

"My guns—?" Riker commenced timidly.

"Your guns are on the earth," Dilliard jeered. "Let 'em stay there. Don't blame me. You threw 'em there. Better get slopin', you hombres. My forty-five might throw lower next time I let go. Get!"

Helplessly, angrily, the two men turned their horses and departed from the vicinity at a fast lope. Neither said anything for a long time, until Dilliard had been left far to the rear. Then, Dangler spoke, "Mitch, I don't think we better tell Scabbard what happened."

Riker nodded sadly. "We'll just say that Dilliard wa'n't there when we come to serve the warrant."

"I reckon that's the best way."

The two men loped on. . . .

Meanwhile, Dilliard watched the law-officers' forms grow smaller in the distance. Glancing around, he saw several *vaqueros* arrayed at his rear, Tony in the lead.

Dilliard grinned, "Looks like you buckaroos was all set to back me up, Tony."

Tony's teeth flashed whitely. "No, Señor Dilliard, eet was the othair two from El Vaca I'm plan to make the back up—'way back!"

Manuel Estudillo came riding among his *vaqueros*, ordering them to return to work. The horses scattered. The gathering of cattle was resumed. Dilliard turned to Castameto and explained in Spanish just what the law-officers had intended to do.

". . . and had I accompanied them," Dilliard concluded, "it is very doubtful that I would ever have reached El Vaca."

Castameto smiled a bit hopelessly. "You are quick with the gun, my son, but I fear we are lost. Now, Drake Scabbard, himself, will come, bringing many men. It is best that you leave here at once."

"*Socorro*!" Dilliard laughed. "Would you have me put my tail between my legs and run like a coyote? Have no fears, *patrón*. Scabbard will require time to think this out, before he makes his next move. By then I should be well on the way to San Diego with the cattle. Scabbard won't come for a few days, if I read his type correctly."

"But when you return," Castameto persisted. "Scabbard will come for you then—"

"When I return," Dilliard said meaningfully, "I won't wait for Scabbard. We'll have part of your troubles cleared up. Then, I figure to go see Scabbard myself. What we *Americanos* call a show-down will be due."

"A show-down." Castameto repeated the words slowly, fixing them in his mind. "And then what?"

"I don't think," the Texan said grimly, "it will be necessary to plan beyond that. There won't be any more—not the way I'm figuring it."

22

THE HERD MOVES SOUTH

True to his word, the *mayordomo*, two days later, had two thousand cattle ready to start south at dawn. The previous day, Dilliard had spent in fixing up a chuck wagon such as he had known back in Texas. Hitherto the *vaqueros* were accustomed to being accompanied, on long herd drives, by a heavy wagon drawn by big work cattle. Dilliard made it his own job to rig up a conveyance that could be drawn by a team of horses, which would be enabled to make better time and thus keep ahead of the herd on march.

Dilliard encountered his next difficulty when he learned there was no regular camp cook for accompanying drives. During the round-up, food had been brought from the house for each meal. To offset this, Dilliard pressed into service two Mexican women from the Castameto kitchen, who would ride in the wagon.

The starting of the herd was an event that chilly dawn, before the sun had lifted above the eastern horizon. Several members of Castameto's household had driven out to the range, or saddled ponies and mules to get there, and were gathered in a small knot at one side, waiting. The sky to the east was graying rapidly, commencing to be tinged with thin crimson streaks.

Vaqueros rode busily to and fro in the vicinity of the two thousand cattle bedded on the earth. Now and then came a lowing from the beasts. A few lurched to their feet. Gradually, by twos and threes the remainder of the herd stood up.

At one side, near the little group of watching people and horses, Castameto sat his mount, straight and silent, trying not to believe too strongly in the hope that insisted on rising within his breast. Dilliard reined nearby. Behind the *patrón* were two shadowy figures seated, side-saddle, on horses. As Dilliard approached, his ear caught Teresa's quick laugh, mingled with Tony's. Tony was just remounting, ready to return to the herd. At Teresa's side sat Mariposa, clothed in a riding habit of some dark material, cut according to the Eastern fashion of that day. Her honey-colored hair, piled high on her head, shone in the early sunlight.

A horseman cut across Dilliard's line of approach: Manuel Estudillo, in a high-peaked hat and tightly-fitting breeches, like his *vaqueros*. A cap-and-ball gun was slung at his right hip. The *mayordomo* stopped at Castameto's side. The two men talked. Dilliard rode up and joined them, hoping for a word with Mariposa before the departure. He glanced over Castameto's shoulder, toward the girl's averted face. Castameto's voice fell on his ears:

"Manuel informs me all is ready for the start, Señor Branch."

The Texan nodded, smiled at the *mayordomo.* "I guess there's nothing more to say, except our good-byes."

"May good fortune attend you, *mi amigo. Que vuelva pronto.*"

"I'll return as soon as possible," Dilliard replied, and added, "with the money, Don Salvadore. Jim Hawkins promised to have the cash on hand. I'll guard it well, or turn it over to Manuel to give you, should anything prevent my prompt return."

"The money I shall guard with my life, *patrón*," Manuel promised dramatically, "regardless whether I or Señor Dilliard carries it."

"I believe you, Manuel."

Castameto looked steadily into Dilliard's eyes, then put out his hand to meet Dilliard's in a warm, firm clasp. Castameto said unsteadily, "I haven't told you what all this means—"

"There is no need of that," the Texan said quickly.

Manuel saw the embarrassment on Don Salvadore's features and quickly turned the conversation into other channels: "*Mi patrón*, shall I say to Don Alvaro that we can furnish another herd in the fall—?"

Castameto considered, then, "I think it best, Manuel, not to push Don Alvaro too greatly. This is a new business to him. We must not appear too greedy for profits—"

"But, *mi patrón*, what better time to establish a market for our beef?"

Castameto smiled grimly. "Already, Manuel, you seem to have acquired the enterprise of the *Americanos*."

Manuel chuckled, looked at Dilliard, then back to Castameto. "Sometimes I think it would not be such a bad idea. But, regarding markets, if I were to approach the subject gently and point out to Don Alvaro—"

"I think not, Manuel—"

The two commenced to argue in friendly spirit, Castameto replying with patient negatives to Manuel's proposals, treating the *mayordomo* as he would a child he had taken to rear—which had been, as a matter of fact, the case.

This was the opportunity Dilliard had hoped for. While Manuel and Castameto were talking, the Texan reined his pony past the old Spaniard and alongside Mariposa's horse. Mariposa and Teresa replied to Dilliard's greeting, then Teresa discreetly drew to one side, out of earshot, pretending to seek out Tony's form in the confusion of passing riders.

For a moment, neither Dilliard nor Mariposa spoke. They sat their mounts, facing each other, searching each other's eyes, as though reluctant to turn away. It was Mariposa who broke the contact first: Dilliard caught her quick intake of breath before she shifted her gaze to her father's back.

Dilliard said quietly, "*Adiós*, Señorita Castameto. It was good of you to come out so early to see the departure."

The girl's eyes came back to Dilliard's face and read something there that brought a fluttering sensation to her breast. An expression of pain flitted swiftly across her pale features and as quickly disappeared. She tried to make her tones light when she replied, a certain humor tinging the words: "I'm pleased that you appreciate the honor, *señor*. It isn't for every occasion I'd miss my beauty sleep in such fashion."

"Your beauty sleep?" Dilliard eyed the girl steadily before he said with grave accents, "I'd have *sworn* you'd already had that."

The girl smiled wanly at the compliment but drew back a little. One hand raised a trifle, then lowered again before Dilliard could touch it. "*Feliz viaje*, Señor Branch Dilliard."

"Again you wish me a pleasant journey. Do you remember, *señorita*, the other time you said those words?"

The girl bowed. "I do not think I shall ever forget. It was the day you left to rescue Teresa from her abductors. Señor—Señor Branch—this time you must not return—"

"Not return?"

"—wounded as you were on that occasion."

"Does it matter so much to you?"

"Ah, you are cruel to ask that, Señor Branch."

Dilliard barely heard the whispered words. His low laugh was full of confidence now, "I'll insist on an answer when I return—Señorita Castameto."

Mariposa's left hand came up in sudden protest. "That last, also, is cruel, Señor Branch."

"I don't mean to be cruel—Mary."

The girl had no reply for that. She changed the subject, "There is so much you do not understand—My father—"

Dilliard heard Castameto's voice. He and the *mayordomo* had finished their argument. Manuel was riding away, calling for the start. Dilliard leaned from his saddle, toward the girl's slim form, then caught the warning glance from her eyes. Castameto was calling a last good-bye to his *mayordomo.*

Dilliard paused, backed his horse. Two fingers came quickly to his hat brim, as he swung the animal around, "*Adiós*, Señorita Mariposa."

"*Vaya con Dios*, Señor Branch. *Adiós*."

Dilliard turned, the girl's soft tones making magic in his brain, and saw Don Salvadore watching him. A slight frown creased the *patrón*'s forehead, but it was quickly erased when Dilliard spoke. The two shook hands again, said their final good-byes. Dilliard touched spurs to his pony and loped in pursuit of the *mayordomo*.

Just as the morning sun edged above the peaks of the distant Santa Ana Mountains, flooding the plain with bright, warm light, the herd commenced to move. *Vaqueros* rode about the cattle, getting them strung out in marching form, swinging long *riata* ends at the faces of recalcitrant beasts that endeavored to escape from the rapidly forming line.

In time, the drive straightened out. Ahead rumbled the chuck wagon, with its driver and women cooks. Next came Dilliard and Manuel Estudillo riding the "point" positions, leading the way for the herd. Tony and another *vaquero* were responsible for the "swing" positions, farther back along the line of march. A dozen more *vaqueros*, riding on either side and at the end, occupied the "flanks" and "drags" at various points. Some distance to one side, riding parallel to the strung-out cattle, was another pair of Mexicans in charge of the remuda of extra horses.

Gradually, the cattle fell into the habit of the march, forming a long ribbon of moving backs and horns, almost a mile in length. The sun climbed higher, commenced to throw down scorching rays. After a time, Dilliard reined his pony a short distance to one side and glanced back, past the moving clouds of dust sent up from shuffling hoofs.

The Texan's lips parted in an exclamation of surprise: he hadn't realized he'd already traveled so far. Far to the rear a slim form in a riding habit raised one white hand in farewell. The *vaqueros* and others who remained behind were also still calling their good-byes, but Dilliard had eyes only for Mariposa. Once his gaze strayed to Don Salvadore. His arm too was raised, as he sat erect and silent on his horse. Then the Texan once more faced ahead, settling to the saddle for the long journey to San Diego.

An hour slipped quickly past. Dilliard glanced across the broad expanse of moving backs—yellows, blacks, reds, spotted—and called to Manuel, "Well, we got started without trouble, *amigo*."

The *mayordomo* nodded proudly, before a serious look clouded his features, "Trouble may come, *señor*, when we pass near El Vaca."

"We'll meet it when it comes," Dilliard shouted back, grimly.

Horses and men settled to the pace of the long drive. Hour after hour dragged by, the cattle moving along at, seemingly, a snail's pace—walk, stop, graze a moment, then walk on again only to indulge, frequently, in further stops when they would be urged on by the *vaqueros*. The miles marched past in long, weary procession. Dust raised in thick clouds from beneath the hoofs of the moving herd, spread, and enveloped the scene in a thick, choking haze.

Perspiration trickled into Dilliard's eyes. The back of his shirt was soaked, stuck to his skin. Now and then, he or Manuel loped ahead of the chuck wagon to see that all was well. Before the day's drive was finished, the wagon was to be far in advance of the herd. Now and then, changes of horses were effected from the remuda of fresh animals. The cattle continued their slow shuffling progress.

A *vaquero* moved up to take the *mayordomo*'s position at "point"; Manuel rode back to see that all was well, that stragglers were kept on the move and that the same men weren't forced to swallow the dust of the herd all of the time. Stragglers there were bound to be among the cattle. These must be kept on the march, disciplined with rope's ends, if need be. The beasts at the front of the line gave less trouble.

The herd swung past El Vaca which lay two miles to the northeast. Gazing across the range of rolling terrain, Dilliard could see only the roofs of the tallest buildings. He frowned thoughtfully, having expected trouble at this point, but nothing untoward happened. The cattle moved serenely on; no hostile riders were sighted.

It didn't seem possible that Drake Scabbard was ignorant of the drive; on the other hand it seemed but natural for him to endeavor to stop it. But nothing appeared amiss. Slowly, El Vaca dropped below the grassy horizon at Dilliard's rear.

Toward noon, the foremost cattle scented water ahead and broke into a quick, awkward gait. The remainder of the herd moved faster, quickly closed in to follow. There was less lagging behind now, as the trail led through a wide canyon running between brush-covered hills. The trail swung more to the south, the cattle moving along without urging. Half a mile further on, the dust-covered beasts were watered at some unnamed branch of the Trabuco River.

The sun swung westward. The way led through a lush valley now. Late afternoon saw the herd passing within three-quarters of a mile of a group of low buildings situated across the grassy valley. What appeared to Dilliard to be stone arches, partly in ruins, towered above the lower buildings.

Dilliard spurred up to the head of the herd, rounded the leaders, and reined his pony beside Manuel Estudillo's mount.

"What are those buildings?" Dilliard asked.

Manuel glanced across the valley, then gave answer, "That is the Mission San Juan Capistrano that you see."

"Sort of appears to be falling to pieces."

"*Por Dios*, Señor Dilliard! It's to be wondered that anything is remaining of the mission, established there by Junípero Serra, in the latter part of the last century. The mission had enemies and much trouble. The wall and buildings have passed through earthquakes—not unscathed, as you see; the worst in the year 1812, I have been told. Previous to that there was a fire. Early, during this century, it was captured and held for a time by pirates—"

"No wonder the place is nearly ruined."

"Some of the buildings are habitable. But what I've told is nothing. Back in the year '45, the mission was illegally auctioned off by the Mexican Government. That condition prevailed for many years, but in 1865 your Abraham Lincoln restored the mission to its rightful owners, bringing joy to the *patrón*'s heart—"

"Lincoln, eh?" Dilliard's eyes twinkled. "I don't understand the *patrón*. Seems to me, Lincoln was a gringo."

Manuel laughed. "Already I have pointed out that fact to Don Salvadore, but he stoutly affirms that Abraham Lincoln did not belong solely to the gringo government, but to the whole world."

"What did you say to that?"

"*Diantre*! What was there to say? The *patrón* was right."

Dilliard said seriously, "I guess he was, at that." He glanced again toward the mission. A scattering of figures moved about the ancient buildings, almost too far away to be seen clearly; Dilliard judged them to be Indians. A dark-frocked form moved among them. "There seem to be people living there," Dilliard commented.

"Always there are a few there, these days. Tomorrow being Sunday, that is, doubtless, Padre José Mut we see, come to officiate."

Dilliard frowned thoughtfully. "Didn't I hear there was a river near the mission? Seems as though Don Salvadore said something about watering the cattle there, tonight."

"Further on," Manuel replied, "we'll reach a bend in the San Juan River. I have given instructions to the driver of your chuck wagon to make camp."

The trail sought lower ground through the valley. Brush, trees and the gradual descent blotted the mission buildings from view. Dilliard reined his pony around to the other side of the marching herd. The drive progressed steadily as the afternoon waned.

Abruptly, Dilliard spied the chuck wagon which had pulled ahead, earlier in the day, drawn up beside a big live oak. Wood smoke ascended in the air which had by now assumed a fresh, salty odor. A soft breeze, redolent of the not far distant ocean, had sprung up. The *mayordomo* loped past, shouting orders. Gradually, the cattle were turned off the trail and brought to a halt along the banks of a small stream, not far away.

Dilliard continued on to the chuck wagon. The fragrance of well-cooked food tingled in his nostrils. As he drew rein near the fire, the two Mexican women cooks looked up, greeting the gringo with shy smiles of welcome. The driver of the vehicle had long since unhitched his horses and was busily engaged in gathering firewood.

After a time, the cattle were bedded down for the night. Some of the *vaqueros* came loping swiftly in to the camp. Supper passed. To the west, the sky was slashed with broad streaks of scarlet placed vividly against the deepening gray. The scarlet gave way to deep lavender that, in turn, blended quickly to violet and then purple.

Night enveloped the camp. After a time, small stars winked into being. These, also, spread rapidly. There was some conversation among the *vaqueros* grouped about the fire, for a time. Gradually, the blaze died down. The *mayordomo* appointed guards for the herd; these rose, saddled and rode away, the men whose places they were taking soon arriving back in camp. Horses were unsaddled, blankets unrolled. A long sigh of contentment went through the camp. The talk slackened.

Here and there from a blanket came a faint pinpoint of fire from some *vaquero*'s *cigarito*. These too were extinguished after a short time. Silence descended even before the moon to the east was edging the hilltops with silvery light. . . .

23

WARNING!

Dilliard awoke easily to find a *vaquero* bending above his blankets. It was one of the four men supposed to be guarding the herd.

"What is it?" Dilliard asked quickly. Already he was pulling on his boots and reaching for his sombrero.

"One has arrived who insists on speaking to you, Señor Dilliard. I suggested the *mayordomo*, but the boy insists on seeing you."

"A boy?"

"*Sí*, a *muchacho*—boy."

Dilliard frowned. Moonlight was on his face; the features of the *vaquero* shielded from the light. The Texan gained his feet, noticing that the fire had burned down to faint embers. Blanket-rolled figures were scattered about the camp. From the chuck wagon, in the shadow of the big live oak, came the lusty snoring of the women cooks.

Dilliard caught a movement under some trees a few yards to his left and made out the form of a horse with a slim figure standing near.

"Over there," the *vaquero* pointed, nodding toward the trees.

"I see him," Dilliard said.

"Shall I wait for you, Señor Dilliard?"

"No. Go back to the cattle."

The man mounted and rode away from the camp. Dilliard strode toward the trees. A form in velvet breeches and high-peaked sombrero moved in the leafy shadows. Dilliard caught the glint of silver braid and silken tassels in the moonlight. The horse whinnied restlessly, and Dilliard noted that it was streaked with sweat, its withers foam-flecked.

"You have ridden swiftly, *muchacho*," Dilliard said in Spanish. "You wanted to see me?"

The "boy" took a swift step to meet him. "Señor Branch, I—"

"Good gosh! Mariposa! What brings you here? Is anythin' wrong? The *vaquero* said a boy wanted to see me."

"He recognized me but said nothing."

"But, what—"

"Listen, Señor Branch, Drake Scabbard is moving against us."

"I've been expecting something of that sort."

It was a matter of quick questions and excited low-voiced replies for a few moments.

"You know this Cat-Eye Fremont, then? He did not lie?" Mariposa asked breathlessly.

"I reckon he didn't. It's like he says. He trailed me, intending to kill me. I led him a long chase and while he slept, took his horse and gun."

Dilliard chuckled. "I'll bet he was plumb sore."

"Angry? Yes. But not at you as much as at Drake Scabbard. Cat-Eye remembered that you could have killed him. Instead you only took his gun and horse. It is against Scabbard he holds the grudge. He swears he will even the score—"

"Go slow, girl. Tell it from the start."

"Cat-Eye came to warn you of Scabbard's plans, but you were already on your way. My father was out superintending the gathering of the herd, so when Cat-Eye asked for him, he could not be seen, either, without making a ride. It was Teresa whom Cat-Eye saw first when he arrived at the *casa.* Finally, Teresa brought him to me, and Cat-Eye told his story. He was in a rage at Drake Scabbard—"

"I don't get that part," Dilliard said patiently.

"Scabbard was very angry at Cat-Eye because Cat-Eye had failed to kill you. Cat-Eye waited in El Vaca a few days, hoping Scabbard would overlook the failure. Today, Cat-Eye approached Scabbard again, asking for money that was due to him. Instead of paying the money owed, Scabbard ordered Cat-Eye out of El Vaca and threatened to shoot him. The old man left as quickly as possible. He was forced to leave on foot, as Scabbard wouldn't even allow him a horse. He walked to our place—"

"But what are Scabbard's plans?"

"Tonight—rather, tomorrow—shortly before

dawn, when the moon is gone—Scabbard is sending twenty men to stampede our cattle and kill all *vaqueros*—including yourself. The cattle are to be driven into the sea and drowned."

Dilliard's face was a grim mask of anger. He glanced quickly at the moon. "It's nearly midnight now. We'll be ready for Scabbard's coyotes when they arrive. You'd better take a rest before you start back. I'll send a man with you—"

"Señor Branch! Do you think I am nothing but a helpless woman. You'll need every man. Perhaps the horse requires a rest, not I. Why—I was born to the saddle."

"You shouldn't have come, Mariposa. One of your men, or your father—"

"I wanted to do my part. I slipped on these clothes of Ramon's—my brother who was—who died—to ride more comfortably—"

"Why did *you* come, Mariposa?"

The girl glanced away. A stray lock of hair from beneath the sombrero turned to pale gold in the leaf-shadowed moonlight. Her voice came slowly, "Had I told my father of Cat-Eye's warning, he would have gathered the remaining men and come to your aid. Something of the kind might have suited Scabbard. He could have attacked the house, when there were no men to defend it, burned, pillaged—"

"Why did you, yourself, come, Mariposa?" Dilliard persisted.

Mariposa was silent for a moment. The girl's face was lustrous in the filigreed light, her long dark lashes forming twin fringes against her cheeks. Her low words, when they finally came, were barely audible to the Texan: "You must not ask me that, Señor Branch."

Once again, Dilliard repeated his question.

An expression of pain flitted across the girl's white features and she turned away. Dilliard placed his hands gently on her shoulders. He was standing very near to her now.

Quite suddenly, the girl raised her face to his, eyed him bravely. Her voice was low, steady-toned, when it came: "I think, Señor Branch, I wanted to see you once more. I wanted to tell you that I liked the name 'Mary,' and that you must never again call me Señorita Castameto. Oh, there are so many things to tell you, *mi* Señor Branch, things I shouldn't even dream—"

And then she was in his arms, holding him close, murmuring those other things against his cheek. . . .

After a time, they reluctantly separated. The Texan's voice was husky when he said, "I reckon my sights don't need adjustin', after all." His words came stronger, ringing with new-found confidence, "Oh, there'll be a fiesta this country will never forget, when we—"

"No! No, Branch," shaking her head sadly, "that can't be—ever."

"I'd like to know why not."

"It would break father's heart. You know his feelings where *Americanos* are concerned. He'll call you friend, do almost anything for you, but it would kill him to see a Castameto wedded to an *Americano.* You could ask anything else, and he'd give it gladly, but he'll never consent to our—"

"Señor Dilliard!" It was the voice of the *mayordomo* approaching from the camp. "Is anything wrong? I awoke and heard voices—" He broke off, catching sight of Mariposa, recognizing the girl instantly when he drew near. "*Señorita*—" the *mayordomo* bowed low, "—at first, I did not see you."

"That is all right, Manuel. I came with news."

"It's Scabbard," Dilliard put in. "He plans to stampede our cattle." The Texan continued, explaining matters to the *mayordomo*, then turned, remembering, to Mariposa again: "Is Cat-Eye Fremont at the house now?"

The girl shook her head. "He left right after he'd told his story. He said all that he wanted was to even matters with Scabbard, then he was heading for Northern California. He recognized his horse in one of the corrals. We found his rifle, when he asked for it, in Tony's cabin. I let him have both. I didn't think that would do any harm. Besides he had warned us—"

"The old coot deserves to get his horse and

gun back," Dilliard nodded, "after bringin' that warnin' against Scabbard. . . . Manuel, I have told the *señorita* we can handle this matter that Scabbard plans, and that now she must return to the house. I think it best if one of the *vaqueros* accompanies her."

"That is not necessary, Señor Branch," the girl protested. "You and Manuel will require the help of every man."

"But you might bump into Scabbard's men on your return."

"Could one man with me avail against many? No, Don Branch, do not worry about me. You forget I was raised in this country. I am familiar with every inch of ground, every mountain. I know canyons and hidden trails and arroyos that Scabbard's men have never even dreamed of. For me there must be no concern. I will return safely. That I promise you."

"What she says is true, *señor*," Manuel put in.

Reluctantly, Dilliard nodded. The girl moved toward her horse. Dilliard caught her hand a moment, felt the pressure of warm fingers. There were some murmured words of farewell, no more, both Mariposa and the Texan being mindful of Manuel's presence. Then, Mariposa swung her lithe form up to the saddle, turned her horse and moved quickly off among the trees. In a few moments horse and rider had blended silently into leafy shadowed moonlight.

24
STAMPEDE!

Dilliard turned a face tense with concern toward the *mayordomo.* "Manuel! Do you think she will be all right?"

"Of that I am certain, Señor Dilliard. I remember her, as a small girl, riding through this country. She knows it even better than I, and I would have no trouble evading anyone I did not wish to see. Be assured, she will reach home safely."

Dilliard nodded, feeling somewhat better about the matter. "Then there is nothing for us to do except plan for the attack of Scabbard's men. There will be twenty men to oppose."

"We are nineteen—not including the two women cooks."

"We'll tell the women to stay in the wagon, close to the floor." Dilliard gave further details as related by Mariposa: "Scabbard means to designate half his men to stampede the herd and kill the guards. The other half is to sneak close to our camp and shoot down the sleeping men when they are awakened by the sounds of running cattle. When the killing has been completed, Scabbard's men will follow the cattle and run them into the Pacific. Many they'll probably scatter and rustle later."

Manuel said grimly, "What are we to do? Have you thought of anything?"

"We have until dawn to prepare. Your men are all armed?"

"The *patrón* saw to that before we left, furnishing those who didn't have them, six-shooting cap-and-ball *pistolas*. Some of the older men, with experience, carry extra cylinders, loaded and ready to replace empty ones."

Dilliard and Manuel walked slowly back and crouched beside the ashes of the campfire which still gave off a bit of warmth. A few dried twigs and a dead mesquite limb were placed on the heap. The twigs caught fire after a few minutes; in time the dead limb commenced to blaze. The two men talked in low voices so as not to disturb the sleeping forms nearby.

After a time Dilliard asked, "From here to the Pacific is how far?"

"Probably two miles—perhaps a trifle more—to the beach."

"Cliffs?"

"Not at the point where this valley opens to the sea. Farther back, of course, to the north and south, there are steep cliffs."

Dilliard nodded. "I didn't remember for sure. On my trip to San Diego I didn't stay with the regular trail all of the time. Much of the journey was made in the darkness, too. . . . Well, we can let 'em run, then." This last Dilliard muttered, half to himself.

"What is that, Señor Dilliard?"

The Texan roused himself from certain abstractions, put them into words: "Here's my plan—when the attack comes we will have our men scattered about the brush, in hiding near the herd. When Scabbard's coyotes stampede the cattle, we'll wait until they have passed, before we do any shooting. Then we'll close in on their rear."

"But the cattle?"

"We'll let 'em run. They won't run far after this day's march on the trail and with the ocean in front of 'em. I figure they'll scatter along the beach and up in the hills on either side of this valley. They can be rounded up, later, and the drive continued."

"*Ojala*!" Manuel muttered. "I believe it is as you say. With no one to urge the cattle on, they will quickly grow weary of running. But what of the men on guard?"

"Warn them of what is coming, and tell them to get speedily to one side. Tell them not to follow the cattle, as they would ordinarily do, and as the Scabbard gang plan they will do until shot down."

"Scabbard's men will undoubtedly have *carabinas*."

"What of it? Rifles will do them little good. The moon will be down by then. They'll have to approach closely to do their shooting, anyway, so our six-shooters will be sufficient."

Suddenly, Manuel gave an exclamation of dismay: "*Ay de mi*! What of the men sleeping here? If they are not in blankets, the Scabbard scoundrels will suspect—"

"They won't be in blankets. Instead they will be hidden at various points about the camp, where they can fire at the flashes of guns when Scabbard's men attack—"

"But if they are not in blankets, Scabbard's men will become suspicious—"

Dilliard laughed softly. "It's just another gringo trick I'm planning on, Manuel. It's been used against the Comanche Indians, back in Texas, before this. Look you, it will be dark, just before dawn comes. I plan to have only a small fire burning here. The blankets will be grouped about the fire, but their owners will not be inside them."

"What then?" the *mayordomo* queried blankly.

"I plan to have the blankets stuffed with brush."

"*Diantre*!" A broad smile twisted Manuel's grizzled features. "You are a devil, Señor Dilliard!"

"One must fight devils with devil tricks," the Texan chuckled. "Go now, awaken your men. Order them to move quickly and quietly.

I'll saddle and ride out to speak with the men guarding the herd."

The two men got to their feet. There was a minimum of noise and a maximum of activity about the camp for the next half hour. The *vaqueros* went silently and swiftly about their appointed tasks. Brush was gathered and rolled inside blankets, manipulated into lifelike dummies sprawled about the campfire. The blaze was allowed to die down. The moon swung farther to the west and commenced its downward journey. . . .

An hour before the expected attack, the men were ready. Horses and *vaqueros* were secreted among the brush, not far from the rim of the herd. Dilliard, himself, was in charge of this group. Near the camp, but scattered well away from it, was Manuel with more men, guns ready for the first flash of murderous fire. The two Mexican women cooks had been warned to lie low in the wagon, out of harm's way among the dunnage of travel. The lower sides of the wagon were thick oak and capable of withstanding any glancing bullets that might be flying about.

An hour passed. Slowly, the moon dipped from sight. Darkness again settled over the valley. In the east came the first faint streak of false dawn. A cricket chirped in the brush near Dilliard. Suddenly, not far from the herd came the cry of a mockingbird.

Dilliard stiffened. "That was no mockingbird," he told himself.

A mounted *vaquero*, not far from Dilliard, whispered, "That was no bird, but a man, *señor*."

"You're right," Dilliard said, low-voiced. "It's a signal of some sort. It's Scabbard's men. They certainly moved quiet. Are you all ready, *amigo*?"

Soft whisperings rustled through the brush. In a few moments, the *vaquero* said, low-voiced, "All is ready."

The *vaquero*'s prompt reply was lost in a sudden wild scream, intended to resemble the sound made by a mountain lion. It was a good imitation, at that. The herd was growing restless. Several of the cattle were getting to their feet. Others were up, starting to mill uneasily about. In a minute the whole herd was standing, ready to run.

And then it happened: a horse neighed close at hand. Abruptly, there came a volley of shooting near the herd, the wild yelling of men's voices. The cattle were electrified to silence for one brief moment. A frightened bawling arose on the night air. The rush of hoofs and yelling, shooting men charged nearer. With a tossing of horns and lifted tails, the cattle started frantically to run.

The earth shook to the drumming of the sudden rush. A wild clattering of horns reached Dilliard's ears above the pounding hoofs. The *vaquero* at

Dilliard's side stiffened, spoke a low, impatient exclamation.

"Wait!" Dilliard whispered tensely. The *vaquero* nodded, passed the word along to his companions.

From the direction of the camp came a sudden ragged volley of firing. It was answered immediately by a second, savage outburst. But the sounds were almost drowned in the mad, demoniac rush of fear-frenzied cattle that swept past, through the night. Dilliard caught a quick view of a vast sea of surging backs and agitated horns plunging past in the gloom. Already the cattle were being swallowed by the darkness beyond.

Behind the herd came a group of yelling, shooting men, flashes of gunfire momentarily bringing in sight certain fiendish faces. The firing near the camp had died down now. Scabbard's stampeding riders rushed on, their shooting slacking a bit as they slowed to reload guns.

Dilliard spoke quick orders along the line of waiting *vaqueros*. Reins were gathered tightly. The Castameto forces swept out from the brush, closing in rapidly on Scabbard's men who were following the cattle.

Suddenly, from ahead, there came a choking yell of dismay, as the Scabbard forces abruptly realized that they were being attacked from the rear. Dilliard's forty-five was out, firing rapidly. Other weapons were speaking now.

The Scabbard riders jerked their ponies about, the cattle forgotten, and turned to face this unexpected threat. Gun-barrels barked savagely, lighting up the night with sharp flashes of orange fire.

A horse screamed and went down. A rider pitched to the earth. A second rider rushed out of the night, appearing suddenly before Dilliard. His face was ugly, vindictive. Dilliard caught the flash of an upswung gun. His own gun kicked in his hand. The man's face faded away in the darkness.

Dilliard realized suddenly that his hammer was falling on empty shells. He punched out the dead shells, inserted fresh loads into his cylinder. A *vaquero* loomed out of the darkness beside him. The steeple-crowned hats of the Mexicans were easy to recognize.

"You, Señor Dilliard?"

"*Sí, amigo*."

"There seem but few of those *cabrones* left."

Dilliard said grimly. "There shouldn't be any left."

The two rode side by side, guns ready. There came a lull in the firing as the barking of weapons was replaced by the cries and curses of wounded men. On all sides, riderless horses were running loose. Dilliard yelled a sudden order, started for the campfire. His *vaqueros* fell in behind him.

A few shots still cracked in the vicinity of the camp. Dilliard and his riders fanned out, approaching from wide angles, using their guns. Sudden yells for mercy rose on the air. The Scabbard faction—that portion which was left—was calling words of surrender.

The *vaqueros* closed in as the shooting halted. Three or four were dragging prisoners at the ends of their *riatas*. The *mayordomo* emerged from the brush, his face covered with perspiration. Wood was heaped on the fire. Other men came into view, their features glistening in the sudden glare of the flames. It had been hot work for a few minutes.

From far down the valley came sounds of the still running cattle. Manuel looked at Dilliard, smiled tiredly when he saw that the Texan was unwounded.

"We've won the day," Dilliard said.

Manuel repeated, "We've won the day."

Dilliard nodded. "The surprise was complete, *amigo*." He felt suddenly weary, as he dismounted stiffly from his pony.

25
CONFESSION

Along the horizon the eastern sky was growing crimson now. The *mayordomo* gave certain orders. *Vaqueros* turned their ponies and commenced to search for wounded at the spot where the cattle had been bedded down.

By sun-up, eleven prisoners, six of whom had wounds of various degrees, had been brought into camp. One of them was Mitch Riker; another, with a bullet through his lungs, was the nearly finished Bart Fustian, who was unconscious and breathing with difficulty. Those of the prisoners who could talk begged to be set free.

"Are these all that are left?" Dilliard asked the *mayordomo*.

"The remainder of Scabbard's men will never ride again," Manuel replied meaningfully.

Dilliard asked if Wirt Bisbee and Clem Corill had been seen. One of the prisoners, anxious to talk, said that Bisbee's wounded shoulder had prevented him from coming.

"How about Corill?"

The prisoner cursed Corill, concluding, "He was too yellow to come, I reckon. Maybe he suspected there might be a fight. Anyway, Clem stayed behind with Scabbard, in El Vaca. Look here, Texas man, how about lettin' me off? I'll get out of this country and—"

Dilliard hardened his face and turned back to the *mayordomo.* "Manuel, any of our own men hurt bad?"

"Three have slight wounds," Manuel replied, "which are not severe enough to keep them from saddles." He repeated Dilliard's words of a short time before, "The surprise was complete. Our men were fortunate."

Tony Aguilar pushed up to Dilliard's side. "I'm think we are put the complete to the Scabbard skonks—no?" Laughingly, he wiped a smear of blood from his forehead, disclosing a wound that was but little more than a break in the skin.

Dilliard nodded, spoke to the *mayordomo.* The women cooks crawled out of their wagon. One started food preparations; the other busied herself with the injuries of the wounded. Five of the *vaqueros* remained in camp. The others, with Dilliard and Manuel leading them, rode in search of the missing cattle.

The sun was high, flooding the hills with golden light when the Texan and his companions rode out of the valley to the west. In front of them lay the broad blue expanse of the Pacific Ocean, sparkling under the warm rays of morning light. Ranged along the beach and near the valley mouth were at least half the cattle, peacefully at ease.

Up from the beach, at either side of the valley, were high bluffs, covered with grass and brush. Manuel pointed toward the top of the nearest bluff. "Doubtless, most of the balance of the cattle will be up there."

He shouted orders to his *vaqueros.* Some of the men commenced rounding up the cattle scattered along the beach. Others accompanied Manuel and Dilliard up the side of a steep bluff. Emerging at the top, Dilliard found himself on an almost unlimited stretch of lush tableland. Cattle were grazing quietly about. The *vaqueros* began to gather the beasts into a compact bunch.

"I doubt we have lost more than a few of the beef animals," Manuel said with satisfaction.

Dilliard nodded, absent-mindedly, and sniffed the fresh salt air rolling in on the morning breeze. From his position on the broad mesa he had an unbroken vista of surf-pounded coast. Huge breakers rolled in to crash with a shower of white spray on jagged clumps of rock. Great combers of glassy blue, formed from slow moving swells, broke on the golden beach and ran far up, putting into orderly rout a small band of sandpipers which retreated with soldierly precision, only to wheel and pursue the wave out as it receded.

Above the sky was cloudless. Dilliard breathed deeply of the morning air, each breath sending the blood tingling through his veins, making him glad to be alive. The weariness of the long night seemed to dissolve from his lean form. He realized it all suddenly—this was his country; he'd come to stay a long time. The Texan turned slowly to Manuel, mounted at his side, and said, "I don't think I'll ever leave California."

The *mayordomo* eyed him gravely. "It is like coming home, Señor Dilliard?"

"Like coming home," Dilliard nodded. He stiffened reluctantly in his saddle, gathering his reins. "Work ahead, *amigo*."

Leaving the *vaqueros* to their business of gathering the herd, Dilliard and the *mayordomo* returned to the camp. They found Tony just preparing to mount and ride after them.

Tony explained to the Texan: "Eet is this man, Gage—" he commenced.

"Who is Gage, Tony?"

"One of Drake Scabbard's raiders. I forget you do not know hees name. Only recent I'm learn heem—"

"What about him?"

"He is die—feenish! It is you should see heem—"

"Oh," Dilliard said patiently, "one of Scabbard's men, named Gage, is dead—"

"Not yet, hees die, but ver' quickly now. But before he die, he is ask to talk weeth you, Señor Branch."

"Where is this Gage?"

Dilliard was led to the wounded Gage, who lay on a pile of spread blankets. One of the *vaqueros* spoke to the dying man, held a cup of water to his lips. Gage opened his eyes, searching for the Texan. He was a long, thin man, looking little different from any of the Scabbard's henchmen whom Dilliard had seen before.

Dilliard bent near. Already death was laying a gray finger across the man's brow. "You been askin' for me, Gage?" Dilliard said quietly.

Gage tried to nod, his lips moved slowly. "Wanted to talk to one of my own kind—a white man. Me, I'm snuffin' out. I know that. Reckon I ain't got any regrets, exactly, only—I might have lived—cleaner—"

"It was just bad luck that got you in with Scabbard," the Texan said, not unkindly. "Where you're goin' now, maybe you'll get a fresh start."

"Yeah—I hope so. Drake Scabbard was to blame. But I took his money. It come easy. He's a dirty hound—Scabbard is. Out to wipe Castameto off'n the map—figures to steal him blind—and then let him hang—"

"You mean for the killing of Lucas Reardon, the man who murdered Ramon Castameto."

"That's it—but old Salvadore Castameto didn't murder Lucas Reardon, as the arrest warrant charged."

"I know that, Gage. It wasn't murder. Castameto

killed Reardon in fair fight. The murder warrant was Scabbard's doin's."

A ghost of an ironic chuckle passed Gage's lips. "Hell! Old Castameto didn't even kill Reardon. He shot Lucas in fair fight, like you say, but the doctor said Reardon would live."

Dilliard nodded. "But Lucas Reardon bled to death that night."

"Sure—he did," Gage stated feebly. "But only after Clem Corill went into Lucas' room—found Lucas unconscious. Corill did somethin' to Lucas Reardon. Something that opened the wound and made it bleed. Reardon died. Castameto was accused of murder."

"Good Lord! Gage, what are you saying?"

"I'm speaking truth, Dilliard. Corill acted on Scabbard's orders. Corill told me hisself—after it was done. Lucas Reardon had some money. Scabbard and Corill split it between them, after Lucas Reardon died . . ." The man's voice failed.

Dilliard held the cup of water to Gage's lips. After a moment he said, "Gage, are you sure of this?"

"I'm—sure," came the weak reply. "You see, Dilliard, you're square. I'm askin' you to—get Scabbard for me. I'd figured to kill him—myself—when things came right, but I can't do it—now. You get him."

"I don't understand, Gage."

"Don't call me 'Gage.' My real name is

Reardon. Lucas Reardon was my son. I came out here—years ago—when Lucas was just a babe in arms. There was a reason—for leavin' my home—back in Kentucky—those days. You see, I'd killed a man. When Lucas growed up—he traced me out here—come lookin' for me—but didn't recognize me as his father when we met. I'd taken the name of Gage. By that time I was workin' for Scabbard. Some of the things I done weren't nice to think on. I never let Lucas Reardon know who I was. Then, after he died, I planned to rub out Scabbard—and Corill—but now—now—"

The man stopped speaking, his eyes became glassy. Dilliard called his name, gently shook his shoulder. The pallid lips moved feebly, "You get 'em—Texas man. You're white. . . ."

Dilliard rose grimly to his feet, spoke one word, "Dead."

Manuel nodded gravely. "It is a strange story he told."

The Texan nodded, lost in thought. After a moment he said, "Manuel, I'm going to El Vaca. It's time for a show-down with Scabbard."

"Alone, Señor Dilliard?" Manuel looked worried.

"I can take care of myself. If things can be settled with Scabbard now, it will make things easier on this drive and the ones to follow. Scabbard will be suspecting, before long, that his scheme to wipe us out has failed. He'll try something else if I don't stop him first."

"But the herd?"

"You and your men keep pushing on to San Diego. If I don't catch up with you, after I've seen Scabbard, you can collect the money from Jim Hawkins. You know Serrano, don't you?"

"*Sí*, I know Don Alvaro very well."

"Good. These prisoners and the wounded Scabbard men you better take to Capistrano Mission, after you've buried the dead. At the mission, the prisoners can be held and taken care of until we get around to them. We'll settle with them later. You'd better leave one *vaquero* to act as a guard—"

"But, Señor Dilliard—"

"You don't need me, Manuel. Not right away. I'll go to El Vaca, see Scabbard, then return and overtake the herd, if possible. If I don't catch up with you," grimly, "well, you know what to do."

"*Sí*, Señor Dilliard."

The Texan remounted. "*Adiós*," he said.

"*Adiós*, *amigo*. *Vaya con Dios*. Go with God."

Dilliard turned his pony and settled into a fast lope that carried him swiftly along the valley floor. When he looked back, a few minutes later, the camp was lost to view around a bend in the trail. He jabbed in his spurs, urged the horse to greater speed.

26
SHOW-DOWN

The sun showed two hours before noontime, when Dilliard loped into El Vaca's single, dusty street. There weren't any *Americanos* in sight along the winding thoroughfare—only Mexicans and Indians. Dilliard pulled to a walk, his eyes alert for both sides of the roadway. To the rear of the town, a mountain sloped steeply to the south. High on one of its narrow shelves moved a man and horse, too far away to be recognizable. Dilliard wondered if by chance it might be Scabbard, or Corill.

The tiny figure on the slope disappeared around a bend. It wasn't moving fast. "Ten to one it isn't anybody I know," Dilliard mused. "Probably some Mexican, cutting across country." His gaze ranged across the surface of the slope, took in another shelf of rock lower down. The horseman didn't reappear.

Dilliard again gave his attention to the street. Nearing a saloon, he pulled to a sudden halt, having spotted Wirt Bisbee's red beard on the saloon porch. Bisbee's shoulder was still swathed in bandages. He looked up suddenly, spied Dilliard, then, thinking he hadn't been seen, withdrew quickly to the interior of the saloon.

Five minutes passed, while Dilliard waited. Bisbee didn't show up again. Dilliard spoke to his pony, moved on, passed the saloon without anything happening. The town seemed to have grown strangely quiet all of a sudden. There weren't nearly so many pedestrians abroad as when the Texan had first entered El Vaca.

"Must be," Dilliard chuckled grimly, "the Mexicans and Indians realize I've come for a showdown with Scabbard. They're keeping out of sight until they see what happens."

A saddled horse stood at the hitch-rail before Scabbard's house, whether Scabbard's or someone else's Dilliard didn't know. He rode up, dismounted, flipped his reins loosely over the rail, and turned toward the house with long, even strides.

The door of the house stood open. Dilliard glanced both ways along the porch. No one was in sight. A board creaked slightly under foot as Dilliard mounted the steps, but there came no sound from inside the house.

Softly, Dilliard crossed the porch floor, peered around the edge of the casing. The Texan hesitated but a moment, then pushed on through. He saw Scabbard before Scabbard realized that anyone had entered. Scabbard was seated at his table and appeared to be computing some figures on a sheet of paper. In the corner, at Scabbard's rear, the door of his iron safe stood partly open. Account books were piled at one end of the table on which Scabbard worked.

Scabbard's head lifted a trifle as he wrote down certain figures. Dilliard caught the gleam of greedy satisfaction in his pale eyes, just before the man's gaze fell on the Texan.

Scabbard's thin smile faded swiftly. "Dilliard!" he exclaimed, rising from his chair.

"Sit down, Scabbard!" Dilliard stopped, half-way to the table.

Scabbard eyed the gun at Dilliard's hip, settled reluctantly back in his chair.

"Surprised to see me, eh, Scabbard?"

"Somewhat. I thought—"

"You thought—hoped—I'd be layin' dead about this time, didn't you, Scabbard?"

"Well, er, no—why do you say that, Dilliard? I've intended looking into your affairs. You know there's a warrant out for your arrest—"

"Yes, your men tried to serve it. Their tails were between their legs when they left—"

"What's that?" Scabbard looked startled. "I don't see—"

"It doesn't matter. Your scheme didn't work. Your schemes are all through working. Your plotting against Castameto is finished. That drive's going through, clear to San Diego. You'll get repayment on the loan you made Castameto, but much good it'll do you—"

"That's fine. I'll need that money. But that doesn't help you." Scabbard had regained some of his composure. "You know, Dilliard, that warrant for assault and battery against Bart Fustian will have to be served—"

"Forget it," Dilliard said scornfully. "Bart Fustian may be dead by this time. He was hit bad. Mitch Riker was wounded too—"

"What are you talking about?" Scabbard had gone white. He was commencing to tremble.

"The man you knew as Gage is dead, Scabbard," the Texan continued relentlessly. "He talked a heap about certain things before he died. And get this, Scabbard, we didn't lose a man. Your raid was a failure."

"You—you're talking in riddles," Scabbard gulped. "You don't make—make sense—"

"Listen, and you'll get it all. We were ready when your coyotes come attacking. We wiped 'em out. Does that make sense? You've played your last hand, Scabbard. You're done!"

Scabbard's face was deadly white. Twin spots of crimson burned angrily against the pale flesh. "I repeat," he snarled, "I can't make head nor tail of what you're trying to say. I have no more time to waste. You get out of here at once or I'll send word for the deputy-sheriff to come after you. I'll give you this last chance. You'd better get started—"

"Scabbard, you're not talking to a friendless

Spaniard now. That bluff don't go down. I know this country and I know its people. And I know that the gringo isn't half as dirty as your actions have led Castameto to think. From now on, there'll be a square deal for him. No, Scabbard, I don't bluff easy. I'm dealing the cards now—and they're bein' dealt from an honest deck!"

Scabbard got control of his emotions. His voice was dangerously quiet as he asked, "Dilliard, just what are you after?"

"Castameto's papers," the Texan said promptly.

"What papers?"

"Don't squirm away, Scabbard. I want Castameto's land grant to Rancho Sicamoro and the deed you forced him to make out in your name. The paper regarding the loan you made him, you can keep until the money is repaid."

Scabbard laughed harshly. "Why, you can't have those papers—not until the loan is repaid. The deed and grant are security—"

"I'm taking those papers. You tricked Castameto into that business, making him think he was a murderer. It's you and Clem Corill who will swing for the murder of Lucas Reardon."

"Bosh! You're talking riddles again. Do you think for one minute I'll hand over those papers?" Scabbard's voice trembled.

"I know damn well you will!" Dilliard slapped the gun holster at his hip. "Unless you want to argue the matter."

"You mean you'd take those papers by force?" Scabbard's eyes narrowed nervously.

"If you don't fork 'em over."

"That's unlawful."

"No more so than the things you've done. If you like we can have a Deputy U. S. Marshal sent down here to investigate. You'll get the return of your money, but I want those papers now."

Quite suddenly, Scabbard laughed. "All right, if you feel that way about it." He moved his chair back a few inches, slid out a drawer in the table, reached one hand inside.

Dilliard saw the derringer before it was clear of the drawer. His six-shooter leaped out, covering Scabbard.

"Hold it, Scabbard! It's the papers I want—not your gun. Now, get them *pronto*! I figure them to be in that safe back of you. Will you get 'em or will I? Think fast!"

Scabbard shrugged his shoulders in baffled rage. "Just as you say," he surrendered angrily.

Rising from the table he turned and threw wide the safe door. Then he returned to the table bearing a sheet of paper and a square of heavy parchment, yellowed with age. These he tossed on the table before Dilliard.

Warily, tense for some trick, the Texan kept his gun trained on Scabbard while he examined the papers with a quick, efficient scrutiny. Both were written in Spanish. Castameto's name was signed to the paper. The parchment also carried the name Castameto, was covered with legal verbiage in faded ink, and bore the great seal of the Spanish Throne.

Dilliard backed away, thrusting the documents inside his shirt. He eyed Scabbard steadily, caught the gleam in the man's cold gaze. Something was wrong. This was too easy. By all rules, Scabbard shouldn't have surrendered without more of a fight. Dilliard tensed, as the most cautious of movements from the doorway to the rear, caught the Texan's ear.

Dilliard whirled to see Clem Corill just raising his gun for a murderous shot in the back. Like a flash of light, Dilliard whirled to one side. Corill's gun roared. Scabbard leaped for the derringer in his table drawer.

Dilliard righted himself, his gun swinging in a half-arc that bore on Corill. The weapon barked savagely as Corill unleashed a second shot. Corill went crashing into the wall at Dilliard's left, dropping his six-shooter.

Scabbard's gun cracked viciously. Adobe plaster thudded from the wall behind the Texan. The room was suddenly swimming with powder-smoke. Dilliard jerked to one side as Scabbard fired a second time—missed again. The Texan's weapon crashed loudly, shaking the roof beams of the ceiling.

A sharp cry of pain was torn from Scabbard's

throat as the derringer went spinning from his hand. Scabbard backed away, crying for mercy, shaking his pain-numbed fingers.

Dilliard laughed grimly as the man struggled to get his arms in the air. "You're lucky, Scabbard, my slug didn't land where it was intended to go. That's freak shootin'—knockin' that derringer out of your hand. Keep 'em up!"

Scabbard backed against the opposite wall, arms high in air, his face contorted with fright. Corill was down, groaning with pain, sprawled full length on the floor. The drifting haze of powder smoke commenced to clear from the room.

Steps pounded heavily on the porch. Deputy-Sheriff Luke Dangler burst into the room, gun in hand. He stopped short, looked surprised at seeing Dilliard in command of the situation.

"Wha—what's goin' on here?" he demanded.

"Kill him, Luke!" Scabbard shrieked. "He shot us down without a chance!"

Dangler glanced at the gun in Dilliard's hand, then looked uneasily at his chief. Before he could speak, Dilliard said sternly, "Dangler, Scabbard's game is up. Yours will be, too, unless you make a fast choice. Are you swinging with Scabbard—and that means swinging from a gallows—or do you want a chance to go straight and enforce the law? Quick! Make up your mind!"

"Luke!" Scabbard wailed. "Don't you listen—"

"We-ell," Dangler commenced uncertainly, "I'd like to be on the side of the law, like always. I want the straight of what's goin' on here."

"You got it," and Dilliard's gun bore on Dangler. "I said you'd have to think fast. Gage has made a confession. Corill and Scabbard are due to hang for the murder of Lucas Reardon. We've got plenty witnesses. There'll be other charges, too. What's it to be, Dangler?"

Dangler didn't look at Scabbard as he said to Dilliard, "I figure to string with you, Mister Dilliard. I've had enough of Scabbard's game—"

Scabbard cursed Dangler viciously. Dangler told Scabbard to shut his mouth. Dilliard ordered the deputy to examine Clem Corill. Dangler knelt by Corill's side, arose after a few minutes to state that Corill would live if he received medical attention.

"There's a doctor in town," Dangler said eagerly. "Want I should go for him, Mister Dilliard."

"In a few minutes. We'll put Scabbard in your jail first. I'll hold you responsible to see he don't escape, Dangler. Got handcuffs with you?"

"Yessir, Mister Dilliard," producing the steel bracelets.

"Put 'em on Scabbard."

Scabbard cursed some more. Dangler approached warily.

"Go ahead, Dangler," Dilliard ordered. "I'll plug him if he resists arrest."

Dangler blustered, "No more of your resistin', Drake. Your game's up! And high time too."

"Damn you, Luke!" Scabbard snarled. "*You* won't get out of this so easy. Better think twice."

Dangler paled but persisted in following Dilliard's orders. "You hold out them wrists, Drake. I don't want none of your talk."

Angrily, Scabbard extended his arms for the handcuffs. Dangler came nearer. The next instant, Scabbard had dashed the cuffs from the deputy-sheriff's hands and made a dash for the doorway. His shoulder struck Dangler. Dangler staggered back, and sat heavily on the floor, mouth gaping open.

Scabbard was through the doorway, now, crossing the porch, intent only on making an escape. Dilliard leaped to the porch, gun raised, in time to see Scabbard mounting his horse. Scabbard was frantic with fear, as he whirled the animal savagely away from the tie-rail to the open roadway.

There was one moment when the escaping man presented a favorable target for Dilliard's gun, but the Texan couldn't bring himself to shoot a man in the back. Swearing softly, Dilliard ran out to the other horse standing at the tie-rail.

Even as he started to mount, he caught the sharp crack of a rifle, from back of the town. The

Texan turned just in time to see Scabbard throw both arms in the air and pitch from the running horse's back.

Sprinting out to the center of the roadway, Dilliard glanced up at the mountain slope, rising behind the town. There, perched high on one of the rocky shelves, well out of six-shooter range, Cat-Eye Fremont was sitting his horse.

The old scoundrel let out a wild yell of triumph that carried faintly down into town. "I swore I'd get him!" Cat-Eye yelled, shaking his Spencer rifle in the air.

The next moment he had put the horse into motion and was riding at break-neck speed around the mountain trail.

"Cat-Eye!" gasped a voice at Dilliard's side. It was Luke Dangler, looking considerably ruffled.

As though by magic, many Mexicans and Indians had appeared on the street now. A group had gathered around the silent form of Scabbard, stretched full length in the dusty road. A Mexican had caught the horse on which Scabbard had attempted to escape and now approached leading the beast.

Dangler at his side, Dilliard went to examine Scabbard.

Dangler said unfeelingly. "Right through the head. That dang Cat-Eye sure can shoot straight when he draws a bead."

Dilliard said sternly, "Dangler, you've got a

chance to make somethin' of yourself, now. You better go straight. Scabbard's finished. You take care of this body. Better see to Clem Corill first. See that he gets medical care. I'm holdin' you responsible to see that he comes to trial."

"Yessir, Mister Dilliard—and—and thank you. And say, Wirt Bisbee's still hangin' around town. Want I should arrest him?"

"Suit yourself. I'd warn him to leave town, if I were you. Then you better get on Cat-Eye's trail."

"Shucks, there ain't nobody could capture that old varmint now."

Dilliard smiled. "I think I could—but I don't intend to try. I don't expect you to catch him, either, but you can show your good intentions by trying. Fact is, he deserves to escape, I figure."

"Me, too. Scabbard was pretty low."

"And you were tarred with the same brush, Dangler. You've got your chance. Run a lawful town and you'll keep out of trouble as far as I'm concerned. I'll be back in a coupla weeks to see how you're living up to your new resolutions."

"Yessir, Mister Dilliard," Dangler said humbly.

Dilliard turned to find his horse, mounted, and pounded out of El Vaca. The outdoors seemed fresher and cleaner now than when he had entered the town a short time before. A square of parchment and a sheet of paper crackled inside Dilliard's shirt. Resolutely, he turned his pony's head toward the Rancho Sicamoro.

27
FLAME OF SILVER

Midday had passed when the Texan reached the Ranch of the Sycamores. The big house and its smaller buildings seemed locked in the lull that comes with the daily *siesta.* Dilliard dismounted near one of the corrals. A small Mexican boy came sleepily from a nearby shack and took his reins.

From another house there was a startled cry, and Teresa came running to greet Dilliard:

"Señor Branch! What is it?" she gasped. "My Antonio—?"

"Take it easy, Teresa. Tony is all right. We're all, all right."

"That is ver' good," the girl smiled, relaxed suddenly.

"Did the *señorita* return safely last night?"

"Sooner than even I expected. She was worried. Those raiders of Scabbard's—?"

"Were beaten off. We have nothing more to fear from Scabbard."

"Thank the *buen Dios*!"

"Is Don Salvadore out on the range with the round-up—?"

"He is at the house, Don Branch, having arrived but a short time back for some business or other. He returns to the round-up shortly. You'll find him inside before he leaves. . . . And, Don Branch—"

"Yes, Teresa."

"I think the *señorita* will be very pleased to see you."

Dilliard left the girl, strode on toward the house, his step light and springy. He passed through the entrance to the patio, crossed quickly to the *corredor* and entered an open doorway.

Don Salvadore was pacing the floor in the center of the big main room of the house. The gray-haired old Spaniard stopped short in surprise.

"Señor Dilliard! What is wrong?"

"All is well, *mi patrón*."

Dilliard related quickly all that had happened, pressed a certain square of parchment and written paper into Castameto's hands. The Texan turned quickly away, so as not to see the moisture in the old man's eyes. After a few minutes, Castameto's hands found Dilliard's own, shifted to grip the younger man's shoulders. The pressure of his fingers was firm, more than friendly.

The old Spaniard's voice wasn't quite steady, "I think," he said, "I have found a son, to stay with me—always—"

"If you will have me, *patrón*."

"All that I have shall be yours, Branch. Only for you—"

This was almost too much for the Texan. He turned toward the doorway.

"Where do you go, my son?"

The Texan tried to hold his tones careless. "I planned to overtake Manuel and the herd."

"But wait. First you must see, talk to Mariposa. She is in her room, taking the *siesta.* This morning, she told me many things before I rode away. It seems she had been up all night, thinking of those many things that had to be put into words for my ears. I've wondered if last night she hadn't ridden to see you, once more, before you got too far to the south."

"It was Mariposa who brought us word of the raiders, *patrón*."

"*Madre de Dios*! She didn't relate that. She is brave—a fit mate for the eagle that has come to our nest." Castameto's lips curved a trifle ruefully. "Perhaps, if I try very hard, I may learn the ways of the *Americanos.* I think, most of all, I want that, now that you are to stay with us . . . But wait."

Castameto hurried from the room. Dilliard moved across the *sala*, stood gazing out on the flowered patio. Castameto returned after a short time. He placed both hands on Dilliard's shoulders and was glad when the Texan didn't try to evade his steady scrutiny.

"No," Castameto said, half to himself, "I do not lose a daughter. I gain a son. Go to her,

Branch. She does not sleep. She waits for you."

It was difficult for Dilliard to keep from running. He brushed past the old Spaniard, stepped out to the *corredor.* Beneath the great, wide-flung limbs of the sycamore, the patio was fragrant with roses and honeysuckle and jasmine.

The Texan paused before an open doorway. Dim coolness, a movement, within. He hesitated but a moment more before he saw Mariposa's slim form, waiting like a silvery flame in the dusky room. She was nearer now, as Branch stepped across the threshold. The girl's face was lifting to his own. He felt warm arms raised about his shoulders. There was a misty fragrance in his head . . . either the honeysuckle . . . or the yellow rose of Monterey. . . .

About the Author

William Colt MacDonald (December 2, 1891–March 27, 1968) was an American writer of Western fiction born in Detroit, Michigan, whose work appeared both in books and on film.

His many novels include *The Gun Branders*, *Guns Between the Suns*, *Law and Order, Unlimited*, and *Showdown Trail*.

His film credits, all for character writing, are for his most famous, The Three Mesquiteers—Stony Brooke, Tucson Smith, and Lullaby Joslin. They first appeared together in the 1933 novel *Law of the Forty-Fives*, which was adapted into the movie, *The Law of the 45's*.

Between 1936 and 1943, Republic Pictures released a Three Mesquiteers film series, starting with *The Three Mesquiteers*. Among the 51 movies of the series, eight have John Wayne as Stony Brooke: *Pals of the Saddle*, *Overland Stage Raiders*, *Santa Fe Stampede*, *Red River Range*, *The Night Riders*, *Three Texas Steers*, *Wyoming Outlaw*, and *New Frontier*.

Center Point Large Print
600 Brooks Road / PO Box 1
Thorndike, ME 04986-0001 USA

(207) 568-3717

US & Canada:
1 800 929-9108
www.centerpointlargeprint.com